Adopting a cat doesn't sou  meets Harinder Mangal, the loves animals and hates cu: inspires more than simple motion for an absurd game ∪₁ ᴜᴇᴄᴇⁱ that ʙoasts a fluffy cat named Dumpling as the prize.

Harinder hates Jericho's attitude, especially when it comes to owning a pet. He attempts to chase the other man from his store and is shocked when Jericho overcomes every obstacle, no matter how bizarre. Not only that, but he generates some of his own wild inconveniences that leave Harinder seething in his ugly sweater and mom jeans.

Before either man can get the other to crack, Harinder finds himself unexpectedly homeless. Despite their mutual antagonism, Jericho invites Harinder to crash at his place. The increased proximity makes it difficult for Harinder and Jericho to maintain their respective ruses, not to mention stopping themselves from actually *caring* about their pet-parenting rival.

CAT'S GOT YOUR HEART

Jem Zero

A NineStar Press Publication

www.ninestarpress.com

Cat's Got Your Heart

Printed in the USA

Print ISBN: 978-1-64890-102-7

First Edition, October, 2020

Also available in eBook, ISBN: 978-1-64890-101-0

WARNING:
This book contains sexually explicit content, which may
only be suitable for mature readers, abuse of a MC
(past), parent death (past), racism (present), housing
instability (present), use of slurs (present), and non-
graphic mentions of animal death and drug
use/overdose.

Yes, Mum, you're first! To the woman who always believed I'd eventually Get Here; to my wife Tora, who held me during panic attacks and fatigue drops; to my writing comrades, particularly Skye, Lisa, and Jami; to Tamara Lush, who has been holding my hand for years and who made sure I never gave up, even when plans A-thru-Y didn't succeed.

Chapter One

Jericho Is Not Prepared

There's a Petco another half hour down the bus line, but it's snowing and Jericho doesn't have that kind of time. Well, he does. But his phone is only at thirty-seven percent battery, and he's not patient enough to go that long without entertainment. Fortunately, there's a small hole-in-the-wall ten minutes from his apartment.

Aquariums & More doesn't have a website, but according to Yelp, the "more" includes live pets. Half the Yelp reviews complain about hostile and unwelcoming employees, but that's none of his business.

The pet store looks even shittier in person than it did in the picture. Multiple neon signs have been added since the pixelated, overexposed image was captured—probably somewhere in the early 1800s. Combined, they shine so brightly they distract from the puke-green awning, torn from years of weather, with faded navy font that looks like it's trying to be Comic Sans but isn't quite.

The visual assault is such that Jericho briefly overlooks the grime on the windows and how there seems to be something alive inside the trash can.

Any animal bought from this place is guaranteed to have three kinds of rabies and possibly congestive heart failure in addition to being intellectually dishonest and a kleptomaniac. It's perfect for his sister, Shiloh, so Jericho spits a wad of tasteless gum into the cigarette disposal (he isn't going near that trash can) and steps inside.

The bell on the door jingles merrily, but upon passing the threshold, there's no one in sight: no customers, no pimply teenage employees, not even a grizzled old man to regale him with stories of putting live mice in freezers.

Alrighty then.

Along the entire front wall is what must be a six-foot-long, gargantuan tank full of...sand and wood? Jericho looks closer, blinking when he sees some small things skittering through the thick foliage. Oh, hermit crabs.

"They're not for sale," a rough voice says behind him.

He startles, but not enough to make a fool out of himself. Instead of swinging around to face whoever came up behind him, Jericho casually rolls his back. See? He isn't bothered in the least.

"There's a sign right there." He points down at the far corner of the tank where **Hermit Crabs $5 per ea**. is written in Sharpie on an off-white piece of cardstock. It's placed away from the reach of the fluorescent tank lighting as if someone doesn't want it to be noticed.

A dark hand reaches into his line of sight and unceremoniously rips the sign off the tank. "That was a prank," the other person says. "Feel free to ignore it."

"Okay," Jericho says—because sure, whatever—and turns toward the speaker. The voice made him expect someone at least moderately intimidating, but the fluffy hair, round cheeks, and full lips are suspiciously cherubic despite the rather genuine scowl. Also, this guy is, like, five feet tall, give or take a few inches. "Do you work here?" He's dubious about whether or not this is customer service or an attempt at stealing his lunch money.

The guy rolls his eyes—which makes Jericho think the answer is *no*, and he's about to be held at gunpoint in a pet store—and then he grabs the front of his mustard-yellow sweater and tugs the wrinkles straight to reveal a worn laminated tag that reads: Hello, my name is Harinder. The first thing Jericho notices is that his nails are painted black, although heavily chipped. The second thing he notices is the bottom of the nametag where the phrase How may I assist you? has been cut off at the bottom and heavily frayed.

Harinder drops the sweater and reaches up to brush his overgrown bangs out of his eyes, then folds his arms over his chest. It turns him into a puffball of rumpled wool and flyaway hair, which Jericho fails to find either professional or impressive. A hissing alley cat, at best.

Speaking of. "Do you have any kittens?"

If Harinder's face looked offended before, now it looks straight-up murderous. "If you want a kitten, I invite you to look into one of the mills of inbred, abused, unloved, soon-to-be-abandoned, backyard-bred animals. Might I suggest Craigslist, or some cushy chain pet shop balanced on the rusty, beloved seesaw of quality photography and appalling ethics? There're at least three of them downtown.

"If you want to pay five hundred dollars for an animal you'll only care about until it stops being small and inoffensive, be my guest, but I'm afraid I can't fff— I can't help you."

Jericho blinks very, very slowly. He didn't miss that aborted f-bomb, but as with the Yelp reviews, that isn't Jericho's problem. He tries again. "Do you have any... cats?"

Hunching his shoulders around his ears, Harinder jabs a thumb at the wall behind him. "Cat kennels are through that door."

"Thanks."

There are, in fact, no kittens. However, the eight kennels filling in one side of the room give him enough to choose from. The moment he catches the attention of the room's inhabitants, there's a chorus of noise as all the cats come to the doors of their steel prisons to bat fluffy paws through the bars in a sordid appeal for pets.

Jericho obliges the nearest one, threading his fingers through a gap and allowing the animal to smash its head into them, purring enticingly. He wiggles his hand as best he can to facilitate a more effective petting motion. This one is a skinny tabby, and the note on the front of its—his—cage says he's two years old and calls him Princeton.

It's such an obnoxious yuppy name that Jericho can't help but snort. What a terrible name for a cat. He shakes his head and moves to inspect the next prisoner.

In total, there are nine cats. Two green-eyed, gray longhairs inhabit one of the lower cages. They remain curled around each other, staring dispassionately at Jericho from the back of the kennel.

"Fuck y'all too," Jericho comments, leaving both "Lacey" and "Casey" to their own shitty devices.

A ten-year-old Abyssinian boy going by the name of Sir Charles immediately becomes his favorite. Jericho loses about five minutes trying to cram his whole hand through the tight bars so he can stroke his sleek honey-colored fur.

He doesn't think giving Shiloh a pet that might die soon is the best idea, and he isn't prepared to take on his own cat, so he moves on.

He ends up two cages to the left, shoulder pressed against the wall, studying a creamy Siamese point. She has a shaggy medium-length coat, faint textured stripes, and piercing blue eyes, with which she regards him coolly before padding over to give his extended fingers an inquisitive sniff.

Her body is long and lanky. *Regal,* Jericho thinks for all of thirty seconds before he looks at her infocard and discovers that her name is Dumpling.

A short, surprised laugh bursts from his chest; Dumpling's ears flick backward in disapproval. She's perfect. At a solid four years, she's old enough to know how to use a litter box and, hopefully, a scratching post, but isn't quite aged enough that he has to worry about being strong-armed into frequent vet-related errands.

The adoption fee is sixty-five dollars. A little steep, but manageable. Before he can do anything about it, the door to the kennel room bursts open and Beethoven's Sixth Symphony Performed Entirely by Cats nearly deafens him.

Harinder snarls. "What the f—" His teeth settle for a moment on his bottom lip. "—are you doing?"

"Just looking," Jericho says, pulling his hand away from the cages and shoving it in his pocket as if he was doing something wrong, although he's pretty damn sure petting cats in a pet shop is not actually illegal.

"I've heard people use their eyes to do that," is the surly reply. Of *course* this jackass would go there.

"Gonna call the cops?" he asks, rolling his eyes. Jericho is used to threats of police intervention in his simple existence. No innocence when you're Black. Even being albino doesn't change that.

Harinder's face clouds. "I wouldn't." Then he wraps his whole fist around a cable lying against the room's back wall and gives it an unnecessarily forceful yank. A thick brown curtain rolls up to the ceiling, exposing a greasy window. Harinder doesn't say anything more, but the message of "I can see you and will rain unholy hellfire down on anything that displeases me about your conduct" is clear.

Jericho doesn't respond. He only finds his voice when Harinder turns toward the exit. "Hey, wait. I want to buy a cat."

Harinder stops dead, spine stiffening. Again, Jericho imagines some kind of small, furry creature raising its hackles in a misinformed attempt to look threatening.

"We don't sell cats," Harinder says, voice gravelly.

"Uh, what?"

He turns around, jaw clearly set. "I. Said. We don't *sell* cats, you—" He clamps his mouth shut.

"What are these here for, then?"

Harinder's eyes flick to the kennels, then back to Jericho. "They're up for adoption."

Jesus fucking Christ. Jericho rolls his eyes again. "Fine. How do I '*adopt*' a cat?"

Although he looks very much like he'd rather rip his own eyes out and smash them on the floor, no more than ten seconds tick by before Harinder mumbles, begrudgingly, "Right this way." He turns on his heel and doesn't spare Jericho so much as a disdainful huff before thundering toward the counter.

Jericho follows at a much more resigned pace, hands still stuffed in his pockets. The cat chorus expresses disapproval at being ignored, but he closes the door behind him and wanders out before they can make him feel bad about it.

Harinder is rummaging around in some file cabinet, so Jericho takes the opportunity to glance around the rest of the building. Along the wall beside the cat room, there's a small rack of fish tanks, three high and six across. Though the glass is scratched and old, the walls are bright and clean of algae, water clear, and fish healthy.

Not that Jericho would know what healthy fish look like. He's just guessing.

The next row of tanks hosts an assortment of creepy crawlies. Reptiles and some arachnids. The surfaces of these, too, are immaculate. A glass-faced fridge, the door of which advertises everything from bloodworms to brine shrimp to frozen rodents in varying sizes, stands between the two structures. At least this one looks properly nasty.

Past the reptiles are bins full of live crickets, framed by cups of assorted worm species. He turns right when he reaches the door to the back room, past the aisle of fish and reptile accessories sitting opposite the two racks. The remaining aisles hold nothing more interesting than various bird cages lining the back wall. His ears are glad for the lack of live birds.

The store quickly turns boring, containing nothing else but shelf after shelf of aquariums and vivariums. He completes his lap around the building. The only remaining thing of interest is a large ferret cage tucked beside the register. Fifteen seconds into a stare down with one of the slinky weasel-wannabes, a voice cuts through the silence like a rusty axe.

"Do you want the cat or not."

Sighing, Jericho says, "Yes, I want the cat. How many liters of blood do you need?"

"You can start with this," Harinder says, sliding a thick stack of paper across the counter.

Jericho stares. "The fuck is this?"

"An adoption form."

"I can read," he says, inspecting the top page. "What's the rest of it?"

For the smallest instant, Harinder almost looks gleeful. He waves his hand at the stack of paper. "It's the adoption form." His voice rings with a badly muffled note of triumph. "Fill it out and return it at your convenience. We only hold animals after a form has been submitted, so the longer you wait—"

"You've got to be shitting me."

"The management of Aquariums & More does not take chances on the safety of our animals, sir." It's the most professional thing Harinder has said thus far, and also the most smug.

"This is at least twenty pages," Jericho says. "I've had final exams shorter than this."

Harinder leans his elbows on the counter. "Your underachieving academic performance isn't really any of my business. The adoption form consists of twelve pages of questions that are all highly successful in matching up pets with qualified caretakers. You have as much time as you need to complete each and every section." Beat. "Unless you're no longer interested."

Jericho snatches the form, wrinkling all twelve pages in his overly tight grip. "Thanks for your help."

Snow hits his cheeks when he storms out the door. It melts on contact, leaving his face wet. When the bus arrives finally, the form is a sodden mess, wilting in his hand.

Chapter Two

Harinder Probably Hates You

A bag of dog food lands on the counter. It's a decent brand, so Harinder's glare isn't as potent as usual when he greets the person buying it.

"Did you find everything you need?"

"Yes, I did," says the woman, flashing a distracted smile as she rummages in her purse. Harinder scratches at the nail polish on his thumb while waiting for her to locate her card. "I just had one question. Are those ferrets for sale? I didn't see a price tag."

"They're store pets, actually," he responds smoothly. "Your total is $23.84. Is there anything else I can help you with today?"

She shakes her head and mumbles no, already swiping her card. The receipt prints, and Harinder hands it to her, boredly reciting, "Here's your receipt. Have a nice day, and thank you for shopping at Aquariums & More."

The bell on the door chimes, and he's alone again.

"Fucking finally," he says, dropping onto his stool after the noon rush. "Rush" is a generous term—it's normally a loose chain of customers coming in to buy crickets and aspen chips on their lunch breaks. Most of them aren't particularly demanding, but it divides his attention from everything he'd rather be doing.

Harinder leans back against the bulk bird seed bins and pulls his notebook from under the counter, then shoves a bag of fish gravel out from where it was obscuring his phone, propped up against the back of a large fixture full of dog treats.

Thanks to the myriad of junk cluttering the cashwrap, he's able to pass his free time relatively obscured, and is easily able to hide his stuff before a customer makes it far enough into the store to see him. He presses play on the indie thriller film he's analyzing and settles down, ready to shiver through the next scene.

The doorbell chimes.

Harinder tries not to groan too loudly as he throws his notebook back under the counter and pauses the video. He ignores the approaching footsteps while tucking his phone behind the gravel.

"Can I help—"

"Hey, do you have reptiles?"

Harinder stares reproachfully, then admits, "Yes. We do."

"Where are they?" The skinny white kid looks like some kind of tweaker, with an oversized Slipknot hoodie and long hair that probably hasn't been brushed since 2013. It's matted into an approximation of dreads, but only somewhat.

Harinder doesn't have an emergency button (because who the fuck is going to shoot up a pet store?), though he does carry a pocketknife and a passport in case he has to flee the country unexpectedly.

Pushing the swinging door to the cashwrap aside, he says, "Right this way," and shuffles to the far aisle where the live pets reside. The white kid shoves past him, immediately pressing his hands to the tank fronts Harinder just windexed an hour ago.

"Do you have any, like, tarantulas?"

"Sold out."

"Is that a scorpion?"

"Yes. Have you ever been stung by one?"

"Holy shit, that's a big lizard."

"He'll grow bigger," Harinder hisses through his teeth, toes digging into the bottom of his shoes.

"I want that one."

Tilting his head, Harinder examines the tweaker, on his knees with his finger jabbed at the bearded dragon enclosure sitting closest to the floor. Three juveniles occupy the space. In about six months they'll have to be separated. Maybe he can clear the gravel bags out from under the hermit crab tank and put one under there, which means he still has to find responsible owners for the other two... But definitely not this guy.

"Do you know what that's called?" he asks, affording a thin veneer of patience.

"Ummmm..."

"It's a bearded dragon. Do you know how big they get?"

"Well—"

"Are they desert or tropical?"

"The carpet is brown like a desert, so—"

"Do you know the requirements for a desert enclosure? What temperature should the basking spot be? What's the purpose of full spectrum lighting?"

"Uh, I don't..."

"What's the recommended diet for a juvenile dragon versus an adult?"

"Dude."

Harinder crosses his arms. "Go home. Do some research. Come back. Or better yet, don't come back.

These animals deserve better than some punk who thinks it's a good idea to get a pet he doesn't even know the name of."

The white kid frowns hard at the enclosure, avoiding Harinder's eyes. It makes him feel twitchy in the feeling places, so Harinder runs a hand through his thick hair and sighs. "Okay, look. Come with me."

The kid stands up mutely and follows him down two aisles, then to the right.

"See this? This is a three-hundred-dollar reptile enclosure. This is the minimum space requirement for a single adult bearded dragon. If you don't have that kind of money or space, this isn't the right pet for you. Got it?"

The kid nods.

"Okay, hey," Harinder says, grabbing the front of his shirt and dragging him back to the reptiles. "Let me tell you some things. Leopard geckos are good reptiles for beginners. They don't get too big and are easy to handle if you train them right and respect their boundaries. Remember, there's no easy pet, and the concept of throwaway pets is a cruel myth, but."

He reaches toward a file on the side of the reptile tanks and pulls out a sheaf of papers.

"This is a care sheet for leopard geckos. Read it all. Memorize it like it's your new Bible. Hush, don't speak. I'm serious. There's a nonnegotiable supplies list in the back complete with prices and tax factored in. In two weeks, if you still want a pet, come back and talk to me. No more looking like your hopes and dreams have been crushed by a rampaging herd of near-extinct rhinoceroses; this is about an animal's life and comfort, not anyone's hurt feelings. It's not personal or anything."

When the kid continues to look dejected, Harinder shoves the care sheet at his chest, cheeks heating. "Just take it. If you come back in two weeks, I'll let you hold one, okay?"

"Can I see which one is the gecko?"

"Leopard gecko," Harinder corrects because they also have cresteds, and then, "Sure. This tank has the juveniles, and there are two adult females the other one." Before Harinder set up the 125-gallon tank in the front for the hermit crabs, he was forced to sell the juveniles before they matured enough to cause problems with the others. Now he's gleefully able to hold on to his favorites.

He waits generously as the guy stares in wonder as a tangerine juvenile sips from his water bowl. "How much is that one?"

"We'll talk about pricing once you've done your reading," Harinder says firmly, taking the opportunity to physically manhandle the stack of papers into the kid's hand. "Now get out of my store."

Then, to his absolute horror, the tweaker wraps his lanky arms around Harinder's stiff shoulders in a crushingly tight hug. He smells like weed, body odor, and... lemon curd? The fuck. "Thanks, friend," he says, sporting a lopsided grin.

"You can thank me by leaving," Harinder says, taking deep breaths as he tries to push the kid away. He's going to leave cooties on his favorite sweater, and Harinder's blood pressure shoots up at the thought.

Finally, the guy makes the bell go ding, but before Harinder can relax, a voice calls his name from behind him.

"Harinder?"

Shit.

"Um, yes, Mr. Kulkarni?"

Harinder's boss usually doesn't come out of the office. He enters through the back door, does paperwork for a few hours a week, then leaves, often without talking to Harinder, unless he's done something wrong. Today, Harinder hadn't even heard him enter.

Ajit Kulkarni, who owns Aquariums & More, is a medium height, stocky Indian man who looks exactly like the kind of person who would throw all his free time into making glass boxes for a living. Most of his money is made through his custom tank commissions; the store was more of a formality to get his business off the ground.

"I was looking through some of your order forms. You haven't ordered tree frogs in three months."

"We haven't sold any," Harinder says, glancing in the direction of the herp tanks as if he can see through the multiple shelves in front of them. "If I ordered more, the tank would be overcrowded. Sir."

"Overall animal sales are down ten percent from last holiday season. I received a call from the animal shelter yesterday, asking when we'd need more adoptees. When was the last time a cat actually left this store?"

"People would rather get free kittens from their irresponsible cousin-in-law than pay to adopt adult cats in need of homes," Harinder grumbles. "That's not my fault."

"No, it's not, but— Why is the sign off the hermit crab tank again?"

"It keeps falling," Harinder says quickly, glancing at the enclosure. "I was just about to make a new one, sir." If that pathetic drugged-up white kid hadn't distracted him he would have heard Mr. Kulkarni walk in and had time to return the sign to its place.

Mr. Kulkarni inspects him critically. Although Harinder's been the best pet care associate this store has ever had (in Harinder's own opinion), he mostly got the job because Mr. Kulkarni felt bad for him.

At the time he was living on under-the-table cash from a shitty delivery company—the only place that would hire him after he escaped foster care. During a particularly disastrous delivery mix-up, in which Mr. Kulkarni's pad Thai had been replaced by two Double Whoppers, Harinder had broken down in tears in front of the man. Normally that would be the point where someone told him to get the fuck away, but instead, Mr. Kulkarni asked if he needed a better job. The pay is only a bit over minimum wage, but he's full-time with benefits, so he doesn't complain.

"Fish sales are doing good," Mr. Kulkarni says finally. "Try to get those ferrets sold. I'm sick of the way they smell."

"I'll try, Mr. Kulkarni."

Then he's gone, and Harinder lets out a whoosh of air, stumbling back to cashwrap so he can sit down.

It's not that he doesn't want people to have pets. Rather, he hates seeing animals go to bad homes. It was two years ago when he started. Back then the store was still carrying birds. He sold a parakeet to someone who, three hours later, attempted to return it because they left the tote in a hot car and the poor thing died. It was one of several traumatizing events that established his new life's purpose of refusing to let a single animal through the doors without unerring assurance they would be properly cared for.

Also, well. He just can't stand seeing them go.

"Speaking of ferrets," he says to himself. Their cage needs to be cleaned.

Harinder is bent over a garbage bag full of used paper bedding with a harnessed ferret running across his shoulders when the dreaded bell alerts him to the arrival of yet another customer. He doesn't move to greet them because he's fucking busy, and they can help their own self; if they need something, he's making enough noise, and they can ask like an adult. Footsteps walk up behind him, then stop. He waits for a voice, but all he gets is silence.

The ferret starts rummaging through his hair, trying to locate an ear to chew on.

"Popcorn, quit it," he says, rising and plucking the furry troublemaker off his shoulder.

"What's with you and these dumbass pet names?" someone asks. "Like, I assume you're the one who thought it was a good idea to name a cat Edwina."

Chapter Three

Harinder Ferrets Out a Plan

Already scowling, Harinder spins around and is met with the sight of a white boy in a Teenage Mutant Ninja Turtles hoodie. He's not white as in Anglo-anything; he's bedsheet-white, albino with colorless hair, wide gray eyes, and Afrocentric features. A thick white Afro hangs low on his forehead.

In his hand is a heavily water damaged stack of paper.

"I finished your stupid form. Almost. I just need the ID number for the cat. Forgot to get it last time before I left."

It's not the first time someone has completed the form. Harinder's best friend, Sam, is the one who compiled material for the excessive questionnaire. It makes quite a formidable opponent, but some people are obtuse enough to not question why the number of dependents on their W-2 form is relevant to a cat adoption.

Still. Harinder remembers this guy from a week ago, and he looked pretty pissed when he left. Harinder was certain he'd managed to gently convince the customer to take his business elsewhere.

No such luck.

Harinder sneers. "Forgetting the information on the cat you wanted is exactly the kind of responsible behavior

I look for when adopting out an animal. How did you know."

"I didn't forget shit," he says. "Her name is Dumpling." He holds out the adoption form like proof, and when Harinder checks, all the information on her is correct except for the identification, which, technically, was Harinder's job to fill out.

Harinder snatches the form from—looks like...Jericho Adams? And he has the audacity to complain about Harinder's naming habits—Jericho's hand and walks around to the entrance behind the counter, shoving the squirming ferret under one arm as he goes.

The swinging door bumps into the edge of the ferret pen where Lucille and Tomas are resting and trying to chew through the bars, respectively. After distractedly unclipping the leash from Popcorn's harness and returning Popcorn to the others, Harinder edges around the large pen until he can reach the file cabinet. He barely manages to wrangle the thick adoption binder from the drawer in the limited space, but triumphs at last. Slamming the binder onto the counter, Harinder proceeds to dig for Dumpling's file. When he locates it, he pens her number in on Jericho's form, then shoves the wad of badly wrinkled pages into the binder, snaps it shut, and jams it inside the file cabinet.

"We'll review your responses and call you back with the results in two to four weeks," he says blandly, dipping down to scoop Lucille into his arms so he can tickle her adorable sleepy belly.

Jericho's face flickers through several not-quite-expressions. "Two to four weeks? Dude. I can't wait that long."

"Then go somewhere else," Harinder says, hoping he will. He likes Dumpling. He doesn't like Jericho.

"How many customers do you get a day? Why can't you look at it right now?"

His jaw clenches, the back of his neck prickling with anger. "Because my manager needs to look through the form before I can continue with the adoption process, and he isn't here every day." It's true, too, though Mr. Kulkarni would take five minutes to approve the adoption and technically doesn't know about the form of doom anyway...

"Okay, so why doesn't that take a week? Maximum."

"He's on vacation," Harinder blurts out, face turning red. Lucille squirms in his grip, which he loosens apologetically.

Jericho seems to sag after that, running his fingers over his hair. "Shit."

Harinder is about to spin the least sympathetic response he can muster when there's a sudden clatter behind him. He whirls around to see two ferrets blinking in surprise after their combined efforts to scale the side of the pen managed to undo the closure linking the panels together, loosened when Harinder accidentally bumped into it. The panel hangs open, resting where it banged against the swinging counter door, and then there's only one ferret.

Harinder manages to scoop Popcorn into his free hand, but Tomas is already under the door and out of cashwrap, bolting like an employee trying not to be crushed by a wave of overzealous Black Friday shoppers. Harinder looks around frantically, but his hands are full with two other ferrets, and he has no idea what to do.

"He's right there," Jericho says, pointing down aisle two.

"Where?"

"He's, look— Shit!"

Harinder bursts out from behind the cashwrap, narrowly missing Jericho as he runs past. Jericho reaches the aisle before Harinder does, his hands raised halfway into the air like he's trying to catch a bird instead of something that only stands an inch or two off the floor.

The only thing Harinder can think of to say is, "Be careful! Their bones are very fucking delicate; you could crush him!"

He hurries after Jericho, still clutching Popcorn and Lucille. He arrives just in time to see Tomas disappear under one of the shelves.

"Shit, oh god," Harinder says, dropping to his knees and trying to peer under the very large unit in hopes of finding one very small ferret. It's impossible to see through the shadows and thick layers of unswept dust, and to make matters worse, he can't stand up with both of his hands preoccupied with the other two ferrets.

"Here," Jericho says, and Harinder blinks up to see the Ninja Turtles hoodie half unzipped and held open in front of him. Absurdly, his only thought is that he can't believe this idiot is wearing a tank top in November. Then he shoves Lucille and Popcorn into the pocket made by Jericho's sweatshirt and only stays long enough to see Jericho zip it up to trap them inside before he books it into aisle three to frantically search for his loose charge.

"Tomas," he cajoles. "Come on you stupid shitting troublemaker, come to Hari. You really don't want to be lost in here, where someone clumsy and terrible could step on you and break your awful little adorably bendy spine. Come on, please don't— Ah!"

Tomas is halfway up the screened front of a chameleon cage, but he gets spooked and scurries off as Harinder approaches. He attempts to wriggle his way between the bird food bins.

"No no no! Don't do that!" The bins are heavy, difficult to move, and there are surely fucktons of dust and spiders behind them. Wrangling him out of that area would be near impossible.

Tomas rounds to the right, making a beeline for the gap between the fish tanks and the freezer, but before he can get his nose into the space, a flat object intercepts his progress, blocking him from his escape route and giving Harinder the precious seconds needed to sweep Tomas into his weak and trembling arms.

Jericho coolly returns the lid to a tub of dog treats, his left arm wrapped protectively around two writhing lumps under the fabric of his hoodie. He looks suspiciously calm, not even breathing hard. "Anything else?" he asks after a moment.

Harinder stares down at Tomas, covered in dust bunnies and cobwebs but otherwise safe in his hands, and resists the urge to scream and/or cry.

"What's all the shouting for?"

"Mr. Kulkarni! I, uh." Harinder shoots a nervous glance at Jericho, who is staring at him oddly. His face goes hot. "I didn't realize you were still...here..."

"I'm going to be away for a few days, so I need to get the orders sent in today, so they'll arrive on time next week," Mr. Kulkarni says.

It takes every single ounce of strength Harinder has to not start relief-sobbing on the spot. He forces a weak, triumphant half-smile. "Right. Well, before you go, I have a favor to ask..."

"Yes, ask away, but you still haven't told me what the noise was."

Jericho takes that moment to unzip his hoodie, catching a ferret in each hand and holding them both up like a sacrifice to the sun god. "Uh, not to interrupt, but what can I do with these?"

Mr. Kulkarni blinks. "Is this young man buying the ferrets?"

"No!" Harinder shouts, then clears his throat. "No, he just. Helped me catch them."

"Catch them?"

"One got out," Jericho says, gesturing with Lucille toward the one still curled against Harinder's chest. Her lower body flops obligingly with the movement.

"Give that to me," grumbles Harinder, loading his arms up with all three precious terrors and carrying them over to the mostly clean cage.

He pointedly ignores Mr. Kulkarni thanking Jericho for his help while he carefully wipes every single inch of dust from Tomas's fur. He's nervous about what Jericho will say to Mr. Kulkarni. Harinder's well aware that he pushes the boundaries of acceptability, but he is also extremely careful to ensure the worst of it never reaches Mr. Kulkarni's notice.

He doesn't know whether it's because he's more scared of losing his job or looking like he's taking advantage of Mr. Kulkarni's trust. It's probably some combination of both, which would then be overshadowed by fear of what would happen to all the animals without him there to care for them.

Upon hearing his name, Harinder flinches, then squints warily past the ferret cage.

"What was it you wanted to ask me?" Mr. Kulkarni enquires.

"Oh." Harinder latches the cage good and tight, then lets himself behind the cashwrap, avoiding the still-splayed panels of the ferret pen as he navigates over to the file cabinet. The drawer is still open, adoption binder sticking out awkwardly. "I was hoping you'd look over this adoption form before you left..." Before walking onto the sales floor with the disaster of a form, he quietly rips the bottom ten pages straight off the staple and drops them all in the trash.

Normally, he puts the entire thing in the trash, only noting down the phone number to call so he can tell the person they've been rejected. This time, he feels he owes it to Jericho, after what just happened, to give him at least a tiny glimmer of hope before Harinder brings down the ultimate, final "hell-the-fuck no."

As expected, Mr. Kulkarni scans the first page of the form in about twenty-five seconds tops and doesn't even bother looking at the second page before he hands the form back. "Looks good to me. If you have everything under control, I'll be going back to the office. I have to be out of here and on a plane by five o'clock."

"Have a good trip, Mr. Kulkarni," Harinder says to his already retreating boss.

The back door closes, and the store descends into silence.

"So," says Jericho.

"I'll call you with information on the second part of the adoption process before the end of the week," Harinder says begrudgingly.

Jericho's face twitches, but only a little. "What? There's more?"

Harinder snorts. Almost laughs, but not quite. "You bet your stupid Ninja Turtles hoodie there's more. You need to call and set up an interview."

"What more could you possibly need to know?"

"The interview," Harinder says, absently picking at his nail polish, "will focus more on husbandry and the individual feline's needs rather than suitability. We've determined you're capable of being a good caretaker, but I still have to decide whether or not you'd be a good match for Dumpling, specifically."

Jericho is silent for at least half a minute, then says, "Fuck you, man."

The only reason Harinder allows himself to smile is because he's confident there's no way of interpreting it as a nice smile, under any conceivable context or from any physically possible angle. He brushes the dust from the day's chase off his sweater and steps behind the counter, then throws the rest of the adoption form away. He doesn't care if Jericho sees.

The bell jingles, and someone walks through the door.

"Hi there, welcome to Aquariums & More." Harinder turns from Jericho, hoping he feels properly dismissed. He even puts on his fakest customer service voice—just to rub salt into the wound. "Can I help you find anything today?"

Instead of simply leaving, Jericho slides one lanky arm through the swinging door, reaching just far enough to retrieve his discarded form from the trash bin. He keeps Jericho in his peripheral vision as he tells the woman information on pricing for custom tanks and stand options. Before he's finished, Jericho walks around the corner and slides the rumpled paper over to him, now folded in half. The door chimes once, and he's gone.

Harinder spends the next quarter hour helping the woman debate between getting a tank tailored exactly to her space availability or rearranging her entire living room to accommodate an existing model. She thanks him and leaves without making a decision. He wanders back to the counter and idly picks up the abandoned adoption form, now sporting a few greasy fingerprints.

He's halfway to returning it to the trash when he notices writing on the back, inside the fold, and curiously opens it to reveal the back of the paper.

"i fucking hate you," it reads, followed by a list of weekdays with availability scribbled beside each one. Harinder huffs a barely audible laugh, folds the paper, and shoves it in the still-open drawer of the file cabinet.

Chapter Four

Jericho's Sincerity Is Not Very Sincere at All

Every instinct Jericho has tells him he shouldn't be putting up with this shit, and yet here he is, jamming the jack for his shitty brand-name earbuds into his phone while his feet approach his shoes in a similar fashion. The back portion of one shoe gets stuck under his heel, and he trips trying to adjust without taking the shoe off, but if no one is around to see it, did it really happen?

The reason Jericho needs a cat so bad is complicated. He really didn't mean to let his sister's cat out the back door when he burst inside. Yes, Shiloh had told him to be careful coming in because Mephi (short for Mephistopheles) was an escape artist. She had recently changed him from indoor/outdoor to exclusively indoor after reading something about songbird deaths, and Mephi wasn't happy about it.

Jericho should have been more careful, the fact that he was wildly excited about meeting the latest Patreon goal for his webcomic notwithstanding.

His computer bleeps at him, plaintive. Longing. His followers are pissed that he cut his usual livestream short, and unless he churns out some solid fanservice, he's going to be hearing about it.

Thing is, it's not his fault. He wrote down his availability for the adoption interview, but when Harinder called him back (finally), he said the only time he had available was at the ass end of Jericho's weekly Thursday stream and blandly reminded him he was welcome to void out his application and find a cat elsewhere if he couldn't make it.

It's a lie. It's obviously a lie. Jericho isn't quite creepy enough to stalk the company's weekly traffic, but he knows there's plenty of downtime during the average work day at Aquariums & More, and Harinder probably selected a time that interfered with Jericho's schedule just to test him.

Which is the problem.

Yes, Jericho could give up and go to Petco. Yes, he could be defeated by some shitty retail pawn with a bad attitude. Or, he could step up to the plate and catch every damn curveball Harinder throws at him. Jericho wants to beat Harinder at his own game. Jericho wants to *win*.

Also, sunk-cost investment is a whole bitch.

He slings a jacket over his shoulders and pulls a red knit beanie over his ears. It's getting a bit cold to wear just a hoodie, and besides...his TMNT one hasn't smelled the same since the last time he was at the pet store. Jericho is pretty sure one of the ferrets peed on it, but he hasn't yet gotten desperate enough to do laundry, so. Jacket.

He puts his computer to sleep and leaves his apartment in blissful silence for about thirty seconds until his phone catches the next alert and pings. Jericho sighs and meanders out to the bus stop, at which point he silences his phone and refuses to succumb to despair.

Aquariums & More's glaring storefront gleams at him like a bad omen: a beacon promising naught but unpleasantness and discomfort. Somewhere in that greasy exterior is a heart full of warm, fluffy cats, and it is guarded by a pissy five-foot-tall dragon who has a vendetta against combs.

Jericho makes a point to approach the front from an angle, avoiding the demon-infested trash can. The chime of the door opening is becoming a physical manifestation of Jericho's pride and sanity coursing down the drain, but it's cool. It's not like talking to Shiloh is any different—or not talking, as it were. After Mephi ran out the door, a black cat into a black night, Jericho had spent several hours looking for him, to no avail.

His humiliated apologies fell on unwelcome ground. At three in the morning, when he was still panicking about Mephi's disappearance, Shiloh finally told him to go home. The sharpness in her voice shredded him like junk mail. He texted her begging her forgiveness, not trusting her terse, *It's fine*. Of course it wasn't fine.

Shiloh's responses dwindled to nothing, and when Jericho finally passed out, he woke up to a curt text from Shiloh's fiancée, Layla.

> *Shiloh doesn't want to hear about it anymore. Stop messaging or I'm going to block you.*

The fact that his sister abandoned him over a fucking cat weighs on his chest like an anchor, but he can't do anything about it. What's done is done. His only hope now is to get her a replacement friend by her birthday on December thirteenth. It's drawing dangerously close to the end of November, so Jericho has to get this Dumpling situation squared away, like now.

When he steps in, he sees absolutely no one, and an eerie sense of déjà vu settles over him, but Jericho is getting the impression this is pretty normal for the business's aesthetic.

"Hey," he says, loud enough to be heard through the empty aisles barely visible behind the heavily cluttered cashwrap.

"Back here," calls a voice in response. Jericho follows it to the reptile unit. He sees the giant, electric-blue lizard first, then Harinder, looking completely natural crouched over an open tank with a dinosaur lounging on his shoulder.

"Do you have a thing for making me chase down your merchandise or something? Because I'm not fucking with the large reptile market. I did a whole report in middle school about the ways a Komodo dragon can fuck a person's shit up."

"This is an iguana," Harinder says, pulling his arms out from the large tank and wiping his hands on his jeans. "And Machiavelli would never bolt like that."

Jericho almost snorts. "You and those names, man."

He watches as Harinder pulls the iguana carefully from his back and sets it on his lap, patting its flat head in front of the trail of spines that extends down its back. Eventually, Harinder eases the reptile, who seems rather reluctant about the affair, back into its enclosure.

"Not that finding out you're a reptile whisperer isn't fascinating, but I'm kind of on a schedule here." He really isn't. He doesn't have anything to do today aside from appeasing his followers for the earlier slight. They may pay his bills, but they sure as fuck are demanding as hell about it. Harinder doesn't need to know that though.

"How am I supposed to believe you'll have availability for a cat if you can't wait five minutes? Pets are not predictable. What will you do about vet visits?"

Harinder locks the enclosure then stands up, frowning. Jericho gets distracted thinking about how

Harinder's been wearing that same mustard-yellow sweater every time he's seen him. He wonders if the guy ever switches it up, maybe to a less grating color.

"I'll schedule cat stuff in," he says, even though it's a lie because the cat isn't going to be his. He somehow doubts Harinder will be receptive to the "gift" part of acquiring Dumpling, so he conveniently leaves it out. "Right now, I don't have a cat, so it isn't on the menu. Funny thing about menus, though, is they can change. They evolve. I don't eat Kraft mac 'n' cheese all day every day just because I made four things of Easy Mac one Sunday night when I lost control of my life."

Harinder contemplates him. "That was more information than I ever needed to know. Follow me."

Jericho does, but when Harinder steps behind the counter, he pauses, then goes around the front to the register.

Harinder doesn't seem to notice until he looks up and doesn't see Jericho around. "Are you capable of following basic instructions?" he asks acerbically, inspecting Jericho over a box of cat toys. "Get over here."

Reluctantly, Jericho shuffles back the way he came and steps through the swinging door, letting it fall behind him. It catches his thighs on the backswing because he didn't step away quickly enough, but Harinder is too busy arranging a foldout chair to notice, so Jericho doesn't make any indication that it happened.

"Are you always here alone?" Jericho wonders, more acutely noticing the lack of other employees or even a manager to watch the front while Harinder performs the interview.

"Customers happen," Harinder says.

"Yeah, no shit. Where are your coworkers?"

Harinder frowns at nothing, then plops into a beaten-up desk chair. He tucks his short-ass legs onto the end of the chair and balances a notebook on his knees. "Don't have any. Sit down. This is about your shitty life, not mine."

"Wow," Jericho says, settling himself in his place much more coolly. "How do you get away with insulting customers as often as you do? Genuine question."

"So, your application says you're twenty years old. Is that true, Mr. Adams?"

Um. "Um. Yes?"

Harinder squints at the notebook, then squints at Jericho. "Are you sure? You sound like you're thinking about it. Are you nervous?"

"Holy shit," Jericho says, running his fingers over his hair. "This is an adoption, not an interrogation. Yes, I'm twenty. My birthday is December twelfth. Do you need it described in graphic detail?"

"Moving on. In your own words, describe your motivation for adding a feline companion animal to your life."

Jericho pauses. A similar question had been on the application, but it's much easier to bullshit on paper. He doesn't really want a cat, but again, telling Harinder that he lost Shiloh's beloved pet and now has to find a replacement so she'll stop shunning him sounds like a one-way road to Denied-ville. Shit out of luck, out of gas, and out of sisterly companionship for the near and far future.

He's quiet, like he's seriously contemplating a good answer instead of panicking, and when he finally opens his mouth, all that comes out is, "I live alone."

Just when he's sure he blew it, something that looks suspiciously like understanding flickers across Harinder's face for a split second. He scratches something on his notebook, then moves on without another word on the subject. "What about Dumpling's care card made you think she'd be a good match for your household?"

Yet again, Jericho doesn't know how to answer. "I dunno, she was soft and kind of bitchy? It made me think of my sister."

Harinder's face is much less understanding this time around. "Are you taking this seriously at all?"

Jericho doesn't waste time thinking about it. "I think this is a crock of shit, to be honest. I don't need to offer some philosophical breakdown of why I want a cat, or why I want one cat in particular above the other equally nice cats. I don't have any roommates or other pets. I know how to put food and water into bowls. I know how to jiggle a string. There's literally nothing else I can say. I'm not going to engage in some quasi-intellectual horseshit just to prove to you I've thought hard enough about the reality of courting a creature that shits in a box seven days out of the week.

"Do you need to know where in my apartment I'd keep that box? Because I actually don't know the answer to that, and maybe *that* would be a useful thing to ask me, instead of whatever-the-fuck you're currently doing."

Sputtering, Harinder growls back, "These are important compatibility questions—"

"No. They're not." Jericho continues, careless about interrupting him. "That's the thing. Here, let me save you some time. I work at home. I don't go out much, and all my friends are online. If this cat needs any amount of love and support, I will be there to provide it. I will nurture the fuck out of her. I don't sleep very deeply because I have nightmares, so if she starts howling at two AM, I'll deal with it. I have enough disposable income to provide her with a cat castle and whatever fancy-ass specialty food you recommend. My apartment only has one bedroom, but it's pretty big, so if she's one of those cats who do that manic run-around-for-no-reason thing, she's got plenty of space to not accidentally hit any walls or whatever. I'll let her sleep in my bed."

He pauses. "If she wants to, I guess."

Jericho clears his throat and shoves his hands into his pockets, head dipping down so he can study the stitching on his pants. "So there's that. Anything I missed?"

Harinder stares at him like he just confessed to being made of playdough, or born into a family of ostriches, or having a fetish for fucking the exhaust pipe on strangers' cars. Without looking away, Harinder grips the corner of the page he was writing on and slowly tears it from the rest of the book. He crumples it in his hand, then tosses it across the small cashwrap space into a trashcan. Despite Harinder not sighting anything, it goes in, which is surprisingly...cool. For a dork like him.

Still not talking, Harinder sets his chin on his knees and inspects his fingernails critically. It looks like the black has been repainted, though it's horribly messy, especially on his right hand. Finally, he drops his hand to his side, and frowns at Jericho over the tops of his knees.

"If that's all the information you want to provide, then I think we can consider this interview finished."

"Cool."

"You can go now," Harinder adds, finally looking away.

Jericho does similarly. "Cool." He stands up, brushes invisible dust from his thighs, and turns to leave.

"Don't put the litterbox near where you keep the food." Harinder hasn't moved and is now studiously avoiding eye contact. "I shouldn't have to explain why something might not want to eat right by where it shits."

"I'll keep it in mind," Jericho says absently, giving Harinder a weird look. "Does this mean you're letting me have the cat, or."

"No," Harinder says aggressively, shooting out of his chair. "It means that if you do get a cat, maybe from here, maybe from somewhere else, at least now you know where to put the box. When someone helps you with something, the polite response is to say thank you."

Jericho snorts at the thought of this loser, of all people, giving tips on etiquette. "Thanks, man. When do I get my, uh, results?"

Harinder scratches the back of his neck. "I'll call you. I have to go over my notes with my manager."

"You threw your notes away."

"I'll make new ones."

"Need me to stick around?"

"No. God, no. Please continue to leave."

Jericho only half obliges. He does exit the cashwrap, wandering around the length of the counter and noting the dust on some of the box tops. It's weird. Many areas of the store are run-down and filthy, contrasting severely with the obsessively manicured animal enclosures. He passes the exit on his right, tracking two fingers through the dust covering the far corner of the counter, right across from the immaculate ferret cage. Jericho wipes his hand on his pants, then jams it against the grate to see if he can entice any of the weird cat snakes to come near him.

"What are you doing?" Harinder asks. "Why are you still here?"

Although he knows they all have names, Jericho can't tell them apart, but one does eventually walk over to chew on his fingers. It doesn't hurt enough to bother him, so he doesn't take his hand away. "This is a public place," he offers blandly. "I have as much right to be here as you do."

"Incorrect," says Harinder, but Jericho ignores him, pulling out his phone with his free hand.

"Okay, so. It's the eleventh. It took you over a week last time to contact me. Obviously, genius can't be rushed, so I won't expect results by tomorrow."

Confusion fills Harinder's face. He was obviously expecting an insult, but Jericho likes to keep people on their toes.

"Then there's the weekend, which usually isn't included in the typical 'response zone' for business days, so we'll give you that too. Monday, eh, you're shitty and tired from the weekend. I get it. Tuesday though." Jericho clicks out from the calendar app and sets his phone down. "I think I can reasonably request details on the nature of my fate by Tuesday. Deal?"

"Not a deal," Harinder growls.

Jericho raises a hand to silence him. "Or I can hit up your boss, unless he's still on vacation." Harinder closes his mouth. He looks genuinely afraid, which prompts Jericho to generously add: "Look, I'm not trying to get you in trouble. I'm just trying to adopt a fuckin' cat, and if you need to drag me through some annoying and frankly nonsensical hell gauntlet before you're comfortable entrusting me with the care of furry sentient life, fine, but at least be timely about it."

The plan is to give Harinder some processing time before driving the final nail through the coffin, but Jericho's rapid-fire one-liner selection is interrupted by a curt, "Fine. I'll call you by Tuesday."

Jericho blinks. He hadn't actually expected that to work. A thrill runs the length of his spine when he realizes he just managed to counter Harinder's bullshit. Yes, Jericho Adams has conquered the first level of Retail Hell. He is that much closer to winning.

"Will you leave now? I have shit to do, Adams."

"Don't swear in front of customers," Jericho says absently, watching the ferret paw at the cage bars as he withdraws his by now well-chewed flesh.

"Don't tell me what to fu—" Harinder clears his throat. "You're not my boss."

"Yeah, okay." Jericho stuffs his hand into his pocket and walks back around to the front of the counter. "I'll talk to you on Tuesday, then."

"Yeah."

"Looking forward to it," he adds, resisting the urge to smirk a little.

"I can't say the same," Harinder sneers, but it seems halfhearted. He knows he's lost, or at least Jericho's projection of his hypothetical internal monologue knows he lost.

It doesn't really matter, because Jericho knows the truth. That comfort alone gets his ass out the door and to the bus stop without any more nasty quips or pointed barbs. Harinder put up a good fight and has earned the luxury of being able to recuperate before what will hopefully be their last interaction.

Chapter Five

Jericho, Uh...Gets Hit by a Bus

Jericho spends the bus ride musing about Harinder's weird and defensive behavior regarding the care of the animals, halfway wondering if there's a reason for it while simultaneously not wanting to become creepily invested in other people's personal issues. Despite his hesitation, Jericho is buried so deeply in thought he doesn't notice the fire hydrant coming up on his side until the bus has already swerved into it.

There are some details about a biker and a wayward smart car that float down the line of bus passengers, but Jericho is mostly dazed after having been thrown against the seat in front of his. Nothing feels broken, and after a few minutes, his brain returns to a somewhat solid state that allows for rational thought.

His first thought is to call Shiloh and ask her to take him to urgent care to make sure he doesn't have a concussion or whiplash or a severed spine. His second thought is, *What the fuck.*

There's no phone in his pocket.

Jericho runs through his recent memory, but he doesn't need to go back that far. He's betting on it being right where he left it—on top of the damn ferret cage when he was squaring off with Harinder.

Fuck.

A sensible person would borrow someone's phone to call a cab, but Jericho is far more antisocial than most people realize. He's no Harinder, but stripping away the guy's overt hostility might expose a similarly vulnerable fleshy filling.

Jericho's head is mostly clear by the time he starts making his way to the bus exit, only stumbling a bit. The bus driver asks him if he's alright, but he needs to escape. Jericho doesn't remember saying it, but he must have because next thing he knows, there's cold almost-winter air hitting him in the face. Just in time, too, because the flashing lights of a police vehicle begin to flicker in his peripheral, and the scream of an ambulance siren seems close. Fight-or-flight response triggered, Jericho forces himself to put as much distance between himself and the crash as possible, one step at a time—stiff, ow, pain, head spinning, okay, okay, okay.

It takes him twice as long as it should. He might have spent twenty minutes asleep on a bench, but by the time Jericho gets back to the layer of hell that captured his poor phone, he feels fine. Sore, but fine. So maybe his head hurts? Whatever. He'll get his phone, call...someone. Yeah.

What happens next is obscured in confusion when Jericho looks through the grime and sees Harinder with a customer, looking...not unhappy? Not full of hatred? What?

There's an animal carrier on the counter next to where Harinder is setting a sheet of paper—just one, Jericho can't help but note. He's stunned, because some facts are universal, and the pet store employee's bad mood was supposed to be one of those things, and he just got hit by a bus (kind of), and now he feels lied to.

It could be the closed-head injury talking, but shh.

Harinder doesn't look concerned when he hears the door, but upon seeing Jericho, he balks. "What the fuck are *you* doing back?"

"Forgot my phone," Jericho says, looking around as if he doesn't know exactly where it is. "What's going on? I thought you were physically incapable of contorting your facial muscles into anything that in any way resembled a smile."

"I wasn't smiling—" Harinder begins, which would be hilariously defensive considering the accusation was "being pleasant for once," but his protest is cut into by a loud yowl, and that's when Jericho notices the Asian girl standing across the counter from Harinder.

To clarify: The girl didn't produce the yowl, but she does respond to it by pressing her nose up against the box. which Jericho had forgotten about. She shoves her finger in one of the holes and purrs, "There, there, Mister Charles! It's okay. You'll be out of the box soon."

"It's *Sir* Charles," Harinder corrects without hesitation. His eyes flick to Jericho a moment later.

He suddenly understands.

"Y'know," Jericho says, forced casual, "When someone adopts an animal, they usually get to pick what they're going to name it."

Harinder at first looks ashamed and then looks indignant. "Yeah, well. Some people actually care about their pet's comfort zone and realize that familiarity—"

"Are you accusing me of not caring? Is that what this is about?"

Charles's new owner stares between each boy curiously, momentarily distracted. It's pretty pathetic to be emoting about cats in front of a stranger—or anyone, really—but Jericho just got slammed into a plastic bus seat, so he's feeling a bit keyed up.

"I seriously hoped it'd be obvious I give a shit by now after all the fuckshit you've put me through—"

"I'm going to sign this," the girl says, not quite interrupting. She reaches over and grabs the pen from Harinder's fist. His brown skin had gone white with how hard he was clenching it. She scribbles something on the paper he'd presented before Jericho barged in. "Anything else I have to do?" She glances at Jericho under her eyelashes before looking back to Harinder.

"No," Harinder says, sounding strangled. "You're all set, Mint."

"Thanks! I'll bring pictures!" She lifts the box containing Sir Charles from the counter, blows Harinder a kiss, and avoids looking at Jericho as she slides around him and out the door.

Ding!

The store descends into silence.

"If I wasn't at least ninety percent sure you had no idea who I was before I came in here the first time," Jericho says, "I'd think this was personal."

"It's not—"

The door opens behind Jericho. He steps aside quickly and is unprepared for the headrush that follows. A short, reedy man shuffles around him, not sparing so much as a glance, and makes his way to the counter.

"I need one hundred large crickets," he informs Harinder, who grunts as a way of response and exits cashwrap, leaving Jericho standing with the strange man in the front of the store.

Jericho takes a few steps backward, then disappears around the ferret cage, slithering through an aisle and around the back so he comes up on Harinder from behind.

His voice is a hissing whisper. "What exactly is your fucking problem?"

Harinder looks startled but recovers quickly. He's funneling some truly massive insects into a clear plastic bag, face scrunched, presumably counting them as they fall. "I don't have a problem. You're the one getting possessive over a cat adoption. Possessiveness is a precursor to abusive behavior within a relationship. You should see someone about that."

"Thanks, Dr. Phil. I'll keep it in mind." Jericho crosses his arms and leans against the door to the back room, acting like he doesn't care. He doesn't. He just wants his sister to talk to him again, is all, and he lowkey wants to defeat Harinder at whatever game he's playing. There's no way Jericho is invested in getting a cat, and this is not being interpreted by his brain as a personal injury. As far as Jericho knows, Harinder and Mint could be long-time friends who'd had this arranged for a while.

Then again, Harinder doesn't seem like the "friend" type.

"Not that it's any of your business," Harinder says in a savage voice that is trying to be a whisper but failing, "but Mint was far ahead of you in the adoption process. She already filled the requirements and everything."

"What requirements?" Jericho asks, exasperated. He's still managing to keep his voice much lower than Harinder's. "You've never told me what's expected of me. It's all just some garbled clusterfuck where I'm stumbling around desperately trying to guess the right thing to say and do. If I wanted that kind of interaction, I'd become an actor on a high school drama where my abusive girlfriend could emotionally manipulate me to the delight of a socially unaware audience. It'd be great; I'm sure I'd make a lot of money and have a lot of fans, which is more than I can say about this situation."

He takes a moment to swallow before continuing. "It's been two weeks, and I don't even have a furry companion to comfort me as I grapple with despair and try to reconcile the scars from my past. I'm not asking you for your liver or your virginity or anything, just tell me what I have to do."

Harinder looks...stunned, and there's something else Jericho can't exactly parse. Before he can examine it, Harinder blurts out, "There's a community service requirement!"

Anything Jericho was prepared to say dies on his tongue. His tongue is now a literal and metaphorical graveyard. Bury everything he's said in his entire life in the fleshy wasteland that used to be his mouth. Jericho Adams may never produce sound again.

"Community service."

"Yyyyes."

"What. The."

"It's to make sure you're giving back to the community!"

"The cat community?"

Harinder rolls his eyes, dumping the crickets remaining in the funnel back into the bin before he ties up the bag with a rubber band. "We need to make sure you have an appropriate level of investment in contributing and enriching the lives of those around you! A pet is a serious commitment, and if you haven't had an animal companion before, you might not be as selfless as you think you are when push comes to shove. To avoid a situation in which a cat needs to be removed from their adoptive home, we require the would-be adoptive parent to provide documentation proving an investment in interests other than ones that directly and primarily benefit them!" Harinder finishes in a rush, face gone red.

He turns on his heel and stomps back up to the front of the store.

Jericho gives chase. "And, let me guess... This chick totally went with it and scrubbed a bunch of graffiti off government buildings or some shit? Just to get a cat?"

"As a matter of fact, Mint already had a diverse volunteer history, and pet experience. Her portfolio was much more rounded than yours."

"Fuckin' portfolio," Jericho repeats. "Is this me attempting to give a needy animal a loving place to call their own, or trying to get into some pretentious-ass Ivy League college?"

He'd forgotten about the cricket guy. The reedy man gives Jericho an odd look. Harinder manages to appear the exact combination of hassled and innocent necessary to exonerate himself from all blame; he slips back behind the counter and starts to ring the customer up, looking very much like he has nothing to do with Jericho's deranged rantings.

Not wanting to look like some intimidating Black dude harassing a helpless store employee (ha), Jericho about-faces and makes his way over to the fish wall, which he proceeds to study with distracted intensity. His head is starting to hurt, and the tropical fish swishing idly through the water serve as visual white noise, a filter for his polluted thoughts.

How invested is he in this? For what reasons?

Nothing's been hard for him for a while. He started his first webcomic when he was twelve, and by the time he turned eighteen, Jericho had a massive following and a

Patreon netting several hundred dollars every month. The original comic has been running for eight years, and while it became more involved over the years, the art growing more refined and unique, it's never been particularly difficult.

He turned up the heat on a few side projects, but competing with his own inferiority complex isn't exactly the best mental exercise.

Being social is pretty much Jericho's worst nightmare. He chats with a few regulars online, but he sorts them neatly into "followers" or "fellow professionals." His whole life is a pattern of pseudo-professionalism. Aside from Shiloh and Layla, he doesn't have actual friends.

There was Maxx—a childhood best friend he still chats with on occasion, but they've drifted significantly apart. Maxx goes to school. Jericho doesn't. When he left the mediocre, mid-sized Arkansas city where they grew up, Maxx stayed in the area for college. Now he's got finals and works at a legal office filing papers or something, and his Discord setting usually stays on Do Not Disturb.

So maybe Jericho's just feeling a little desperate now that his only tether to the real world has been snapped. Maybe that's why he's still entertaining Harinder's nonsense.

"Twenty hours," a voice says behind him.

Jericho spins around and nearly faints. He catches himself against the tanks, ignoring Harinder's weird look. He didn't even hear the other man leave. "What?"

"You need to sign off on twenty hours of community service," Harinder repeats.

"Are you shitting me?"

He frowns. "Do I look like I'm shitting you?"

It must be either the boredom or the loneliness because Jericho spends a good handful of seconds studying Harinder's face. Tired and stubborn is a given, but there's also this weird flavor of sincerity. Something inside Jericho demands to be free of this garbage, but he squashes it down. He's okay with losing this one for now. The universe is free to retroactively claim his earlier victory.

Right now, all Jericho wants is to stagger home and sleep for a week. "Is there anywhere specific I have to go? Any volunteer activities you don't accept?"

Harinder thinks about it. "No, not really. Just, you know." He shrugs.

"Gotcha. Alright. I'll get on that, I guess."

Nodding, Harinder steps back, looks at the crab tank, then returns his sulky gaze to Jericho. "Here's your phone," he says at last, holding it out.

"Thanks," Jericho answers neutrally. He accepts it and shoves it in his pocket. "I'm gonna go now."

"Cool," Harinder says and hurries to the cashwrap like a scared beetle.

"Cool," Jericho echoes before hurrying his own way past the counter and into the cold outside. Not knowing where else to go, he stumbles to the bus stop and sits on the bench for about five minutes, feeling numbed by more than the cold.

Then he calls for a fucking Uber, because to hell with that.

Chapter Six

Harinder Has a Complicated Relationship with Windows

"I'm sorry you think the price for Pedigree is too high, but that's the lowest-quality dog food we sell. Walmart probably has it cheaper because they have more lenient sell-by dates. Well, it's great that you've been feeding her that for nine years; congratulations on meeting the lowest quality of care for your companion animal. I'm sure she'd be thrilled to know that her lifetime of friendship and support was being repaid with the least possible effort on your part. Yes, you have a good day too."

Harinder slams the phone back into the stand, scowling down at the grody plastic. His quiet moment of hatred is interrupted by a good-natured voice saying, "Excuse me?"

For a moment, he feels exposed and a tiny bit embarrassed, but his resolve hardens. He's not ashamed about what he has to say; he'd tell it to someone's face if need be. Still, his nastiness is cautiously selective. A good customer gets good service. He doesn't want the business to go under. Still, when he offers a sheepish, "How can I help you?" the customer only smiles.

She's a familiar old woman, though he doesn't recall her name. "Could I get one hundred small comets, please?"

Peering through the bins at the tanks, Harinder responds, "I don't think I have that much in there. I could probably do sixty. Is that okay?"

"Oh, yes. I'll just come back. When's your shipment due?"

"Wednesdays are our live-animal delivery," he says, making his way over to the feeder tanks.

She casts her eyes down at her phone. "That's only two days from now. I'll come then from now on, so I can get enough." Harinder is quick about netting all the available fish, minus a few that escape by hiding in the corners. "You can stop at fifty. I wouldn't want to leave you with nothing."

Harinder pauses, then resumes counting, plopping each fish into the specimen cup with a silent apology. When he's reached the desired quantity, he bags the fish quickly and meets the lady at the counter.

"That'll be seven dollars and ninety-five cents," Harinder says before he's even gotten to the register. He's got the prices of most common quantities memorized— like ten and twelve, fifteen, twenty- and thirty-five, up to one hundred and thirty-three—because there's a customer who comes in and orders twenty dollars' worth of smalls, which usually means Harinder has to dip into the backstock tank early, or sell out both minnows and goldfish, depending on what day the guy decides to show up.

The lady reaches into her purse, and Harinder takes the time to key the order into the register. "What're you feeding?" he asks as a reflex, not remembering whether she's told him before or not.

"Convicts, mostly," she says, pulling out a ten-dollar bill.

Pausing as he accepts it, Harinder muses, "That's a lot of fish for a smaller cichlid. They get vegetables too, right?"

Unsolicited advice on animal husbandry is not always appreciated—not that that stops Harinder from offering it—but the lady's smile grows brighter. "I breed convicts as a hobby; feeders are only half of their diet, but I still need quite a few. One hundred goldfish lasts my adults about two weeks, once you include my flowerhorn and Jack Dempsey. Those I don't breed; they're just for fun."

"Oh," Harinder says, not unimpressed. "Will fifty be enough for your fish? I could get the rest, or, uh, there's a Petco down the street."

She lets out a small, exaggerated shriek of what Harinder can only assume is horror, and then giggles. "You would never catch me buying fish from one of those places." She says *"those places"* like it's a bad word, her laugh-lined mouth tilted conspiratorially.

"I live just past the intersection by that strip mall," she explains, accepting when Harinder mutely hands her the change, "but I drive all the way out here to get my feeders. You don't have to worry about getting any more; my babies aren't that greedy. I'll be back on Wednesday."

"Thank you for your business," he replies, not sure what else to say.

Tucking the bag of fish against her chest, the woman winks with one starry green eye. "Thank you for keeping the healthiest and best cared for feeder fish out of any pet store in the county. I swear, your feeder tanks are cleaner than my breeders."

Harinder tosses a look at the fish wall, as if he doesn't know that he scrubs the walls of each tank every other morning, in addition to weekly spot cleaning with a toothbrush in corners and over ornaments. By the time he remembers what he was doing, the bell has already chimed, and there's nothing to see but a tan coat disappearing behind the sign-covered door.

Reflecting on the encounter puts him in a strangely charitable mood through the remainder of the morning, but all good things must pass, and happiness is transient.

In other words, Jericho Adams shows up.

The winter air stings Harinder's face when he bursts out of the store, forgetting to grab a scarf or a coat. "What the actual, fire-shitting fuck do you think you're doing?"

"Does being outside make swearing any less unprofessional, or have you just stopped caring?" Jericho doesn't smile—doesn't make any expression, doesn't even hesitate in his movements—but he exudes such a smug sense of accomplishment that Harinder can pick up on it despite Jericho's voice sounding neutral as always.

"I'm calling the cops," says Harinder.

"Do you promise?" Jericho sets the window scraper in the bucket by his heels and straightens his spine, crossing his arms over his chest. "What're you planning on telling them? 'There's a suspicious Black male washing windows outside my place of employment, officer.'"

"You're trespassing," Harinder snarls.

"I have permission from the landlord, actually, so I'm pretty sure the only thing I'm doing is those community service hours you told me to work on."

The next minute contains approximately two million years of tectonic activity shoved through the head of a single needle. Harinder is but a hapless victim to this process. Time passes without him. Language becomes a long-lost luxury. His fragile, mortal form is unmade and reforged in a vat of pure rage.

He doesn't take his eyes off Jericho, but he's sure his hands have bled white and red from how hard he's clenching them, nails digging into his palms.

Jericho matches every second of Harinder's infuriated stare, not moving an inch until, using the last of the moisture hidden under his barren tongue, Harinder rasps out, "What."

"Do you need to see my papers, or."

Harinder doesn't need to see any *goddamn papers*. He spins around and wishes for the ability to slam the door behind him without hearing the damning sound of its judgmental chime.

This is not what he wanted to happen. Yes, he'd made up the community service requirement—in part to stall, in part to save his ass. Harinder doesn't owe Jericho anything, and he's not ashamed of his decisions, but he does feel pretty bad about having been caught in a lie like that. Really, he was hoping Jericho would just decide it was too much work and give up, but Harinder's starting to believe he's picked a more difficult opponent than he initially realized.

He spends the next twenty minutes brainstorming, scribbling new excuses and lies on a page in his notebook, which he then puts through the shredder. Watching the lined paper disintegrate into strips, Harinder tries to gain some perspective on the situation. It's not the end of the world. The windows needed to be washed anyway, which is probably how Jericho got permission from the landlord to do it. Who is the landlord of this place, even? Harinder has no idea. Mr. Kulkarni deals with that kind of stuff.

Really, he's reacting more severely than he needs to. After all, Jericho is outside, and he is inside, and he has work to be doing, and if Jericho gets cheated out of his time, that's not Harinder's problem. His fault, yes, but his problem? No.

Jericho should have considered this before walking into Harinder's store and acting utterly intolerable as if Harinder would simply let that go. *Not a chance, Adams. Not a chance.*

Taking a deep breath, Harinder returns to the sales floor and steels himself. He won't look at the windows. He'll shove himself in the farthest corner of cashwrap with the most obscured view and try to take his mind off the plague outside the store with the goriest indie horror he can think of. It'll be fine.

Except, once he gets to the front, the first thing he does is glance through the heavy signage behind the hermit crab tank. The window certainly doesn't look any cleaner, although that could just be his side. Harinder doesn't get paid to take care of things that aren't animals, so he estimates nothing has been tended to since he moved the 125 gallon in front of the mess. He'd tell Jericho to wash that, too, but Harinder doesn't think he can stand being around him long enough for the job to get done.

In fact, Harinder can barely walk to the counter door without craning his neck to catch a glimpse of the asshole beyond the clutter, already getting angry just thinking about him being out there, whether visible or not.

He makes it another twenty minutes, approximately, before hurling his notebook across the cashwrap and storming back outside.

"Who the hell do you think you are?"

"Jericho Adams," he answers automatically, wiping a rag over the...window-scraper thing.

His sass does nothing but fuel Harinder's incoherent rage. "Why are you doing this? You could have gone anywhere."

"Maybe I missed you," Jericho says, continuing with his methodical strokes over the filthy storefront. "Thought this'd be a good way for us to hang out."

"I don't want to fucking hang out with you."

Jericho pauses his scraping to clutch a hand to his chest. "Aw, Hari. I'm crushed."

Harinder narrows his eyes. "Don't call me that."

There are a few seconds of silence. Jericho's mouth might twitch a little. Harinder is filled with intense dread which is fully validated when Jericho opens his stupid face and says: "Should I make a joke about calling you late to dinner and then explain it, or—"

"I hope a jet crashes into this building and takes us both straight to fucking hell." Harinder is ashamed to let Jericho see his unprotected back a second time as he retreats, further solidifying his place as an embarrassing black smudge on his family tree.

Though he just cleaned the reptile enclosures Thursday, Harinder retreats to the back of the store where he can stop himself from trying to glare out the window at Jericho. The cat room would be safest, but he cleaned the whole adoption center this very morning before the store opened, so that would be redundant. Harinder aggressively scrubs down every available surface, telling himself that reptiles carry a lot of bacteria, so this is totally fine and rational behavior.

It's still a fairly early Saturday, so customers are sparse. They'll pick up in a couple of hours, but in the meanwhile, he's wrangling sticky tree frogs into totes so he can hand-feed them crickets because their enclosure isn't even pretending to be dirty.

Someone enters the store, just as Harinder is scowling at an uncooperative cricket that won't hold still and allow itself to be tweezed into a frog's hungry mouth. He pauses to listen, hears multiple sets of footsteps, and sighs as he sets the tongs down. As he rounds the corner, he's already opening his mouth—*Hi there, welcome to Aquariums & More*—but he stops.

Rewinds until he's back around the corner. Tries to be quiet as he bolts into the back room to see if Mr. Kulkarni is here or not.

The back office is dark and empty. Harinder represses the panic rising like fire in his chest.

The unfortunate nature of his living situation is compounded only by the people his roommate considers friends. Would that Harinder had been more sensitive to the absolutely deplorable lack of quality in any of these persons before he decided to rail against one of them for the improper use of a choke chain on his badly trained pit bull. Previous to the altercation, he'd been unpleasant to them at best, but issuing a personal challenge managed to poke at all the wrong kinds of dominance displays in this particular troglodyte.

Slurping greedily from his family's many silver spoons doesn't consume enough of this douchebag's time, so he learned (presumably from the roommate) where Harinder worked and now makes random appearances solely for the purpose of harassing him. Mr. Kulkarni shoos them away when he's around, but Harinder is genuinely scared of being alone with them.

His spine is cold as he stalks over to the reptile racks, grabs a frog in each hand, and returns them to their enclosure, which he closes and locks. The footsteps are approaching, loud voices raised and mixed with laughter.

"Yo, anyone home? Helloooo."

Harinder puts on a stubborn face and grabs a bottle of Windex. He can't fight worth a damn, but with all the biking he does, he's very fast, so he could probably blind them and get a head start running away. The cat room has a lock on the door. He could totally call 911 in there.

They reach the fish wall before Harinder can, blocking his passage to the paper towel holder (and the entrance to the cat room). He swallows but refuses to show any fear.

Chapter Seven

Harinder's Literal (But Only Kind Of) White Knight

"Welcome to Aquariums & More," Harinder growls, trying not to look like he's brandishing the Windex bottle.

"Hey dude," says one guy Harinder doesn't recognize. He's the shortest of the group but still taller than Harinder. "We almost thought the place was empty."

The irresponsible dog owner (whose name is probably something like Brendon, although Harinder has never committed it to memory) snickers. "That's shitty customer service, man. I'm gonna give you bad reviews on Yelp."

Harinder sneers. "Be my guest." Half their customer reviews already complain about the service, which Harinder doesn't care about because Mr. Kulkarni doesn't seem to know the page exists. (The rest of the reviews praise the quality of the animals and products, giving the business a respectable 3.5 average rating, which Harinder is content with.) He cares even less knowing that, if he were so inclined, he could probably ask Sam to find a way to strip the bad reviews from the page.

"I wanna talk to your manager," Brendon says, taking a step closer. He knows full well Mr. Kulkarni isn't around because if he had been, Harinder would have gotten him the moment he saw them. Likely, he just wants Harinder to admit that he's alone.

"He's busy," Harinder says instead. "Though, if you managed to forget since the last time you were here the location of the garbage-quality dog food you always buy...it's aisle three. You're welcome."

With that, Harinder lifts the arm holding the Windex bottle and makes a barrier between him and their bodies as he slides past. Brendon lets it make contact before he steps out of Harinder's way, which sends revulsion through his skin, pooling thickly in his stomach. Defiant, Harinder turns his back to them and starts spraying down the tank fronts, wadding a paper towel in his fist as if he could scrub away the scratches using spite alone.

He pretends not to have noticed how Brendon's chest is solid with muscle Harinder can't match. He delves into his task so he doesn't lose himself wondering if Brendon could pop his skull against the acrylic like a soggy grape.

Harinder is only imagining the hot breath on the back of his neck. He knows this because none of them are short enough to get close without stooping, and he's also wearing a turtleneck under his sweater.

Just ignore them, and they'll go away. Ha.

"You'd better be careful with that shit you're spewing," says the third guy, whom Harinder recognizes as his roommate's fraternity brother. His generic white-boy name is one Harinder has also refused to memorize.

"Yeah," adds Brendon. "Besides, you'll be delighted to hear that I'm not feeding Rex that shit anymore." Rex. Such a typical hypermasc name for a bully dog. "I'm switching him to raw meat, starting today."

"Vital Essentials is stored in the fridge on the right," Harinder says, not turning around.

"Does it come in Mexican flavor?"

"Yeah, got some El Paso in that fridge?"

Though he grits his teeth, Harinder keeps moving along the line of tanks, keeping his voice as normal as possible. "Most of the spices in Latin American cuisine are dangerous to dogs, sorry."

A body hits the space in front of him, cutting off his progress. "We'll have to find an alternative. Rex's got a refined palate."

"Give him something you brought over the border illegally," Brendon jeers. "My family maid says that stuff tastes best."

Harinder fists a hand at his side, pulling the Windex up near his chin. He doesn't want to look small and vulnerable, but he desperately does not want to be touched by any of these assholes. "If you like salmonella, sure. It's not like your personality would be all that different while suffering from mad cow disease. Would your girlfriend even notice a change?"

Grating laughter spews from the space behind them. "Ooooh," the other two crow. "He got you good."

"I'll get his foreign ass good, too," Brendon says. "Hey, puta, if I called the cops right now, would they bust you for having a fake ID?"

"I bet he gets paid under the table."

"Twenty dollars a day to feed your family back in Mexico, am I right, puta?"

He doesn't bother correcting them even though he has trouble fathoming how they're interpreting his features as Mexican. They probably don't even know that India is an Asian country, so he skips that fight entirely.

"Mix it up, asshole. Call me a pendejo while you're at it. God, at least google Spanish insults before embarrassing yourself."

A hand shoots out, grabbing Harinder's shoulder and spinning him around. There are bodies, all boxing him in, and maybe he could bash in one of their eyes with the plastic spray handle, but Harinder doubts he could disable all of them in time to make a safe getaway. Fuck. Fuck fuck fuck.

"You think you're tough shit, don't you, estupido?"

"That's better," Harinder wheezes. He can barely breathe from how tight his lungs are.

Brendon sneers. "How about this: Yo el beato tu ass, bitch."

It's the moment before he dies, and the only thought Harinder can wrap his head around is horrified awe at such profound bastardization of a romantic language. He tries to remember the actual verb for "beat," but high school Spanish class was a long time ago, and there's an angry white boy about to fuck his shit up.

"Hombreeeee. Didn't expect to see you here."

Harinder blinks in confusion at the new voice—was there someone else who came in with them who he didn't notice? He tries to look, but Brendon's body blocks his view.

"¡Qué sorpresa! I didn't know you knew Spanish, buddy."

The wall of douche parts, and Harinder blinks to see...

Jericho. Holding his window scraper, one hand in his pocket, smiling. Harinder hasn't seen Jericho smile before.

"¡Hace mucho que no te veo! ¿Como estas?" Jericho nudges the tool on Harinder's left with the scraper, avoiding direct contact.

Brendon looks gobsmacked. "I think you got the wrong guy, man."

"¡Ni hablar!" Jericho exclaims with more inflection than Harinder's heard him use before. "¿Tu estas seguro?"

"Dude." Brendon looks between Jericho and his friend, who's doing nothing to help. "You really got the wrong guy."

Jericho's expression doesn't change. "What? No way. Kyle, right? From the bar, like, right off the interstate. You're not Kyle?"

"No man, I'm not. My name's Chris; I don't even know any Kyles."

Ah, Chris. That's his name.

"That's a shame, man, you look just like him. You could be twins. You sure? Seriously, él y yo somos como hermanos."

Chris shoves Jericho's window scraper out of the way so he can step around him, sharing the other's bulk like they're about to combine their powers and become Captain Fraternity. "I'm sure, dude, and I don't speak Spanish, alright?"

"Coulda sworn I heard one of y'all speaking it when I came in," Jericho says, coolly surveying all three of them.

"It was a joke."

"Damn," Jericho laments, seeming disappointed but in a completely insincere way. He switches the scraper in his hands, shrugging widely enough that the coalescing white boys have to shrink back to avoid being hit. "Here I was hoping I'd found mi gente. Hey, if you ever want to kick it, though, my schedule's totally open. I could get you into some sick places." He doesn't elaborate on what kind of places.

Harinder doesn't believe what he sees when the three start moving toward the door. Jericho turns measuredly, watching them every step of the way, posture neutral and disarming. Welcoming, even.

"It's fine, dude. It's fine," one voice volunteers while the other says, "Hope you find Kyle, man; good luck."

The door chimes. The footsteps are gone.

The store descends into silence.

Jericho's face is no longer pleasant, or even neutral. It's blank. His shoulders are tense, hunched up toward his ears.

"I didn't know you spoke Spanish," Harinder says, focusing on that rather than his atrophied manners suggesting he thank Jericho for his help.

Turning back, Jericho scrunches his nose a bit but is otherwise expressionless. "I don't."

Harinder blinks. "What?"

"I grew up in De Queen, Arkansas." He fiddles with the window scraper. The edge of his sleeve is damp where it dripped. "The population there is over half Latino, and I learned some basic conversation skills. That's all."

For a second, Harinder thinks he might laugh. It doesn't feel like the right response to the situation, so it's fortunate no sound emerges. His brow furrows. "Do you usually freak out racist white boys by pretending to be Latinx and calling them the wrong name?"

A shrug. "Making people uncomfortable is easier than trying to scare them off." Jericho coils defensively like he's expecting to be mocked.

Harinder doesn't blame him. He's not enough of an asshole to mention Jericho's appearance, but in the context of knowing how to escape from bullies...well, Harinder doesn't doubt that an albino kid would have to get good at fending off dickweasels.

"Are you gonna tell me how stupid I am?" Jericho's voice is oddly aggressive.

Frowning, Harinder says, "No? What do I look like, a braindead fetal goat with no hope of a normal life? Don't fucking answer that, I swear to god." Jericho's lips might twitch, which sits better with Harinder than the blank tension. "Believe it or not, I have basic knowledge of how the world works. When you aren't visually intimidating, it makes sense to..." He shrugs, not wanting to repeat what Jericho said. It's as close to agreement as they're going to get.

Harinder forces his stiff, uncooperative fingers to release the Windex bottle so he can tear off a clean piece of paper towel and wipe the sweat from his hands. Heaving a sigh, he stares at the shiny surfaces of the worn tank fronts. They were never dirty in the first place, and he truly has nothing left to clean.

"You look like your head is empty," Jericho says, not unkindly.

"Normally if someone said that to me, I'd arrange for them to misplace their spleen." Harinder rolls his shoulders, trying to loosen the rock-hard muscle. "Right now, however, you're more on-the-nose than I'd like to admit."

Jericho nods. "After listening to those chucklefucks, I'd be surprised to hear your id *didn't* overtake your higher brain functions."

A bitter laugh escapes. "This Saturday, featuring the new Hollywood blockbuster—*Death of a Superego*, starring Hari Mangal." The crappy signage manifests in his imagination clear as day.

"It'll make millions."

They stand there after that, not speaking until Harinder finally picks his feet up and drags himself to the sink to put the Windex away and discard the damp paper towels. Jericho stays where he is, staring emptily at the fish, scraper hanging limply from his hand.

"So, uh," Harinder hazards. "How'd the windows go?"

A crease forms on Jericho's brow, but only for a second. "There was, like, ten years' worth of buildup on those windows. It doesn't look like I did jack shit. Reminded me of trying to cleanse my sins in Catholic school."

Huffing out something that's almost a laugh, Harinder asks, "You went to Catholic school?"

"Nope." Jericho stretches his arms above his head and appears to wince. "For smooth-brained lugnuts, those guys were remarkably easy to freak out." He drops his arms with a deep sigh.

"They're not exactly complex creatures."

"Yeah, but they didn't even call me an albino freak or anything." Jericho proceeds to roll his neck. "They were almost goddamn cordial."

Harinder shrugs. "Losers like that are walking cases of erectile dysfunction. They act like they can tear shit up, but when it comes down to it, they can't even put it in."

Jericho laughs. Not a snort, or a breathy puff of amusement, but an actual chuckle, low in his throat. Just two notes, framed by the upturned corners of his full lips. It's gone before Harinder can make a big deal of it, but the sound lingers in his memory.

"I'm not complaining," Jericho says. "If the great dicks of vengeance decided to have it out for me, I'd probably be too fucked up to fight back. Sorry, dudes, my punch quota is filled for the week; the city bus got my shit first."

The comment has Harinder's head turning, mouth halfway open in muted shock. "You got hit by a bus?"

Suddenly bashful, Jericho shrugs one shoulder. The corner of his lip tightens. "Does it count if I was in the bus when it hit me?" Suddenly the stretching and the grimacing makes a lot more sense, now that he can't attribute it to soreness from scrubbing windows for a paltry forty minutes.

Harinder wonders if the thought of dark bruises on paper-white skin bothers him more now that Jericho risked worsening them to save his ungrateful ass. He didn't even thank him. Holy fuck, Harinder's entire life and disposition need to be put in a blender and pulverized; he's such a goddamn tit.

"What the fuck are you doing here, harassing me instead of staying at home and, like, resting?"

Jericho tries to provide free labor to improve his workplace, and Harinder calls it harassment. He showed up after being hit by a bus, and Harinder managed to turn it into a personal slight. And now, his mouth has somehow decided that ranting at him is a suitable replacement for expressing gratitude. If some god could just go ahead and strike him down, that'd be great.

"Resting alone in my apartment while you're lustfully searching for someone, possibly anyone else, to throw cats at before you stoop low enough to make something easy and painless for once?"

Harinder doesn't exactly reel, but he does take a step back, offended. "I don't know why you think you'll gain my trust by constantly complaining about my efforts to keep these animals safe."

"I never did anything to compromise your trust in the first place." Jericho's face almost—*almost*—shows a flicker of pain.

Harinder ignores it.

"That's not how it works! Trust is earned. You think you're the first stranger to waltz in pretending to be the next virgin birth attempting to get an animal from me?"

"No, of course not. This is a pet store."

"Wrong," Harinder snaps. "This is a tank store. Animal sales make up less than twenty percent of our revenue. I don't have to sell anyone jack shit, especially if I don't think they're capable of providing a suitable home."

Jericho rolls his eyes. "And you know what? I fuckin' get that. Just do me a favor and stop acting like I'm some blood-drinking succubus here to steal and torture your beloved fuzzy inventory. Goddamn, like— You're so paranoid I'm starting to get suspicious of myself just from the contact high of being around you."

"You would be the worst succubus ever." It comes out before Harinder can stop it. Upon processing, he is immediately and intensely overtaken by shameful embarrassment.

Jericho has his lips pressed into a tight line. Not unusual. The corners tilt down, dimpling his cheeks, and that's when Harinder realizes he's trying not to smile. "Can't argue with that," he murmurs, shaking his head. Without sparing Harinder another look, he stalks toward the adoption center and disappears behind the flimsy door.

Several minutes pass before Harinder follows him. He silently enters the room amidst the usual chorus of mews as the cats recognize him and immediately beg for food and pets. Normally he would immediately go to console them, hands pressing into two different cages to greet furry, purring bodies. Right now, he's too distracted. Arms crossed tightly over his chest, Harinder studies

Jericho, slumped against the wall in front of Dumpling's kennel, frowning intensely as she sits far enough out of reach that he can barely glance her forehead with his fingertips. She looks on coolly, ambivalent to his struggle.

This absolutely cannot be guilt that Harinder is feeling. He refuses.

"Thanks for helping me not get my ass beat," Harinder says eventually because giving in to basic politeness is easier than sacrificing his stubborn pride.

Jericho glances at him, then looks back at Dumpling without so much as a twitch. "Don't mention it. The atrocity they committed against the Spanish language was incentive enough."

Harinder's face scrunches. "Right." Very faintly in the background, the door chimes. "I...have to get that."

"Yeah, man," Jericho nods. "Do your job." He doesn't seem interested in moving.

Harinder opens his mouth, but nothing he might say feels appropriate. Unable to summon anything witty or caustic or—though he would deny it before a jury of every justice-inclined pandimensional deity to ever birth itself like some fucked-up inverse ouroboros—*decent* enough, Harinder leaves without a word.

The customer doesn't greet him as they walk distractedly into the cat section, staring at their phone. Harinder doesn't bother to offer them any help. He goes to sit down behind the counter, feeling numb. He needs processing time. He needs a hot bath. He needs...he needs...

When the adoption center door opens, Harinder doesn't know how much time has passed. He vaguely remembers mechanically checking the customer out, but he doesn't remember what they bought. His eyes follow

Jericho as he shuffles around the cashwrap and out the front, not offering so much as a "later." Harinder is halfway to feeling terrible when Jericho stops just before stepping entirely out and letting the door fall behind him.

"They stole my fucking bucket," Jericho says in a voice that is somehow twice as deadpan as usual.

Harinder slaps both hands over his face because some exhausted, worn-down part of him wants to laugh, and he absolutely will not indulge it, no matter how tempting it is. "Fucking twats," he manages to squeak out past his fingers.

"At least I don't have to take it on the bus now."

"That's like being glad when the bank forecloses your house because at least now you can't accidentally burn it down."

"That analogy only works if I have to carry my house on the bus."

"I've seen stranger things."

Jericho stares for a second longer and then says, "I'm really gonna go now. I got more windows to wash tomorrow. I signed on to do the entire strip."

Part of Harinder tells him to get shitty about the information that Jericho will, in fact, be back, but he simply doesn't have the energy. "Don't die on your way home," he says, unable to summon anything else.

"I'll try," Jericho says.

"Just think," says Harinder, leaning forward on his elbows over the counter. "If you die today, you won't be able to show me up by performing hours of menial labor just to trick me into entrusting you with a dependent."

"God forbid."

"Yeah. Good luck, by the way."

Brandishing the window scraper in an awkward half wave, Jericho finally melts through the doorway. Harinder pretends he doesn't watch his retreating form through the (still filthy) window until he's out of sight.

Chapter Eight

Jericho Defends Portmanteaus

Using someone else's sound system to blare Lil Nas X across the whole of the apartment building is far from the typical model of politeness, but Jericho's neighbor is out of town for the weekend, and he's watching her dog for free.

He was about to head out for his usual bout of harassing Harinder, which has become something of a ritual in the past week when the little sixty-year-old Black woman knocked on his door. He's picked up dog food for her before, usually when he went to the grocery. Earlier in the week, he offered to get some from a real pet store.

Jericho has never owned a pet in his life, but somehow, Ms. Watson decided (unlike Harinder) that being able to buy dog food made him a capable pet sitter, and thus.

It's a pretty cute dog as far as dogs go. Her name is Kimchi. Ms. Watson said something about an old Korean girlfriend, but Jericho isn't sure if she meant it in the gay way or the old-person-gal-pal kind of way. He didn't ask.

Now he's trying to figure out how much distance walking a dog is meant to entail since Ms. Watson said, "Walk her twice daily," but didn't extrapolate any further. He googles whether or not he's allowed to take a dog on the bus because he really has to get his ass down the bus line before his ruse goes sour. It's amazing he's been able to keep it going this long.

When Jericho awkwardly leads Kimchi to the bus stop, he's thankful he returned the scraper to the store for his money back last Sunday and thus doesn't have any equipment to bog him down.

Not that Harinder needs to know that.

Jericho resists the urge to ask the bus driver if he has to pay twice the fare if he has a dog, and shoves Kimchi under his arm while he's boarding, trying to look as inconspicuous as possible. No one says a word, so he sits with the dog on his lap and reaches for his phone.

"You're late today," Harinder notes when he walks through the door, only sparing him half a glance. "I had hoped to spare myself the daily aneurysm."

"Yeah, the windows down at the dollar store were encrusted in the physical essence of poverty, which, as it turns out, is pretty hard to get rid of." Harinder isn't the only one who can pull absurd shit and get away with it. He doubts the guy will actually hunt down the building landlord to make sure the signature Jericho forged on his photoshopped community service log is legit. "Also, I had some pretty distracting company."

Harinder does a double take, then issues a third, sweeping glance around Jericho's general vicinity. Jericho sees the exact moment Harinder spots the dog.

He doesn't squeal, but his mouth drops open, and his eyes go wide. With great amusement, Jericho watches him try not to trip over literally everything as he bursts out from behind the counter, only slowing his purposeful stride when he approaches the chunky amalgamation of fluff at Jericho's side, dropping to one knee and extending the back of his hand.

"Hey there," he says quietly, like it's a private conversation between just him and the dog.

The leash hangs slack in Jericho's hand. "Her name is Kimchi."

"Oh my god. Hey, pretty girl," Harinder croons.

Jericho can't suppress the amused snort. Of course that would be the shitty flavor of pet name Harinder would eat right up. It's like a switch has been flipped. Rather than guarding his every gesture, Harinder makes shmoopy sounds and scratches Kimchi's ears, not seeming to notice any of his surroundings.

Jericho has long since figured out that Harinder likes animals more than he'll ever like people, but the confirmation is as fascinating as it is...uncomfortably intimate.

"What innocent person did you kill to get custody of this flawless animal?" Harinder wonders. "Has the FBI been informed?"

"Yeah, they already set up cameras in my apartment and everything. No, she's my neighbor's."

"You stole a dog from your neighbor?"

Jericho bobs his head and gestures expansively with his empty hand. "I couldn't control the urge. I needed something fluffy in my life. I'm going through actual withdrawal and turning to a life of crime because of it."

"I'm calling CPS," says Harinder decisively. He moves to stand but halts when Kimchi snuffles and paws at his pant leg. He freezes, powerless to resist her doggy witchcraft. "What kind of dog is she?"

"Porgi," Jericho says without missing a beat.

"Fuck you," Harinder says just as quickly. "Fake fusion breed names are the result of a sycophantic society that doesn't know how to value something without ascribing it a shitty title that's meant to indicate worth but is ultimately impossible to quantify." Kimchi rolls onto her back, allowing Harinder to scratch her belly with an air of vicious self-satisfaction. Jericho rolls his eyes.

"Whatever. Porgi is an ingenious portmanteau, and if you're too consumed with hate to understand that, you'll have to deal with calling her a boring old corgi-poodle mix."

"She is not boring," Harinder scolds, giving Jericho a venomous look he's probably not faking. "She is a noble, sophisticated individual."

"She has short, dumb legs."

Harinder sighs, put-upon, and sits on his heels. "Thank you for being the biggest idiot I've heard speak all damn day."

Jericho salutes. "No prob. How's your day going?"

"Only about half an hour left. Which is as good as I could hope for."

"Is it really that late?" Jericho wonders distantly, looking at his bare wrist as if he expects a watch to be there even though he's never worn a wristwatch in his life.

"If it wasn't," Harinder says, pushing himself to his feet, "I wouldn't have commented about it being late when you walked in."

"Well, when you put it that way." The door opens into his back, and Jericho ushers a scrambling Kimchi quickly aside, placating the half-hearted apologies from the woman entering. Harinder issues his rote greeting, not bothering to unslump enough to reveal his worn, barely readable nametag from under the wrinkles of the mustard sweater Jericho has confirmed he wears every single day, unless he has twenty of them like a character in a cartoon.

There's a little rush in the last half hour of business. He barely gets to talk to Harinder and, instead, walks Kimchi around the store idly. It's too cold to spend any prolonged time outside even though there's not much snow, so Jericho only pops out for a second to see if Kimchi has to relieve herself.

When he walks back inside, Harinder is making good on his promise of a daily aneurysm, although Jericho is shockingly not the instigator.

"Why not?" he's asking a bewildered customer. "Why would I not give you a bag to hold one five-ounce item? What reason could you possibly have to hold that thing in your hand instead of carrying it in a harmless shroud of plastic for the forty-five seconds it takes to cross the parking lot and locate your car?"

Oh boy.

"I will tell you why not," Harinder snarls. "The impacted intestines of the magnificent sperm whale that just washed up on one of California's shores is why. Oh, what? You didn't think that your slovenly consumerism might have a meaningful impact on life that isn't directly in front of your face? Of course! How typical. You know what? Here's your bag."

Harinder rips a bag off the pack, snatches up the item before the customer can protest, and violently shoves it inside. "After you get to your car, please do me a favor and drive directly to the nearest beach and stick it directly into a whale's blowhole because that's where it's going to end up anyway. Have a nice night."

The guy staggers off in a daze, gingerly holding his hard-won plastic bag. Harinder huffs through his nostrils, brows drawn so low over his eyes Jericho is genuinely worried he's going to go full dragon and set the dude *and* his bag on fire.

"So, um," Jericho says. "You're a little tetchy today."

Harinder redirects his glare to Jericho. "When am I not?"

"Good point, but that's the third customer you've yelled at in, like, twenty minutes."

"They all suck tonight," Harinder says curtly, winding around from behind the counter and stalking over to the front door, which he promptly locks.

Jericho can't help but notice he's still inside. "Uh, hey?" He looks between the door and the dog at his feet, panting cheerfully and completely unbothered by Harinder's tirade. "I think you forgot something."

"Did I?" Harinder asks as he flicks off the open sign and then stalks down one of the aisles without saying another word.

"I think we just got invited to Harinder's sleepover," says Jericho to Kimchi, who twitches her ears and shuffles up to park her tiny front legs on his shins. He obliges her with scratches, which are apparently inferior to Harinder's because after a second of tolerating them, she drops down and attempts to waddle after Harinder, hauling at the leash. Jericho releases it, figuring that not much bad can happen in a locked pet-safe building.

Chapter Nine

Jericho's Unexpected Access Code

It's weird how familiar this trashy pet store has become. Almost disconcerting how Jericho isn't twitching for the opportunity to escape, to hide alone in his room. That impulse is one reason of many that explain why he doesn't have friends here, and somehow, at some point, Harinder became a palatable alternative to being alone. The thought makes him wildly uncomfortable.

The door to the back room hangs open alluringly. Harinder is nowhere in sight. Approaching the Employees Only area of any store makes Jericho twitchy, but a noise past the threshold draws his attention.

Jericho peeks through and is mildly surprised to see Harinder sitting on the floor, peeling strips of chicken off a drumstick and feeding them to Kimchi. Resting on a cardboard box beside him is a Tupperware container filled with yellow chunks—vegetables, it seems—and a pile of discarded breading.

Shoving his hands in his pockets, Jericho observes the scene. "Not hungry?"

"Not for this," Harinder says, peeling off another chunk of chicken. He gives it a withering look.

Jericho raises an eyebrow. "Why'd you bring it?" A second later, he wonders if Harinder might have an eating disorder—what if being prodded about food is a trigger?—but Harinder seems dispassionate when he answers.

"I didn't."

After a moment of contemplation, Jericho concedes defeat. He opens his mouth, but Harinder continues before he can formulate a question.

"More accurately, I didn't realize some ass-eating cockmonkey thought it'd be funny to put meat in the food I packed for work today before locking myself in my room to escape the carnival of buffoonery that my jackwagon roommate was preparing."

"Your roomie lets his friends get away with that shit?"

Harinder snorts bitterly. "He encourages it, probably. How else would they know I don't eat meat?"

"I dunno, man," Jericho says because he can't help himself. "You're not exactly subtle about your feelings."

Shooting him a dark look under his eyelashes, Harinder goes back to picking the last bits of meat off the chicken bone.

"So, assuming you're a vegetarian, you seem pretty chill touching that."

Harinder throws the bare bone into the Tupperware. He pats Kimchi, stands up, and carries it over to the wastebin at Jericho's side. "I touch raw meat all the time when feeding animals," he says disdainfully. "Cooked chicken isn't going to give me the fucking vapors. I'm just not going to eat it." He upturns the Tupperware, emptying its entire contents into the trash. "Anyway, if you're going to let Kimchi run around unattended, take off her leash. She could get caught on something."

Jericho wants to argue just to argue but obeys instead, winding the leash around his hand as Kimchi shakes her head and shoulders, reveling in her new freedom.

"Sounds like your roommate fucking sucks," Jericho says after thinking about it. If he'd ever had a vegetarian phase, sneaking meat into his food would probably be something his uncle would do. He could totally see that asshole buying cow penis from a butcher and putting a chunk of it into a kale smoothie—or whatever else it is that vegetarians drink—and giving it to him like an evil present.

Not that Jericho would have trusted it, but he'd have done it anyway, just to make him uncomfortable.

"Fucking understatement of the year," Harinder snarls from the sink where he's washing his hands. "I've lived in hovels preferable to the space I share with this cocksore."

"Why do you live with such a jerk anyway?"

Harinder shrugs, looks like he's about to get angry, then deflates as he turns off the water. "The space was nice when I signed the lease. The place I'd lived before didn't even have bathrooms in the apartment, there was just a communal one down the hall. My friend linked me to this ad, and there was this picture of a tiny half bathroom attached to the bedroom."

It's weirdly vulnerable, and yet Jericho doesn't feel compelled to ruin the moment. Instead, he merely nods. "I don't blame you."

"Little did I know," Harinder picks up, aggression back in his voice, "that he was just another frat douche rich kid with more issues than money, which he has a fucking lot of. He has two cars. Two fucking cars. It's good that all I have is a bike because where the fuck would I park?"

As he rants, Harinder begins filling water into a wheeled bucket. The back room is horribly lit, dim and yellow, but the bright red on Harinder's cheeks is still visible. "He doesn't even do his homework, and his parents are literally *paying him* to get good grades. It's not even that fucking hard." He slams the full bucket on the ground, ignoring how it sloshes, and grabs a nearby mop. "He doesn't pay rent. His parents own the house!"

"How much do they make you pay?"

"Enough," Harinder says, gritting his teeth.

Enough that he can't afford a car, Jericho thinks, but he doesn't say it. He knows Harinder is the only employee at Aquariums & More, and the business is open 52 hours a week, which doesn't include the work he does before and after hours. Even on minimum wage, he should make enough to save up for a shitty car. At least enough to take out a loan.

Jericho gives in and asks, "How much?"

"Twelve hundred a month."

Hissing, Jericho says, "For one room? Christ. I don't pay that much for my whole apartment."

"I can afford it," Harinder shrugs. "It's a nice house."

"Worth it though?"

Harinder sets the mop in the bucket, letting the water soak into the tendrils. He pulses a few times to agitate the soap. "I don't really have the ability to move right now," he says finally, and pushes the mop bucket back onto the store floor. He begins angrily cleaning while Jericho hangs back in the shadows.

"My uncle," Jericho says out of nowhere, "was a fucking psychopath. I lived in a studio apartment with him for ten years. Only privacy was in the bathroom." Harinder pauses, mop frozen mid-swipe. "You live alone now," he recalls.

"Yeah," Jericho says, shuffling his feet. "He died."

"Ah," Harinder says. "Parents?"

"Gone."

"Ah."

They don't say anything else for a while. Jericho steals a toy from the discount bin and plays with Kimchi while Harinder mops, and there's silence in the way of voices. The store is illuminated in sounds of wheezing rubber and clacking nails over a slick surface. The churning of aquarium filters. The wet sound of fabric smacking against tile, sliding to and fro.

It's dark outside, but someone sees Harinder as he mops in front of the counter. They knock on the door. He points to the unlit open sign.

"I hate people," he seethes once they've stopped desperately haggling for "just five minutes."

"I got the impression," Jericho says, stepping out from where he'd been hiding.

"I fucking hate that this job makes me deal with people," Harinder continues, fisting his hands around the mop handle as his shoulders shake. "Why can't I just never talk to anyone fucking ever."

"It gets lonely," Jericho comments without meaning to.

Harinder spares him the humiliation of having to explain, or more accurately, blow it off without confessing to feeling things. "Lonely? Do I look lonely to you?" He gestures expansively at the store, not pointing at any particular animal cage, but Jericho gets the point.

It'd be a good time to lay on thick that this is exactly why Jericho wants a cat, but it's so not genuine. Jericho doesn't want a cat, he wants Shiloh to talk to him again, and he wants...

Ha. He wants to not be alone, which is why he's here. Shiloh is the manifestation of that desire. Harinder is a temporary solution.

He doesn't say anything about the adoption, in the end, because Jericho hasn't had a conversation that wasn't eighty-five percent fake in at least a month. The number of lies they've wrapped around that issue can go unprodded, just for the moment.

"Why would I ever be lonely," Harinder goes on, colliding awkwardly with Jericho's silence, "when I'm surrounded by sentient organisms that, unlike humans, are incapable of having shitty intolerable opinions and don't feel the compulsive, uncontrollable need to torture people for fun? Why would I ever prefer anything over that?"

"Do you have pets at home?" Jericho wonders.

Just like that, he deflates. His shoulders sag like a character in a cartoon.

Concern brings Jericho to attention. What if he asked that and his dog had just died, or his roommate killed his cat, what if—

"No," he says finally. Jericho is legitimately shocked.

Harinder pushes the mop bucket away, but Jericho calls after him. "Why not?"

"Pets aren't allowed where I'm living. They're afraid of ruining the carpet." He says it so plainly. Matter-of-fact.

"Caged animals," Jericho says, like he's invested in this outcome.

"What if they escape?" Harinder mimics, obviously not airing his own thoughts. "It's fine." It's obviously not fine. "I've never had a pet in my life."

"Holy shit."

Harinder gives him an odd look over his shoulder. "Were you ever in foster care?"

Jericho shakes his head. "No. I got emancipated when I turned seventeen and moved here to be close to my sister." Shiloh was adopted after their mom...went away. Jericho wasn't. He's gotten over it. "I'd been saving up since I was twelve, and I was fucking sick of him." He pauses, looking away. "Omar died a few months after I left, just before my eighteenth birthday."

Instead of apologizing, or showing any kind of sympathy, Harinder nods viciously. "I was in foster care for five years. I lived with eight different families."

"Christ."

"They bounced me around a lot because I had anger issues," he says without the slightest hint of irony. "When they finally found a fit, I was almost eighteen anyway. It was a white family, but they were nice." Harinder lets go of the mop handle, wanders over to the crab tank, brushes a bit of dust off the hood.

"It was the first house I'd been at where they had a pet. When my dad was alive, we had a hermit crab tank, but that was it. Dad took care of them for the most part."

Jericho's really glad Harinder can't see how Jericho's eyes are riveted on him.

"They had a rabbit—a lop, the kind with the floppy ears. She had a really dumb name, but I called her Kulira. They let me take care of her."

He goes silent.

"This got real," Jericho murmurs, unsure of what else to say.

Harinder laughs bitterly. "Yeah. Sorry."

"Naw. It's all good. Don't worry about it."

Nodding again, Harinder avoids looking at him as he finally pushes the mop bucket to the back room to dispose of the dirty water.

At some point, Harinder stops to reassure him that he usually closes a lot faster than this. Jericho snorts because he doesn't care. Somewhere between the heartfelt confessions about past and present traumas and the ten minutes they spent tossing a ball between them for Kimchi to chase, he got the impression this wasn't his usual afterhours routine.

"Do you like mushrooms?" Jericho asks.

"Uh, yeah," Harinder answers. "Why?"

"I was just wondering because they suck, so I thought you would."

"What the fuck."

Harinder disappears to count money. Jericho lies down on the floor and stares at the stained ceiling until Kimchi gets worried and starts snuffling at his face. Harinder returns, gives him an odd look. "Having fun?"

"Tons."

"I'm almost done," Harinder informs him, like he can't just leave at any time.

"Cool," Jericho answers.

Harinder scoffs and walks away. Minutes pass, and then there's a knock on the door.

"What the fuck." Harinder's voice is muffled from down the aisle. "I'm going to rip someone's face off," he announces loudly, his footsteps making tiny little stomping sounds on the tile.

Jericho sits up. "Nah, it's fine. I've got it."

Harinder pauses. "What?"

He's already reaching into his pocket when he gets to the front door, although it takes him a second to figure out the sticky deadbolt. "Keep the change," he says, handing the guy outside a twenty. The delivery guy thanks him, and the smell of hot, fresh pizza fills the building as

Jericho accepts the box and closes the door. "What?" He innocently regards Harinder's expression of disbelief.

"...the hell," Harinder manages, scrunching his forehead.

"Neither of us have eaten today," Jericho says, including himself to make it seem less like charity even though he's way used to not eating for long periods of time. He tosses the box on the open space next to the register, then opens it to reveal gooey cheese and steaming vegetables. "Do you got any plates or anything?"

Harinder takes a step back, looking weirdly defensive. "What if I'm vegan?"

Jericho gives him a thoughtful look. "Dunno. Are you?"

"No," Harinder says, scowling.

"Then come get some damn pizza. We can use paper towels for plates if you don't have any."

"I have paper plates in the back," he snaps.

"Then go fuckin' get them, god-damn."

He blinks widely, expression close to fearful, then turns in the direction of the back room.

They eat on the floor behind the counter. Kimchi begs, and then curls up at Harinder's side and sleeps when he refuses to give her any of his pizza. Jericho picks the mushrooms off his slice because they really do suck. They eat and talk about nothing, arguing about meaningless details and agreeing rarely. They finish the entire pizza and don't bring up the part where they accidentally bared closely kept secrets to each other without any discernible reason.

Harinder cleans up. "The alarm company is gonna call if I don't get out of here soon." Jericho hooks the leash back to Kimchi's collar. Harinder hovers. "I have to leave out the back," he explains.

"Gotcha." Jericho looks at the front door, gives Kimchi's leash a tug. Harinder doesn't move, studying him with a weird expression. Uncomfortable, Jericho blurts, "Please don't thank me. That makes it gay, dude."

His expression immediately morphs into a sneer. "I wasn't going to fucking thank you, asshole."

"Good," Jericho cuts back, unlocking the front door without waiting for Harinder to do so. "Because—" He doesn't have a reason, there's nothing that comes to mind that sounds neutral enough, nonsensical enough; everything is either too mean or too sincere. He changes the subject rapidly. "I hope the fucking bus doesn't take forever to get here."

"Not my problem," Harinder says, grabbing the door to hold it open, glare affixed to his face as Jericho passes through.

"You would let poor Kimchi freeze?"

"*You* wouldn't let Kimchi freeze," Harinder retorts confidently. "Because then I would form a vendetta against you, and you'd never adopt an animal in this town again."

Jericho rolls his eyes. "We almost went a day without talking about it."

"Buying me pizza isn't going to change my mind."

"Fuck you, I didn't think it would."

"Just making sure," Harinder says and lets the door fall closed.

Jericho's mind scrambles desperately for a retort as he watches Harinder latch the deadbolt. Nothing comes to him. Harinder raises an eyebrow through the foggy glass. Jericho flips him off. Harinder smirks and walks away.

It's starting to snow. Jericho carries Kimchi to the bus stop and waits with her on his lap, warming his hands in her thick fur. He keeps his mind deliberately blank.

Chapter Ten

Harinder Learns a Delicate Dance

Harinder hits the ground running. No, that's not an exaggeration: he literally hits the ground because he just jumped out a goddamn window.

It sounds cooler than it is because the house is built into a hill, so the deck is less than a full story above the grass. Besides that, Harinder has done far stupider shit than jump out of windows to avoid conflict.

He's not absolutely certain the guy he heard talking in the kitchen was the same guy with fuckface who harassed him at work the other day, but he isn't taking any chances. Instead of grabbing food from the fridge and leaving out the side like he usually would, Harinder triple checks the lock on his bedroom door and then launches himself out the window and into the backyard.

He makes a beeline for his bike. His fingers tremble clumsily as he unlocks it from the gate and then tries to wind the chain enough to fit in his bag. In the end, he just stuffs it in and hopes it won't fall out as he zips down the street.

When he gets to work, it's half an hour before he'd usually arrive. His ritualistic eight o'clock punch is already significantly earlier than their ten o'clock opening time, but Saturdays don't allow as much time as Harinder usually needs for tasking. He prefers to get shit done in the morning so he doesn't have to stay late, unlike yesterday.

Not that he minded. The dog was cute. The pizza was good. He refuses to think anything about the company.

Lacking anything else to do, Harinder untangles his bike chain and secures the bike up behind A&M, then walks around to the front so he can meander to the dollar store, hoping to scrounge some breakfast. They might have microwaveable vegetable packs that'll do over the big fat nothing he has otherwise.

For the most part, Mr. Kulkarni lets him arrive as early and stay as late as he needs to get his stuff done. He's not a penny-pincher, and it'd be nonsensical to complain about the amount of care Harinder puts into the store, so Harinder isn't concerned about him freaking out over eight whole dollars. They don't have a machine to track punches; Harinder just writes his hours on a piece of paper outside the office, and he sincerely doubts Mr. Kulkarni checks the video camera to make sure he's actually occupying the store at those times.

Still, showing up two and a half hours early is a little dodgy, even for him.

Harinder finds a microwaveable packet of frozen corn in fake butter and checks the back of the package to make sure there's nothing too disgusting inside. He takes that over the vegetable medley that probably tastes like cardboard and comes completely unseasoned. On his way out of the freezer aisle, he grabs a box of french toast sticks and some four cheese hot pockets to keep in the freezer for emergencies.

By the time he's paid and exited the dollar store, he's killed...less than ten minutes, goddamn it. Going inside to have some breakfast without yet punching in should be okay, right? Again, it's not like Mr. Kulkarni is going to check.

Decimating half the french toast sticks takes fifteen additional minutes. He forces himself to hold back on eating the whole box, and instead stows them in the freezer next to the hot pockets (also tempting). Unable to stand the waiting any longer, Harinder gives in to the urge to be a compulsively attentive employee. He writes the time on his punch card, and when he finally switches the open sign on, he's already completed more than half the things he needed to do for the day.

Shit. It's gonna be a long eight hours.

He should take some amount of pride in his ability to run out of stuff to do in the middle of a building full of poop machines, but mostly, he's annoyed and bored. Usually, he'd be elated to have an undisturbed block in which to analyze the new batch of indie shorts Sam collected for him (even though they hadn't spoken for three days before the zip file showed up in his inbox), but Harinder can't concentrate on cinematography right now.

Forty-five minutes after the store opens, he's only had three customers and doesn't have a single thing to get angry about. No one has challenged him, and instead of having foretold imminent chaos, the morning's hiccup is turning out to be nothing more than a bad omen for completely uneventful bullshit.

By 11:37, Harinder is considering flopping to the floor in the adoption center and willing himself to death. The cats could dispose of the evidence (not that they would since they eat very well and love him). Then, the overpowering stench of weed punches him straight in the nose.

It's so strong he doesn't hear the door open because he's too busy reeling. Now, Harinder is not a virgin, and he's seen "the weed" at least three times before, but this is legitimately excessive.

"Sundance," he says, not that he's surprised, but. "What the actual fuck."

The kid is somehow grosser than he was before. Instead of merely looking like a tweaker, he is blisteringly high—probably on way more than just weed—and isn't even wearing a jacket. Harinder's angry black heart makes an unhappy sound when he sees that.

Sundance walks up to the counter in more of a daze than usual—and, honestly, this is the guy who came back two days later when he said two weeks and was surprised when Harinder said he was twelve days early—but he's smiling like a lunatic, so Harinder is cautiously not terrified.

"'Sup," Sundance says.

Despite Harinder explicitly defining two weeks for him and even putting the date in his phone, Sundance has popped in a couple times since their first encounter. He never stops being awful, which is a problem because Harinder feels sincerely bad for him. He looks far older than his seventeen years, and Harinder's pretty sure no one gives a fuck about this kid aside from, on occasion, himself.

Harinder checks the date. It's been over two weeks. "Why do you smell like a skunk just emptied its entire asshole into your showerhead while you were standing underneath it cluelessly wondering how you arrived there in the first place? To clarify, I'm assuming showering is a foreign concept to you."

"Aw, man," Sundance says, scratching at his arm. He has scabs up and down his scaly, dry skin. "I just got excited. 'm sorry."

"What are you excited about, Sundance." Harinder's tone doesn't even shape a question, and his words are sarcastically deadpan, but he doesn't think Sundance even notices.

"Because, like, I did it. I saved up all the money you said I'd need to buy my friend."

A combination of horror and awe fills Harinder when Sundance reaches into the pocket of his dirty, wide-leg jeans and pulls out a haphazardly folded wedge of paper: The care sheet. The front page is missing, and the staple has been replaced by a literal fucking nail, hammered through the paper until it bent, which is...absolutely terrifying, but it's there. There are even notes written in the margins and things circled and highlighted.

The handwriting is completely fucking illegible, of course, but Harinder regards it with a confused swell of pride. Only problem is, he's still not sending a dependent home with a kid who's clearly fucked up.

"Sundance," he says, much more carefully. He still doesn't know what said kid is capable of, and there's probably a reason he's a ward of the state that no foster parent could handle (or so Harinder guessed after piecing together the nonsense Sundance has told him about his life). "You realize I can't sell you an animal while you're in this condition, right?"

Sundance freezes up. His eyes don't widen, but they go foggy, like he's no longer seeing Harinder or anything around him properly. The care sheet hangs, forgotten, in his hand. His knuckles are chapped and bruised, and his nails need trimming.

"Sundance?" Harinder repeats warily.

Two seconds later, the kid is on the floor holding his head. He makes no sound as he goes down, but when Harinder reaches his side after bolting around the counter, his ears are assaulted by these peculiar wheezy noises.

"Hey, Sundance, it's okay," he says. "This doesn't mean you haven't made good progress or anything. By all rights, you've stuck to your commitments better than half the adults I talk to. You really read that care sheet, right?"

Silence.

Harinder is about to explode from tension when, finally, Sundance nods, still snuffling.

"That's good," Harinder says, encouraging. "Why don't you let me help you pick out everything you need for the enclosure, and then, before you leave, I'll let you choose one. If you promise to come back when you're sober, I will hold the one you want until you're comfortable enough to pick it up." It's unlikely he'd have sold it, anyway, but miracles are known to happen once every other century.

It takes a bit more cajoling, but eventually Sundance lifts his head to look at Harinder, eyes shifting into focus. "You swear?"

Harinder nods enthusiastically. "Yeah, of course. I wouldn't say it if I didn't mean it. Look, you wanna grab that care sheet and look at the materials list? I can show you where things are in the store, and you can start picking things out. Then we'll look at the geckos, okay?"

Sundance nods. His eyes are dry, meaning he probably wasn't crying. Harinder wonders what the whispery sounds were.

Everything goes as expected while helping the kid pick supplies. Sundance reads a bullet point and Harinder shows him where the items are, explains his options, and gives him as long as he needs to choose. It takes the better part of an hour, which Harinder is grateful for. He steps away twice to ring, but when he returns, Sundance has usually found at least one item from the list on his own.

Normally, Harinder would not be inclined to reward such a low-flying accomplishment, but Sundance managing to be semi-semi-functional despite the number of drugs in his system is impressive, so Harinder allows a few nice words to escape. No one else is around to witness it, and no one would believe Sundance if he told, so he's confident nothing bad will come of the lapse.

When the cart is full, Harinder adds up the prices on his phone (plus tax), ensuring Sundance's budget can cover everything he's picked. Satisfied, he suggests they look at geckos.

For the second time that day, Sundance collapses to the floor.

Harinder ends up sitting next to him, playing impromptu therapist and trying to decipher Sundance's babbling. He is scared about owning "a friend," scared that he'll fuck up and hurt his "new best friend." Luckily, Harinder has the responsibility speech down pat thanks to every other person he's sold an animal to during his two years of employment. He leans heavily on that spiel and then has to riff a little bit when Sundance fails to be consoled.

Of course, that'd be about the time Jericho comes in.

It's moderately unexpected. Jericho isn't the kind of person Harinder pegs for being up before noon on a Saturday. Regardless, there he is, shoving his hood back to reveal his pasty face, squinting at where they're sitting awkwardly on the floor. Harinder wills him not to say anything stupid or insensitive.

Jericho mouths, *Are you okay?* and wiggles his phone in the air.

Harinder makes as many "no" gestures as he can think up. He does *not* let himself experience anything in the way of emotions about how ready Jericho is to go to bat for him.

To drive the point home that things are mostly okay, Harinder places a hand gingerly on Sundance's shoulder and gives it a tentative rub. Jericho gets the point. Despite his obvious hesitation, he shoves his phone in his pocket and disappears to the other side of the shelving. His footsteps squeak down the length of the adjacent aisle, then stop, out of sight but still close. (Nope. Still not having any feelings.)

Sundance hasn't acknowledged anything else, so Harinder pulls a face and says, "I'll be back, okay? I'll be right back; you can just...sit here."

Standing, he then moves toward the reptile racks, making eye contact with Jericho when he passes. Sundance had expressed interest in the tangerine, if Harinder remembers correctly, so he unlocks the appropriate row and scoops the bright-orange juvenile into a deli cup. Jericho appears behind him while he's carefully fitting the lid over the cup, making sure not to pinch any delicate baby fingers.

"The fuck is going on?"

Harinder doesn't quite smack himself in the face when he whirls around, but it's a near thing. "Holy fucking shit in a bread bowl, how did you walk up so quietly?"

Jericho shrugs. "Old habits. What's up with the druggie?"

Despite having repeatedly described Sundance as a tweaker in his own internal monologue, Harinder's hackles bristle. "Don't call him that. He's just a kid."

"Yeah, a kid who smells like he just walked out of a Snoop Dogg concert. He's also crying on your floor."

"He's not crying," Harinder snaps before he adds, "Weirdly enough. I thought he was, but he's not. I think he's just seriously fucked up."

Jericho looks speculatively at the gecko sitting on the counter. "And you're about to appease him with a human sacrifice?"

Harinder scowls up at him. "Don't tempt me."

Holding his hands up in surrender, Jericho says, "It wouldn't work even if I tried. I'm not nearly as cute, and it'd be way harder to swallow my fat ass whole."

"I'm sure someone would be willing to try." Harinder refuses to think about the obnoxiously perverse ways what he just said could be interpreted. He also refuses to note how Jericho's lanky form is nearly as thin as Sundance's borderline-emaciated one. Refusing to think *at all* because that way lies danger, Harinder scoops the deli cup into his hands and returns to Sundance's side.

"Hey, Sundance," Harinder says in warning before lowering himself beside the despairing kid. "I brought someone to see you."

Sundance's head jerks. He looks around, panicked, pupils dilated and sclera stained red. Jericho quickly steps out of sight. It wasn't subtle, but if Sundance notices, he gives no indication.

"I didn't call anyone," Harinder says, then snaps his fingers a couple inches from Sundance's face. "Look at what I have in my hands, you ginormous doof." It takes a moment, but Sundance eventually obeys, frowning downwards.

At first Harinder isn't sure he knows what he's looking at, but then Sundance lifts a hand (trembling, ridiculously bony) and draws a single finger over the clear surface of the lid, running over the corrugated air holes.

"Someone like me can't be trusted with someone like this," he says, voice so full of melancholy Harinder almost chokes up himself.

"Listen," Harinder says. "If an asshole like me can be entrusted with an entire store full of helpless captive organisms, anyone can do it. Most people don't care, which is the bulk of the problem. Self-awareness is great. The more you hate yourself for something you dislike, the more you can keep it in line."

Harinder catches a glimpse of Jericho pulling a weird face at him from down the aisle, but it'd be too conspicuous to flick him off, so he just keeps spewing bullshit. "Like, if you're aware of the problem, you can fight it, or some garbage like that. Pets are good rehabilitators."

It doesn't seem to be working. Harinder makes a pained face back at Jericho over Sundance's shoulder.

"Maybe you can focus on taking care of a companion animal instead of doing so many drugs," he hazards.

Sundance snorts and wipes his nose, then starts laughing. It's the harsh gasp of a chain-smoker mixed with raw hysteria, and it is extremely unsettling. Still laughing, Sundance rolls his back. His tired vertebrae crunch like teeth snapping a burnt kettle chip.

Without any warning, Sundance stops laughing, and his head swivels toward where Jericho is peeking around the edge of the aisle, still mostly out of sight.

"You don't gotta hide," Sundance says. "We're doing great over here."

Jericho's face is blank when he slides into full view. He's got his hand in his hoodie pocket, probably clutching his phone. "'Sup," he says.

Harinder watches the space between them. It's not quite crackling, but he suspects they aren't particularly keen on each other, which is fucking fine because Harinder has no investment in either of these assholes. Sundance is a charity case slash business transaction. Jericho...is a nuisance. There's no reason they should ever have to get along or share the same space ever again, especially not in a way that has anything to do with Harinder.

Sundance raises to his full height. His slouch was so profound Harinder failed to notice before this point how tall he is. He's taller than Jericho, who is not particularly short himself. Not quite six feet, by Harinder's estimation. Harinder rarely cares about other people's heights, mostly because his temper thinks he is ten times larger than he actually is.

"So," he says, stepping between them to command their attention. He doesn't give a damn if he's only five foot three; no territorial assholes are going to start shit with each other in his store. Jericho has no room to judge Sundance's breakdown. He's had plenty of his own fits in this store. At this point, the business is practically the pet store of emotional baggage; they should just rename it Aquariums & Tantrums and be done with it.

"Sundance, if you aren't comfortable with taking home a pet, we can put the things back. Don't pressure yourself into something you aren't ready for."

The kid looks at Harinder, a crooked smile on his chapped lips. "No, I get you now." With barely a suspicious glance in Jericho's direction, he says, "I'll just go ahead and, uh." He falters for a second, then keeps going. "I'm gonna get his home set up, right? Then come back when I'm ummm. *Sober*." He spits out the word like it tastes bad.

Harinder scrunches his mouth tight to hide a smile, nodding in approval. "Sounds good. Grab your cart and get your ass to the register before I get sick of dealing with this shit."

Sundance grins and lopes off, still rank and disgusting but looking looser, less manic.

Harinder shoves the deli cup into Jericho's hands when he passes, muttering, "Hold this for me," as he hops behind the cashwrap.

Chapter Eleven

Harinder Regrets to Inform You That He Is Feeling

Money changes hands, and Sundance assures him he can get all this stuff home on the bus just fine, and Harinder doesn't question him (though he does question the damp, sticky quality of the bills). Sundance makes it out of the store without hitting the floor a third time, and Harinder shoves the cash he got from him into a ziplock bag and scribbles a quick note for Mr. Kulkarni that they should be exchanged at the bank and then destroyed. He grabs the hand sanitizer quickly after.

Jericho watches him with an unreadable expression. "Y'know, the most respected prophet in all nine realms could have woken me up in the middle of the night with a blowjob and a vision telling me this was going to happen, and I still wouldn't have believed you physically capable of being so chill to another person. Are you gonna go into cardiac arrest? Want I should call EMS to stop by and check your vitals?"

Harinder takes a deep breath, entreating himself to be calm, and then changes his mind when it doesn't work. "Fuck off. I'm not heartless."

"Obviously not," Jericho says, sauntering around the edge of the counter, still holding the gecko. "You care more about lizards than most people care about their children. That's hardly heartless. I'm just saying, you don't like people much." Pause. "Or has that escaped your notice."

Scowling, Harinder shoves the plague-money bag into the slot in the register. "I'm not gonna be nasty to some stupid teenager who has no idea what he's doing and has problems of his own that don't need to be exacerbated by a random asshole cashier."

"I've literally seen you cuss people out for not wanting to touch bugs."

Harinder slams his fist on the counter. "Look, if people don't want to feed reptiles what they're supposed to fucking eat, they need to get a different goddamn pet; it's common fucking sense."

Snickering, Jericho sets the deli cup on the counter and pushes it over to Harinder's side. "Right, it is. I'm just saying, since when do you care about people's feelings when it comes to dorks who don't know their shit?"

Harinder gathers the gecko against his chest, cradling it lovingly. It proves Jericho's earlier point, but nothing short of Thor himself kicking in the front door and threatening to shit in the aquatic filtration unit could get him to admit that. Instead, he deflects: "Since when do you show up before noon?"

"I got shit to do," Jericho says, shoving his hands in his pockets.

Harinder gives him a skeptical look, pausing at the swinging door.

"Okay," Jericho admits, "I don't have jack, I just pulled an all-nighter and couldn't get to sleep after the sun came up."

Now it's Harinder's turn for a derisive snort. (Though, when is it not?) "Hanging out with friends or something?" He expects Jericho to follow him back toward the reptiles, but when he takes a few paces and doesn't hear any movement, he looks over his shoulder to where Jericho still stands in the same exact spot, staring after him. "Uh, civilization to Jericho?"

"Sorry," Jericho says automatically, "I just thought for a second you implied I had friends, and it was so funny I forgot to laugh."

"What, with a personality like yours?" Harinder wonders. "I'm shocked."

"Oh, like you're one to talk."

Harinder raises his eyebrows and circles back to fully face Jericho. "I have friends," he says, not dignifying the challenge with anything other than that. It's not worth getting pissed over. "I have a lot of friends, actually." Whether he has time to spend with them is not the issue being discussed.

He expects Jericho to say something nasty or witty or insincere or sarcastic or otherwise obnoxious, but his brow wrinkles, and he looks...pretty fucking embarrassed. Harinder is deciding whether or not to feel offended or patronized when it occurs to him that Jericho just sincerely admitted to not having friends, and if he follows that to its logical conclusion, he probably assumed Harinder was the same.

Ouch.

"Shit," Jericho says eventually because he can't just not say anything. "That's cool, then. Good for you."

Trying to give him a minute to recover, Harinder walks away wordlessly, unboxes the gecko, and returns him to his enclosure. He locks the row and wanders back to where Jericho was, only to find him absent. At first, he thinks Jericho has bailed, but he didn't hear the door.

He eventually finds him sticking his fingers in the ferret cage.

"Is there anything in here you don't feel entitled to touch?" Harinder wonders, but it's missing the venom.

"Plenty," Jericho says, not moving otherwise.

With a sidelong glance, Harinder mirrors his position, slumping against the opposite side of the cage and shoving his own fingers up against the grate, wiggling them until someone comes over to chew on them. "So," he says, avoiding Jericho's face. "How come you don't have any friends?"

"This is bullying," Jericho protests.

"You brought it up."

"Ugh." Jericho pulls his hand away from the ferrets to rub at his eyes. "I moved recently to be near my sister, which I might've already told you. Things here are...different, compared to De Queen. I guess."

"It's a small east coast suburb of a city populated mostly by middle class white people too broke to live in the city proper, so I can see where you'd get that impression."

"Fuck off," Jericho sighs. "But yeah, exactly that."

Harinder's gaze drifts to Jericho's pale hands. He shouldn't speculate, but he isn't exactly going to ask either. It seems like Jericho is going to volunteer the information regardless.

"Back in De Queen, I didn't fit in anywhere, mostly 'cuz I was a fucking asocial nerd, but also because no one knew what to do with me. Black kids thought I was weird, white kids thought I was weird. My Spanish wasn't good enough to find other people who might not be put off by my...everything."

Harinder drops his gaze, mouth pursing. "That's tough."

"It wasn't too awful," Jericho says. "In my neighborhood, if someone thought your ass was weird, they'd come outside just to tell you so. It doesn't sound like it'd be better, but at least people paid attention to me. I'd get asked if I'm a ghost or something stupid, and be all, 'Yeah, actually. Most ghosts are invisible but I flunked out of ghost academy so I have to walk around looking like this instead.'"

Despite himself, Harinder smiles.

"See?" Jericho smiles back, though halfheartedly. "They laugh, and even though they still think I'm an albino freak, at least I'm funny, right? I got a chance to defend myself, so I didn't have friends, but there were some guys who wouldn't let anyone fuck with me." He looks distantly between the cage bars. "One time, I was at the bus stop, and this kid asked if I was still Black without any melanin, and I said of course I was. He still didn't like me, but at least he knew I wasn't trying to side with white people."

It sounds weird on the surface, but Harinder nods because when Jericho explains it like that, it almost makes sense.

"Here, though…" Tomas begins gnawing at Jericho's hand, but he doesn't react.

"My sister and I were separated when we were kids. She got got by CPS, and was adopted. I...wasn't. Our uncle ended up getting custody of me. When I left De Queen, I moved here to be with Shiloh. I didn't really think of how different it'd be moving from a neighborhood where white folks were scared to walk to a place where it was...full of them, basically. I didn't expect the cultural difference of living on the East Coast either."

He's taking a while longer to get to the point, even for him, so Harinder assumes there's something he's building up to that's a bit harder to say.

"Here, people don't even wanna look at me."

Oh.

Brows knit, Harinder seeks out Jericho's eyes, but they're closed. His eyelashes are long, ice-white like his puffy Afro, and he has tiny freckles over his eyelids.

"Imagine going to the register to get some Gatorade, and the cashier glances at you, and for a split second, their eyes get real wide, and then they look down and spend the rest of the transaction staring at a screen. It's not incidental. Half of everyone does it because it's impolite to stare, and it's impolite to say anything, so instead, they treat me like I don't fucking exist."

His nose scrunches up in a grimace. "No one gives me a chance to prove myself, no one even stops to call me a faggot. I make them uncomfortable, so they pretend I'm not even fucking there rather than deal with the awkward feelings."

"Fucking...fuck," Harinder says, lost for any other words.

"Yeah," Jericho says without a hint of mirth, even of the self-deprecating kind. "And I'm not exactly the kind of person who approaches someone just because I recognize the band name on their T-shirt, but on the rare occasions where I lose my cool enough to try, it's like..." He shrugs. "I'm still a tall Black kid, I guess."

"People are fucked up." Harinder doesn't know how to process the information. He's not good at sympathizing in the first place, but there's so much more he hadn't considered. As an Indian man who stands at the height of the average thirteen-year-old, Harinder isn't considered threatening. Until he opens his mouth, people hardly notice him. Sure, he's a target for plenty of racism, but no one clutches their purse and has 911 on speed dial when Harinder walks past.

Eurgh. He rubs at his temple and terminates the line of thought. It's insulting to compare experiences anyway.

"Do you really not have anyone?" Prying seems insensitive, but Harinder can't help but ask. Surely Jericho is exaggerating in the heat of the moment.

Jericho snorts softly. "My sister. Her fiancée. I have a couple online friends."

The list ends. Harinder frowns.

"No wonder you want a cat," Harinder says without thinking. Jericho snorts again. Louder, maybe more bitterly.

"I got my reasons, yeah." He wets his bottom lip with his tongue, then pulls his face away from the cage bars. There are tiny red imprints left on his white skin, which he promptly rubs at. He snuffles. "Man, I think I'm allergic to these things."

Harinder opens his mouth to say, *Well, maybe you should stop coming here,* but some bizarre divine intervention has him reconsidering. "You're probably just stuffy because you shoved your goddamn face against their cage, loser," he says instead.

It's not any nicer, but it's also not a rejection. He doesn't think Jericho needs that right now. It's a weird day for Harinder, feeling sorry for so many people, but something prompts him to keep the ball rolling.

"Hey," he says quietly, "so about the—"

"Fuck," Jericho says at the same time, not noticing Harinder was about to speak. He paces several steps from the cage, back to Harinder. "I'm sorry I keep coming here and bothering you. I'm such a sack of shit."

It's so completely unprecedented that Harinder is reduced to owlish blinking. "I've had, like, three customers all day. It's okay." It's nearly one PM, so business will likely be picking up soon. They'll have to stop yelling at each other in the middle of the store.

"That's not the point," Jericho says. "I just—" He gesticulates silently, caught in some private battle. Harinder isn't sure how to help. "I'm so— We're not even fucking *friends*."

Harinder isn't sure how to disagree. He's never said anything nicer than condescendingly neutral to Jericho the entire time he's been showing up, so while his present instinct may be to deny anything Jericho says, he isn't sure that's an entirely honest response.

They *aren't* friends. Jericho really only comes by to harass him about the adoption since it's convenient, what with him washing windows on the strip and all.

"Plenty of my customers aren't my friends," Harinder says eventually.

"I've never bought a single goddamn thing from here," Jericho retorts like he was waiting for it.

"That's fine," Harinder says, starting to get uncomfortable. "It's whatever. I don't fucking care."

"That's exactly why I end up hanging out here," Jericho says, voice suddenly lowered. Harinder almost misses it.

"What?"

"You don't care," Jericho repeats. "You hate everyone equally like a shitty edgelord Facebook meme that's just a pixilated screencap of something that originated on Myspace. It's hilarious how getting constantly screamed at is comforting after being ignored for so long." Before the last word leaves his lips, Jericho is already turning red—over his cheeks and at the tips of his ears. He claps a hand over his face and then makes a beeline for the door.

Harinder doesn't think about the consequences of leaving the store unwatched. He chases him.

"Jericho, wait!"

Jericho stops at the edge of the Aquariums & More property, pulling his hood over his head. "What?" He turns halfway toward Harinder but keeps his face pointed toward the ground.

"Look, I don't know how much community service you've completed," Harinder says, shoving his hands under his armpits to keep them warm. He has no idea how Jericho—who's from fucking Arkansas of all places—manages in just his shirt and a hoodie. "But don't worry about the rest." Jericho's face contorts to one of confusion. "You don't have to come here every day and feel awkward and shit, just. Don't even bother, alright?"

"What am I gonna do about the stupid fucking qualifications then?" Jericho asks, turning his hands out. He isn't usually this expressive, which makes Harinder feel terrible.

Panicking, because after having told Jericho the community service was mandatory, Harinder isn't sure how to justify this, he shouts, "I...can waive it!"

Jericho looks unimpressed.

"If you consent to a background check, I can waive the community service requirement," Harinder finally spits out in one breath.

Jericho goes blank again. Harinder feels even worse. "A background check."

"Yeah, it's just, we do the community service because we need to have the reassurance, that, you know. Most people aren't going to want to do a background check, but it's an alternative, and you won't have to come up here every day, and if the results come back clean, I can approve your adoption." Not that he will. He doesn't even know how to file for a background check, to be honest.

Despite looking like he's about to tear his hair out, Jericho keeps his hands at his sides. He lifts them a bit, then drops them again, pursing his lips and fidgeting. "You know what, fine. Cool. Do you need written consent?"

"No, I can handle it." He knows from the hiring process at A&M alone that he most definitely *would* need written consent to file a background check, but it doesn't matter, seeing as it isn't happening. "I'll just, uh, run the paperwork. And get back to you."

"Cool," Jericho says, not looking cool at all. "You've got my number."

"Yeah," Harinder agrees because he does and has no idea what else to say. "Just. Take it easy, okay?"

"Sure," says Jericho curtly, probably not even looking at him anymore. He jams his hands in his pockets.

"You didn't, uh, forget your phone inside again, right?"

"No," answers Jericho, sliding it out an inch so Harinder can see he has it before pushing his hands back into the worn jacket.

"Do you ever get cold?" Harinder asks.

"Yeah," Jericho says and turns to leave without saying another word. Harinder has no reason to stop him, so he watches his back until he reaches the bus stop. When he finally goes inside, he discovers he's lost all feeling in his face.

Chapter Twelve

Jericho Is Moved to Basic Decency

Jericho tells himself he's only coming back because he didn't realize Kimchi was out of dry food and didn't buy any Friday when he took her to Aquariums & More to meet Harinder. Harinder who wasn't subtle about the fact that he wanted the dog around more than he wanted Jericho.

It doesn't hurt, necessarily—which is not to say that Jericho is upset about Harinder telling him to fuck off. Because he's not. They aren't even friends, like Harinder said. Or he said. He doesn't remember that conversation so well.

He's hooking Kimchi's leash to her collar when his phone rings. That's weird enough, seeing as his phone never rings unless Shiloh is calling him, and that's kind of why he's in this situation in the first place. The number is unfamiliar.

Jericho hesitantly brings his phone to his ear, concerned he's about to discover he has a stalker and this is the creepy first contact predating his murder.

"Yes?"

About a year ago, Jericho signed up for an oil painting workshop. Shiloh predicted he would hate it, but instead, he was enraptured by the whole process; so beautiful and meticulous. It forced him out of the house. It gave him an excuse to pile flowers on top of old animal bones and wrap the whole design around some weird sex toys he nabbed from the sale bin at the grody Lover's Lane two blocks from his apartment building.

More than half the class thought he was unreachably bizarre, but it didn't bother him. He's used to ostracism, and socializing was never his goal. At the end of the course, the teacher approached to offer contact info for a gallery located in the nearby urban hotspot.

Months ago, he decided to give it a shot but never received a response. Not particularly invested either way, Jericho had completely forgotten the brief chapter of his life.

So, when he hears the name of the gallery through the phone speaker, he has to sit down.

When Jericho hangs up, he tentatively pegs the emotion he's experiencing as excitement, but isn't one hundred percent sure. They asked him to bring his work over.

Holy shit.

He removes Kimchi from the leash. He'll walk her later—right now, he has to get to the gallery, which he highly suspects is named Last Minute As Fuck since they asked how soon he could be there. Unwilling to risk taking his paintings on the bus, Jericho schedules an Uber before unearthing the abandoned canvases from his closet.

The gallery lives about twenty minutes out of his city, toward the Petco and its upper-middle class white customers. Naturally, it runs alongside the bus line Jericho follows for his daily trips to Aquariums & More. He fidgets, chews at the corner of his lip, then leans forward to talk to the driver.

Five minutes. Just in and out. Just get the dog food and—

Harinder looks up and his bored expression changes drastically. More overwhelmed on the feelings front than he expected, Jericho averts his gaze, not wanting to spend emotional energy deciphering the meaning of the look.

"Hey. I just need to get some food for Kimchi," Jericho says, staring hard at the hermit crab tank. Harinder's taken the sign off again. They're pretty cool when kept properly and allowed to climb and dig. Jericho had no idea.

Walking out from behind the counter, Harinder asks, "Do you need help, uh, finding anything?"

Jericho turns back to him, brow scrunched. "Dude, I'm here, like. Every day."

Harinder hunches his shoulders and scowls. His chin disappears under his wide, mustardy collar. Jericho wonders if it ever gets dirty. How would he clean a sweater so fast?

"I'm just fucking asking, jeez."

"Jeez," Jericho deadpans in response, leaving for the dog food aisle. He gets the smallest bag he can because he doesn't want to carry it everywhere, but he also doesn't want to stop anywhere else, so this is the lesser of two evils even if he has to deal with Harinder. He takes it up to the register and avoids making small talk, instead focusing on the line of dust around one of the counter displays. He doesn't say anything.

"You're leaving already?" Harinder asks, scanning the bag of food.

The pause that follows is as ambiguous as it is uncomfortable. "I got somewhere to be, I guess."

Harinder snorts, taking Jericho's proffered credit card. "When do you ever have somewhere to be?"

Jericho inspects him until Harinder shrivels with visible discomfort. "I have a meeting with a gallery that wants to show some of my work," he says without inflection.

"...work?"

"Paintings," Jericho says, then he rips his own receipt off the printer and grabs the food without waiting for Harinder to put it in a bag. Harinder doesn't call after Jericho when he stalks out the door, the bell jingling merrily with his departure. Maybe that's for the best.

*

The return Uber cancels on him. This is the Beat-Up Artsy Corner of downtown, and there's a fuckton of construction all around. It's not exactly a huge city, either, so there aren't that many Uber drivers around. Most residents here bike or walk. Getting to the gallery was a pain earlier in the day, but now it's rush hour.

Jericho tries again twice, sighs, then asks the lady at the gallery counter if she has a bag he can use. After storming out of Aquariums & More without a bag for the dog food, Jericho had to carry it awkwardly from the Uber, tucked under his arm alongside the heavy portfolio containing his paintings.

The gallery decides to hang all but two pieces. Less cool is Jericho having to drag those home on the bus, along with the dog food. To make things worse, as he's trying to fit the food bag into the portfolio alongside the two canvases, the bottom splits open, which is very professional and not embarrassing at all.

The lady at the counter gives him two plastic garbage bags and finds a roll of duct tape so he can reinforce the bottom of the bag along with the handles.

If he goes to the nearest bus stop, it'll only be a few minutes' ride before he has to transfer to the right line, so Jericho decides to walk rather than spend the extra thirty cents. He immediately regrets the decision, but as previously established by the whole Harinder situation, Jericho is a poor match for sunk-cost fallacy, so he keeps going.

This turns out to be an even worse decision because dragging his feet through the wet slushy snow in weather-inappropriate sneakers causes him to miss the next bus. He wastes more time calculating the time it'll take the bus after that to arrive at the following stop, decides to walk instead of waiting, and then almost misses *that* bus as well. In the end, Jericho is forced to run an entire block in order to reach the stop right as the driver is about to close the doors, heavy-ass trash bag banging on his leg the whole way.

When he gets on, it's to find said driver laughing at him, which definitely makes him feel good.

Jericho slumps in his seat, exhausted. He doesn't have the energy to adjust the jostled contents of the bag. He doesn't have energy to do more than stare vacantly out the window, barely processing the blurred visual feedback. It doesn't matter. He can die like this.

Fifteen minutes stands between Jericho and his stop, but he doesn't dare close his eyes. Even setting a ten-minute alarm would be a dangerous gamble; he doesn't trust himself not to konk out entirely. To keep himself awake, Jericho forces himself to mumble the names of the businesses lining each dreary strip mall as they slip in and out of his peripheral. He probably looks like a lunatic.

The bus pulls up to the intersection beside a strip mall of more significance. Jericho has become extremely familiar with this intersection over the past few weeks.

Before he started his war with Aquariums & More's grumpy hedgehog of a guardian, Jericho had been completely isolated. Without Shiloh's attention, he would've forgotten how to talk and turned into one of those feral children, never leaving the apartment and surviving on delivery, always leaving instructions for the driver to sprint for safety the moment they released their quarry.

After today, he doesn't have to worry about bugging Harinder anymore, which is disappointing in ways Jericho doesn't know how to deal with. He's not going to get the cat. Shiloh won't talk to him again. On top of that, he still doesn't have any friends. Not that Harinder was a prospective friend anyway, but just hypotheti— *Holy shit what.*

Sitting on the bench at his usual stop is a small body, bent over with hands over their face in clear distress. The person is wearing a mustard-yellow sweater.

Harinder.

Jericho isn't quite close enough to get too many details, but the way his shoulders are shaking makes it look like he's fucking crying. Jericho disbelieves the notion so sincerely that he sits up and smashes his nose against the window to get a better view. Harinder's crumpled pose appears just as despairing in higher resolution.

The bus lurches back into motion. Jericho watches with wide eyes as the bench slowly slides out of his line of vision, taking Harinder with it.

They get one block, and then Jericho hauls on the stop request cord, already scrambling to his feet.

It takes forever for the bus to slow down and longer for the side exit doors to creak open. Jericho waits anxiously, bag in hand. He almost forgot the damn thing and is both grateful and annoyed that a helpful person across the aisle called his attention to it before Jericho could fling himself out the doors. The moment he figures he can fit through the opening without losing any limbs or valuables, Jericho is gone, onto the curb, not caring that he doesn't have a transfer and will have to pay twice if he ever wants to see his beloved bed again.

Jericho runs down the sidewalk, burdened by his goods but not stopping even though he's sure he's working up a hell of a thigh bruise. His pace slows as he makes it over the crosswalk, leaving about half a block between him and the bench. Harinder hasn't moved, trembling visibly with his face still in his hands, and as Jericho's steps (faltering, now) grow nearer, the sound of Harinder's sobs becomes audible.

Jericho doesn't know what to do. He comes to a full halt two pavement squares away from the bench, and stares.

A full minute passes before Harinder's head snaps around, and he snarls, "Find something else to gawk at, assho—oh."

Jericho was probably the last person he expected to see, and it shows. Harinder's shoulders hunch around his ears, and instead of churning up one of his usual caustic rants, he reduces himself to staring at the ground. Tears flow freely down his cheeks.

"Hey." Jericho shifts his weight uncomfortably. He makes a point not to ask if Harinder is okay.

Harinder snuffles loudly and wipes the sleeve of his sweater across his face. Jericho thinks he has some napkins in his pocket—yep, he does. He takes the opportunity to inch closer, holding them out by the very corner so his fingers don't accidentally brush Harinder's while the offering is exchanging hands.

Harinder squints up at him through his swollen, reddened eyes—how long was he crying, even? Shit—but he takes them, then blows his nose messily. "Thanks," he mutters.

Jericho eases himself onto the bench, staying as close to the edge as he can to ensure Harinder doesn't feel crowded. "So," he says, cautious. "Can I ask?"

Huffing a bitter laugh, Harinder says, "If I say no, you'll still be sitting here."

"I can leave," Jericho offers after a brief moment of thought.

"No." Harinder curls his fist around the dirty napkin. "You don't... You don't..." He trembles on the last two words, and Jericho looks up in time to see him burst into tears anew.

"Hey, Harinder, c'mon—"

"My house got robbed last night," he squeaks out, voice constricted.

Jericho feels his own chest go tight. "Fuck."

"Everything they stole belonged to my roommate," Harinder says, wiping his nose and mouth with a second napkin. "I lock my room, so they didn't get anything of mine, except they—" He stutters, hiccuping. "They cut my bike chain and stole my bike. I had to fucking walk to work this morning. I was so dazed. I'd been in my room the whole time, already asleep. Everyone else was fucking around in the basement. Some assholes just walked in and stole shit."

Swallowing, Jericho offers, "At least no one got hurt?"

Harinder snorts. "At least." He rubs his wrists over his eyes. "My roommate called me a few hours ago and had the audacity to blame me. Like I'm the one who fucking left the front door unlocked! That titbaby said some 'thugs' must've followed me from downtown so they could steal my bike, and everything else was opportunity, which is god-damn-fucking bullshit, and he *knows* it." Harinder pauses to breathe, on the verge of hyperventilation.

Jericho clutches his fist around the duct tape–covered bag handles to prevent himself from reaching out. "What a horse's ass."

"Yes," Harinder agrees, nodding viciously. "He fucking is. He really thinks someone followed my broke ass for forty-five minutes just so they could take my shitty bike? And not that someone—probably one of his shit-eating frat brothers—knows he's completely irresponsible about locking doors or having any insinuation of home security, and took advantage of the fact that he is extremely predictable with his beer pong schedule? And fuck, that is so goddamn embarrassing I hate myself for having said it out loud.

"God is punishing me right now. Some medieval torture artists are going to pop out of the sewer and rip out my tongue for the audacity."

"Let's not go that far," suggests Jericho, leaning back against the bench and sighing. "I'm guessing you aren't just rage crying while waiting for the bus though." He throws a quick glance to Harinder. "Not that there's a problem with that. Let it all out."

Harinder squints at him, but the sass dies before drawing its first breath. His eyes water. "Yeah. No. An hour ago, his dad texted me. He flew in with the spare key to my room. They curbed my shit and told me not to come back." Jericho's jaw drops, but Harinder doesn't stop talking. "They're blaming me, and I—and I—" His voice cracks again. "I don't have anywhere to go. That's all I fucking had, and I could hire a van to move my stuff—whatever's left of it—but what would I do with it? I should lie in the street and let my body return to the fucking asphalt where it belongs—"

"Or," Jericho cuts in, "instead of that, I could text the weird guy who lives in my apartment building and ask if he's free to lend his truck to a good cause."

Harinder's mouth opens, but he lets it hang there, processing. He slowly closes his mouth, chews on his lip, then says, "What part of 'I don't have anywhere to go' don't you understand?"

Jericho cocks an eyebrow. "I mean, I figured since he's gonna to go back to our building anyway, we'd just make that a final destination type thing. For now, I mean." It's as direct as he's going to get, which is to say: not direct at all.

As such, it takes Harinder a minute to catch his drift. "Wait. What."

It'd be polite to reiterate the point more clearly, but Jericho wasn't raised like that. He shrugs, self-conscious. "I got a couch, man."

"I'm loud and irritable and a terrible roommate," Harinder snaps, sounding as defensive as Jericho.

"Well, shit, it's not like I asked you to marry me," Jericho says. "But I got a bunch of space in my basement storage where you could stash your stuff until you find a new apartment."

Harinder's face crumples. He looks more broken than before now that Jericho's doubled down on his offer. "Seriously?"

The sound of squealing brakes interrupts what would have been Jericho's response. The bus Jericho usually shows up on pauses at the stop across the street. The doors open with a groan.

Jericho stands up, hauling his bag off the ground. "C'mon. There's another company that runs a bus down this street. There's a stop a few blocks down that we could walk to so we don't freeze to the bench. Tickets are fifty cents more, but I figure it's worth it." He pauses, offering a small smirk. "Unless you got somewhere else to be, in which case." He gestures at the bus going the other direction.

"No," Harinder says, standing up and brushing the wrinkles out of his sweater. "Let's go."

Chapter Thirteen

Jericho Pretends to Be Snow White

Assuring Harinder that he'll be in and out in a minute, Jericho jogs into his apartment building and takes the stairs more quickly than strictly necessary. Fortunately, he doesn't trip. He drops off the paintings and dog food in his apartment—not a moment too soon, considering the pale spot at the bottom where one of the canvases distended the plastic.

He makes himself wait for the elevator for the trip down. The damn thing is glacial, and Jericho rarely has the patience to wait for it. Right now is no exception, especially since Harinder's belongings are likely being pawed through by curbside pickers at this very moment, but the elevator is closer to his next destination than the staircase, so Jericho sucks it up and only fidgets a lot.

In the very back of the first floor is an apartment so creepy it appears as if the fluorescent lighting has been cowed into flickering simply for the sake of atmosphere. Appropriately, the number on the door is hauntingly, inexplicably, a solitary "1."

Jericho knocks, trying to convince himself he's not about to stumble into an unseelie fae bargain. No answer issues forth, so he knocks again. "Hey, Denny! It's Jericho."

The door jerks open violently, stopped by a chain lock. A weathered face sprayed with uneven patches of salt-and-pepper stubble snarls through the gap, a yellow-toothed smoker's rasp. "What?"

It's good Jericho has plenty of practice not showing fear. He merely blinks. "I, uh, need a favor."

Denny is a creepy white guy who prefers glaring to conversation. Jericho spent his first six months in the building heeding advice to give the man a wide berth. Sometime after that, he played unwilling participant to a seventy-two-hour insomnia bender during which he encountered Denny by the vending machines at two AM and could not stop talking while waiting for Denny to finish his selections. Jericho doesn't remember so well, but has been informed by the security guard (the only surviving witness) that his choice of topics had included skin conditions once he noticed the congenital nevus covering a third of Denny's face.

Instead of getting murdered, Jericho gained access to a grunted, "'lo," whenever he and Denny passed each other in the hall thereafter. He hasn't deluded himself into believing murder isn't somewhere on a future menu (hidden in the dessert course, maybe), but for now, Jericho is glad to have conversation rights.

Riding into a nice neighborhood in Denny's rattling death trap of a truck feels like smearing shit on an impressionist masterpiece. Jericho only glances up from his phone a few times, so he doesn't get to fully appreciate the metaphor. Not for lack of inclination, but because he's trying to ignore Harinder's thigh pressing against his in the dangerously small cabin. Heroically, and also because he didn't want to witness a violently negative chemical reaction, Jericho chose to wedge himself in the tiny seat between the driver and right-side passenger rather than let Harinder contend with sitting next to Denny, despite the man being far smaller and thus better suited to the space.

Jericho can't help but notice Harinder has some pudge on him, so maybe their hips aren't too different in width after all. He isn't thinking about Harinder's hips though.

They pull up at an elaborate white house with a snarl of dead, snow-covered branches in the front where there might have once been a garden. Spread out over the front lawn is Harinder's whole life.

The futon is soaked, covered in side-of-the-road slush. They agree to leave it behind. His dresser remains, along with a crumbling plywood desk. Denny offers to take the dresser over the cash payment Jericho offered. Mutters something about it being an antique. Harinder agrees, though the twinge in his expression might be disappointment. Could also be general stress, but Jericho doesn't have time to decipher.

The three of them fill the truck bed with several garbage bags full of miscellaneous items, all belongings haphazardly yanked from Harinder's former room and scattered over the curb.

"Someone took my fucking nightstand," Harinder grumbles. He looks despairingly at his damaged desk.

"I got extra desks at my apartment," Jericho says. "You can have one."

Once Harinder finishes shoving a handful of blankets and pillows into the truck cabin, behind the seats, Jericho asks if he's found everything. Harinder gives him a tight-lipped stare. The answer is in his nonanswer.

The only piece of furniture actually worth taking is the desk chair. Denny jostles the pile of garbage bags aside so he can fit it into the back of the truck and throws a tarp over the accumulated mess.

The return ride to the apartment is tense and silent. This time, Harinder opts to sit in the back with his wet bedding.

Denny pulls up to the loading area in the back of the complex and helps them unload the bags, the chair, and the dresser. They throw everything into Jericho's basement storage to sort through later, still only talking when necessary.

Finally, they help get Denny's new dresser to the hallway in front of his apartment door. Harinder offers a quiet "thank you," but Denny doesn't bother with a "you're welcome." He shoves the dresser into his apartment without asking for further assistance and slams the door.

"That guy is two steps from becoming a serial killer," Jericho tells Harinder as they ride the elevator to his third-floor apartment. A single bag with toiletries and a few clothes hangs over his shoulder. When they get to the landing, Jericho fiddles for his keys, but Harinder hovers a few feet away, hands fidgeting.

Jericho gets the door open and sets the bag down inside.

Harinder still hasn't moved.

"C'mon, Don't tell me you're scared," Jericho says.

"I'm not," Harinder snaps. He finally walks up and peers nervously through the entryway.

"Okay, chill." Jericho kicks off his wet sneakers and grimaces as his socks slosh on the tiles.

"I don't know how you survive up here," Harinder says. He's looking at Jericho's red knuckles peeking out from over the long sleeves of his hoodie.

"Spite, mostly. My sister didn't think I'd make it either."

"You'd have an easier time if you wore weather-appropriate clothes."

Jericho shrugs out of his hoodie, revealing nothing but a long-sleeved T-shirt. "Yeah, maybe. I'm lazy as shit though. At least I don't wear the same sweater every day."

"God for-fucking-bid I not want to turn into an icicle on the way to work," Harinder says sourly.

"Okay, but what's your excuse for (a) not taking it off once you get to work, and (b) wearing the same sweater every single day? Mix it up a little, Mangal. Try some dusky-coral or polka dots. Colorful stripes. Argyle, even."

"Maybe I just like this sweater."

"Maybe you just like looking like a dweeb."

"You are so not one to talk, asshole."

Snickering quietly, Jericho rubs the lingering dampness from snow out of his Afro and shuffles deeper into the apartment. "What, Ninja Turtles not your thing?"

"I haven't seen you wear that since we first met," Harinder comments. "I hoped you'd burned it."

"No such luck, my guy. Your ferret friends peed on it, and I haven't gotten around to doing laundry."

"What?" Harinder pulls a face. "Ew, it's been almost three weeks."

"Yeup," Jericho agrees. "Anyway. Make yourself at home."

Jericho's apartment isn't the worst it could be, but it's definitely still a mess. The front isn't so bad, but his room is worse. He shouldn't give a fuck what Harinder thinks.

If he really wants to bitch, he'll find something to fixate on no matter what. Even the Buckingham Motherfucking Palace wouldn't be immune to Harinder's scathing critique.

"I have to piss like crazy," Jericho says. "There's food in the fridge if you're hungry. Help yourself to anything."

He stays in the bathroom longer than necessary, running his icy hands under warm water, trying to bring some heat back into them. Had he any pigment in his skin, Jericho suspects it would have run for the hills, leaving him just as pale. At last, figuring there's no more improvement to be gotten, he sheds his wet socks, throws them over the shower caddy in the bathtub, and shuffles out of the bathroom.

"Hey."

Harinder jumps, whirling around to face him.

"Whoa there." Jericho holds up his hands in a pacifying gesture. "Settle down, stallion."

"I fucking hate you," Harinder says.

"Yeah, well." Jericho shrugs, then cuts open the garbage bag so he can unload his paintings onto the nearest desk.

When Jericho first moved from De Queen, he didn't have many possessions. After over a decade of having no space and no privacy, the emptiness of his first real apartment started getting...itchy. His solution? Fill it with hobbies.

Four desks have been staggered throughout the apartment.

His simple bedroom has a simple computer desk, in addition to the equally simple bed and nightstand. A drawing desk with an adjustable incline rests by the living room window; directly across the apartment lives the third, which had originally been used for a well-intentioned attempt at stop-motion animation—quickly abandoned once jerkily moving figures started appearing in his nightmares. He repurposed it to be a display rack, filling its high-storage shelves with art, figurines, and pretty rocks. It now sits next to the television.

Neither Jericho nor the apartment needed a fourth desk, but he found a nice one at an estate sale and was embarrassingly attracted to its fine craftmanship and distressed finish. It now lives a glamorous life jammed behind the couch, where the detritus of everyday living might accumulate on its charming vintage surface. Jericho inspects said detritus and frowns.

"Hey, so, I definitely had no reason to expect company today and so am woefully unprepared. If you could find it in you to take like..." He thinks hard for a second. "...a twenty-five-minute shower, that'd be great."

Harinder's shoulders hunch up at his ears. "I don't need to—"

"Listen," Jericho interrupts. "If I have to attempt cleaning with you sitting there watching me, I'm going to end up casting myself into the garbage disposal out of shame. Throw me a bone here."

Harinder scowls. "You're not cute enough for me to throw bones at you."

"We can't all be Kimchi," he says without missing a beat. "Please?"

"Why do you care this much if I shower or not? Am I too disgusting to be on your couch?"

"More like my couch is too disgusting to be worthy of your ass."

Harinder rolls his eyes, but Jericho might see the suggestion of a smile hiding in the corners of his pursed lips.

"I'm serious though," Jericho continues. "Are you trying to get me to beg? Because I won't. You're perfectly welcome to stay cold, wet, and unhappy in my nasty apartment if that's truly your heart's desire."

"It's not that bad," he insists.

"Good to know. Bathroom's on the right. Oh, and I lost the spare key, so try not to lock yourself out. The hardware store is definitely closed by now, and I'm not into the medieval pissing-into-a-crockpot thing."

Harinder muffles something that might be an exhausted laugh and might be an appeal to the elder gods for silence, then makes a begrudging show of kicking off his shoes and walking down the hall. As soon as the door closes, the lock clicks. Jericho's glad he got the message Jericho coded into his casual shit talk: Yes, there is a lock on the bathroom door. No, it will not be mysteriously picked open while Harinder is in there, naked and vulnerable.

The first ten minutes of Harinder's shower are spent frantically picking shit up and shoving it in storage bins that had designated contents before they became emergency junk receptacles. He's going to have a hell of a time organizing them later.

Fifteen minutes left on the clock, and he finally gets the living area sorted. He squints his eyes.

There's nothing wrong with the futon. He spent most of his life sleeping on a futon, which is why he got one instead of a regular couch. It's probably got some crumbs in the folds, but it was brand new when he got it. The frame is sturdy and doesn't require victory in dishonorable combat before converting to or from the bed.

The apartment space is wide and very open.

Jericho walks into his bedroom and strips the sheets off his bed. He tosses them into the laundry basket, which he then moves from the closet into the living room. Everything from the computer desk he might need is shoved in a bag and placed on the futon, while the rest of it, mostly worthless garbage, is swept into a bag and shoved in the nearest accommodating drawer.

Thanks to Layla, he has at least two changes of sheets. Thanks to Omar, he's never actually taken advantage of that.

Jericho is the type of guy who'd throw a blanket over a mattress and sleep on it for a week because he didn't have the executive functioning to struggle with a fitted sheet by himself. It's ultimately good that he never changed them; if he had used both sets of sheets, they'd more than likely still be dirty. Now he digs through the linen closet, selects a plain maroon set, and hurries to make the bed as quickly as his inexperienced hands allow.

He doesn't know how closely Harinder will adhere to the twenty-five-minute suggestion, but he's got no more than five minutes before that time is up, so he's quick about changing the pillowcase to the matching one and doesn't think about how Omar would mock him for incompetence, despite not being any better himself.

In the end, Harinder doesn't come out of the shower until a little over half an hour has passed. Jericho has time to find a tiny travel pack of tissues and sets it on the nightstand along with an unopened water bottle. He decides this is adequately welcoming and steps out of the room, leaving the evidence of his sappy generosity hidden behind a mostly closed door.

Only partially satisfied but having exhausted the extent of his options for the moment, Jericho sits on the futon and stares blankly at the demonic rectangle better known as his phone screen. He does his best not to betray his nerves. (His left foot fidgets. *Stop that.*)

When the door opens, Jericho counts the seconds before he finally hears footsteps in the hall. Harinder's breath becomes audible as he enters the living room. Jericho waits just long enough to not seem overly eager before turning around, peering over the arm of the futon at Harinnnn*whoa*.

He's fully clothed. Not that Jericho expected him to be draped in a silk robe or something equally bizarre since this is a rescue, not a seduction, but he's less clothed than usual. That means something, though Jericho isn't sure what.

Harinder's trademark sweater hangs over his arm, leaving him in jeans and a dark red long-sleeved shirt. He even put his socks back on. The only thing out of place is his hair, obviously having suffered an attempt at drying—judging by the towel draped over his shoulders—but still thick and dripping and brushed back from his forehead instead of hanging low over his eyes like the fringe of a feral beast.

Halfway through a covert study of his exposed face, droplets of water streaming down his temples, Jericho keys in on something and nearly jumps off the futon. "Holy shit. You have facial piercings?"

Harinder's attention snaps to him, and he pulls a face Jericho can't quite identify. "Piercing," he says. "Singular."

Sure enough, his right eyebrow is framed by two spikes. It's the edgiest fucking Hot Topic jewelry Jericho has ever seen. All he's missing is a pair of snakebites and a strong sense of nostalgia for Good Charlotte and MCR.

Suddenly, the black nail polish he's always wearing is put into context.

"I didn't realize you were lowkey trashpunk." Smiling goes against the instructions in his general operations manual, but Jericho finds himself unable to hide a delighted half grin.

"What."

"See, I wondered about the nail polish, and the fact that you never brush your hair, and never smile. But you're also apparently enough of a douche to get a piercing and then keep your hair so long that no one even knows it's there. That's next level, my friend. Good job."

"Fuck off," Harinder says, "There's nothing wrong with my hair." As if to punctuate the point, he reaches up with his free hand and violently ruffles the sodden mass, spraying water everywhere. His bangs fall back into place, but the piercing is still visible through the spiky wet strands.

"I didn't say there was anything wrong with your hair. I'm saying that going through all the effort of getting a needle jammed through your flesh so you could decorate it with metal and then ensuring no one knows it's there is fucking incredible and exactly what I'd expect you to do. I don't know why I didn't figure it out sooner." Jericho crosses one ankle underneath the other to stop himself from bouncing. Discovering a secret about Harinder, even one as simplistic as this, has him excited in a way he can't explain.

Harinder stares at him for several seconds, and then, of all things, he smirks.

"I guess you're right." He looks down at his chipped nails. "Especially considering you haven't seen the rest of them."

Jericho's brain hits the windshield, and he didn't even feel his foot come down on the brake. "The rest? Where—"

"I have to make a phone call," says Harinder breezily, and walks straight past Jericho and out the front door.

Chapter Fourteen

Jericho's Emergency Juice Box Project

Jericho spends the next ten minutes furiously planning what he's going to say when Harinder returns.

It's extremely difficult to gauge how he was supposed to take that last comment, but he's getting some ideas. Where else would he be pierced? Does Jericho really want to think about those possibilities modeled by Harinder Mangal, the shortest marshmallow-shaped misanthrope this side of a young adult novel?

In the end, he has no idea what to say, which isn't a problem because Harinder returns looking much wearier than when he left. He shuffles inside, jamming his phone into his jeans pocket, and sighs through his nose, the rest of his face twisted up in a grimace.

He stands there staring at nothing until Jericho voices a timid, "Hey?"

"Hey," Harinder answers, turning toward him with a blank expression.

Jericho mentally flails, glancing around the room for a convenient conversation starter. "So..."

"Be more awkward," Harinder says nastily. It stings. To make matters worse, Harinder doesn't join Jericho on the futon, instead passing him so he can lean against the wall with the thermostat and carbon monoxide detector.

There, he snatches his phone out of his pocket and resumes scowling.

Jericho does his best to seem unaffected by the dismissal. He stands to resume puttering around the living room, acting as if he isn't the least bit bothered by Harinder's penduluming attitude. If his face is red, if his hands are trembling, it's nothing more than a lingering chill. Doesn't make sense with all he's been moving around in relative warmth, but it doesn't have to make sense in the greasy basement he has for a mind.

Repeating *It doesn't matter* in his head, Jericho reaches behind the couch to grab a discarded wrapper, and his fingers brush the bag of dog food. Right. He still has to feed Kimchi.

"Hey," he says again, lifting the bag. "I have to go feed this dog."

Harinder glances up, then blinks at the dog food until his eyes show recognition. "Huh?"

"I don't know when Ms. Watson will be home; she said she might be late, and I have to drop off the food anyway."

Harinder slides his phone into his pocket for the second or third time, and his posture dissolves into a giant fidget. "Okay. Cool."

Jericho shifts, getting off the couch and onto his feet. "Wanna come with?"

Without his phone to stare at, Harinder is left staring forlornly at the floor. He wrinkles his eyebrows at the invitation and doesn't try to meet Jericho's gaze. "Would that be...okay?"

"Sure," Jericho says with a shrug. "I don't see why bringing a stranger into the living space of someone who entrusted me to take care of their dog would be a problem."

Snorting, Harinder says, "Yeah, nailed it."

Jericho hefts the bag of food under one arm and grabs his keys. "For real though. Coming?"

"Sure. Whatever."

As much as Jericho wants to mock him for pretending he doesn't care, he leaves off. Harinder's emotional baggage storage must be bursting at the seams; he doesn't need an excess of antagonism on top of it. Friendly ribbing is one thing, but Jericho has to remember that even if Harinder's staying with him, there're...boundaries. They aren't friends, he reminds himself. He's just doing this guy a favor in hopes of reaping benefits from a guilt debt.

(*Right. Keep telling yourself that, Jericho.*)

Before Jericho has the key in the lock, Kimchi senses them and starts up a cacophony of whimpering and snuffling, her doggy nails digging furtively in the carpet. A gate prevents her from crossing into the area containing the kitchen and vestibule. Jericho doesn't think to mention this when he opens the door, and so is treated to the delightful sight of Harinder stooping, hands spread, to prevent any excited pup-related jailbreaks.

Harinder doesn't miss a beat. He straightens and quickly crosses the space between the door and the barrier, reaching down to scratch her fluffy ears. He coos quietly.

With Harinder's attention firmly elsewhere, Jericho doesn't have to worry about hiding his smile.

Mood significantly improved, Jericho opens the storage tub Ms. Watson keeps in a low cabinet, empty but for a few brown crumbs, and cuts a hole in the bag of dog food so he can pour the kibble inside. Out of the corner of his eye, he watches as Harinder climbs over the dog gate and sinks to his knees so he's at a better angle to scratch

Kimchi's fluffy, wiggling butt. Jericho grabs Kimchi's food bowl, rinses the crusty remains of the wet food she didn't finish earlier, and portions a scoop of kibble into the dish, topped by a spoonful of wet food. Usually, he'd run it about five seconds in the microwave to get the gravy warm, but he notices both Harinder and the dog have gone quiet.

Kimchi is lying on her side, looking content, and Harinder is on the floor facedown in her fur, one hand idly stroking her chest. His breath comes slowly, so Jericho doesn't think he's crying, but he is crushed under a flood of emotion all the same.

After letting them be for about five minutes, Jericho creeps over to the dog gate, opening it quietly before sliding to the kitchen floor beside them. He sets Kimchi's food on the floor and gives Kimchi a pet between the ears, not making a sound other than the soft click of ceramic on linoleum.

Kimchi sniffs at the bowl, then flops right-side-up so she can eat, dislodging Harinder. He doesn't fuss, just shifts to support his head with his right arm while running the fingers of his left hand through her fur as she munches.

Jericho's attention shifts to the phone. The minutes pass unacknowledged. Left in peaceful silence, with the exception of Kimchi's snuffles, Jericho responds to an email, watches a video without sound, and reads a couple blog posts. When Kimchi licks her chops and moseys away to her water dish, he finally looks up. He half expected Harinder to crawl after her like a toddler, but the other man doesn't move. In fact, Harinder is still facedown on the floor, head resting on his elbow, arm stretched out. Motionless.

He's either dead—in which case, *fuck*—or he's asleep. He's still breathing, so Jericho assumes the second.

It's creepy to watch people sleep, but Jericho does it anyway, studying a small sliver of Harinder's face. He doesn't dare touch him, even to brush away the lock of hair that's stuck against the corner of his mouth. He just looks at him, keeping his breath shallow as if that alone might wake Harinder up and ruin the moment. He doesn't look peaceful in sleep, he looks. Exhausted. Wrung out.

It's been at least half an hour since they popped in, and Jericho starts to get nervous. He doesn't know how to wake Harinder up, especially not without touching him, and no. Not even a tap on his shoulder. He barely touches his own sister.

Jericho is saved from peril by a short fluffy dog who has far less shame than he does.

Kimchi wanders back over to them, snuffling, and shoves her nose right in Harinder's face, then licks him. Jericho watches as Harinder tenses, jerks a bit, then realizes what's happening. He practically melts, laughing quietly, and it might be the first time Jericho's heard Harinder laugh—literally ever—at least from something other than bitterness or spite.

Fucked up how he's never had his own pet, considering how much he relaxes around animals. Harinder would probably feel a lot better if he had constant access to this kind of comfort.

Worried about being caught staring, Jericho averts his gaze and mentally counts down from fifty before he looks at Harinder. He only gets to twenty-three before there's a groan and a "What the fuck?" at his side, at which point it'd be obnoxious to pretend he didn't hear and continue gawping at his phone, so he glances sidelong, feigning disinterest and humming a question.

"I can't believe you let me fall asleep on the floor," Harinder grouses.

"Looked like you needed it" A wave of self-consciousness crashes over him. He tries to avoid appearing concerned or sentimental about people, especially people who have both the ability and the incentive to mock him. Jericho quickly changes the subject. "Anyway, not to rush you, but unless you want Ms. Watson opening that door to find us crashing in her hallway, we should probably move this party to my apartment."

That gets Harinder moving pretty quickly. Jericho picks up Kimchi's dish and scribbles a note while Harinder says goodbye, pressing his forehead against Kimchi's and ruffling her ears. Jericho is at the door before Harinder tears himself away, fastening the dog gate behind him.

They're halfway down the hall when a stern voice calls, "Jericho? Is that you?"

Jericho turns and smiles at her politely. "Hey, Ms. Watson. Just finished feeding Kimchi. She's doing good."

His neighbor approaches the two of them. She's a composed lady with a proud face and a blazer sharp enough to wear to church on Easter Sunday. "Did she behave well?"

"Oh yeah, def. I got her some new food, by the way. You were almost out."

Ms. Watson purses her lips and reaches for the handbag at her side. "Thank you, Jericho. How much did it cost you?"

"That's my secret, Ms. Watson; don't worry about it," he says, holding up a hand. "We're cool. I just enjoyed the company."

Her stern expression softens at the eyes. Jericho's tiny smile gets a bit less obedient and a bit more genuine.

"Well," she says, patting her purse and reaching her hand out for his, a gesture he obliges after a second of hesitation. "Thank you. You're a quality young man." Her hands are wrinkled and soft, and he pulls away as soon as she lets go. Then her gaze falls on Harinder. "Who is this?"

Jericho doesn't know what to say. Who is Harinder, even?

Harinder anticipates him. "I'm a friend of Jericho's. I'm just spending the night."

"It's a pleasure," Ms. Watson says. She nods curtly and moves in the direction of her apartment.

They return to Jericho's living space, but when he walks inside, Harinder, yet again, pauses in the doorway.

"You okay?" Jericho asks.

Harinder doesn't answer for several seconds, then mumbles, "I think I should sleep." He tugs his phone out to glance at it. "I'm going to accept that I'm a fucking hopeless loser who gets tired at nine thirty, but—"

"Nah, man," Jericho says, waving a hand. "Go do your thing. You've had a day." Similarly exhausted, Jericho flops onto the futon.

"Um," Harinder says.

"'Sup?"

"I..." He doesn't look like he knows what to say, and Jericho is obviously running on fumes, too, because it takes him a while to figure out what Harinder's getting at.

"Oh, fuck. I'm a dumbass," Jericho says, standing up. "I didn't tell you."

Harinder squints. "Didn't tell me what?"

Jericho jerks his head toward his bedroom, then thinks better of it and guides Harinder over there personally. He pushes the door open and gestures, now a bit self-conscious about the crummy tissue pack and lukewarm water bottle.

Harinder, though, is staring at it like it's a five-star hotel room or something. "You can't be serious."

"I changed the sheets, dude, no homo, it's fine—"

Harinder rounds on him. "You said you had a couch."

Jericho blinks. "Yeah, and I'm gonna sleep on it. It's my apartment, and I sleep on my futon all the time. You've had a rough day; you don't need to be bugged by me messing around at two in the morning. I told you I have nightmares, right? My sleep schedule is super fucked because of it. I'll be awake for two hours and then sleep for four then wake up for half an hour and pass out again. It's garbage—"

"You're letting me sleep in your room," Harinder says slowly, not caring that he's interrupted Jericho twice.

He shifts. "Yeah, that's what's happening here, I guess. I put your bag over there."

Though it looks like he's about to take a step into the room, Harinder ends up not moving. He chews his lip absently, then asks, "Can I lock the door?"

Bemused, Jericho says, "Whatever you need to do. Knock yourself out." Then he walks away because, holy shit. He thought *he* had issues. They're more alike than it seems at first glance, which is a weird thought that he can't let go of once it's occurred to him.

He meanders back to the futon and hits play on whatever was in the DVD player when he was watching last, which turns out to be *Lady in the Water*. He and Maxx dare each other to watch bad movies sometimes. Maxx was supposed to watch it with him but disappeared midway through and still hasn't popped back in to explain why. It's whatever.

Jericho lets it play, watching mechanically, not really registering what's going on but feeling way too braindead to worry about it or turn it off, or do anything, really. It's mindless. He doesn't think about anything until, halfway through the movie, his bedroom door creaks open.

Turning on the couch, he blinks back at the figure staggering blearily into the hallway. Harinder looks the same as he usually does except he's in sweatpants instead of jeans.

"You okay?" Jericho asks, voice low.

Harinder's mouth tightens, and he pauses his trek. "I can't sleep."

"I feel. C'mon, pull up a seat." He scoots over to give Harinder room to sit down, which he accepts after a moment. "Sorry about the trash film; my best friend and I have this, like, game we play—"

"I love this movie," Harinder says quietly.

Shit. "Well then."

Harinder glares at him, but it's mild. "It's far from Shyamalan's best work, but I enjoyed the magic in the mundane."

Jericho snorts. "Fair enough." He settles back in the couch, letting his attention drift again. Harinder balls himself up at the foot of the futon, wrapping his arms around his legs and resting his chin on his knees. He gazes blearily at the screen and barely blinks. Jericho doesn't think about how he's watching Harinder out of the corner of his eye instead of focusing on the movie.

"Hey, you thirsty?"

Lifting a shoulder in a halfhearted shrug, Harinder mumbles, "Sure."

"Awesome. One sec." Jericho wanders into the kitchen, opens the fridge, and comes back with both hands full. "You want grape or fruit punch?"

When Harinder sees the offering his brows knot. "What the fuck *are* you?"

"Thirsty," Jericho responds. "Haven't you ever had a juice box before?"

"When I was six, maybe," Harinder snarks, but he picks grape. He doesn't open it immediately. At first, he just holds it in his hands, frowning down at the little box like it contains the secret of how to make fire.

"Damn shame," Jericho says. "I always keep juice boxes around in case of emergencies."

"Emergencies," Harinder repeats drily.

"Yep. They're soothing. Meditative."

"You have a weird idea of what counts as soothing."

"I guess. Drink your juice, asshole."

Harinder grumbles, but he obeys, shedding the straw's thin wrapper and jabbing it mercilessly through the tinfoil target. He gives it a dubious look before finally acquiescing and wrapping his lips around the skinny straw.

"Do you also drink milk out of sippy cups?" he enquires acridly.

Jericho snickers. "You're such a prick. Don't you have any stupid shit you do to calm yourself down?"

Harinder opens and closes his mouth. His face is very blank. "I don't like remembering things," he finally says.

"Oh. Sorry."

"You're excused," Harinder says and finally sits down on the futon proper. This time, he looks a little less uncomfortable. He takes another sip from his juice box.

Before the beloved (read: tacky) plot twist, Harinder is asleep again, still upright on the couch with his knees at his chest and juice box clutched tightly in his hand. By the time the credits run, he still hasn't budged.

Jericho deliberates and stretches one sock-clad foot out, barely breathing as he ever-so-lightly bumps Harinder in the side. "Wake up," he whispers, even if that's kind of defeating the point. "I gotta sleep too."

Harinder eventually does get up, mumbling in displeasure as he drags himself and his half-finished juice into the bedroom. The lock clicks behind him.

Jericho swallows.

Then he forces his body back into motion, reaching for the spare blankets tucked into a cruddy ottoman. He drops his crushed juice box on the coffee table, clicks off the television, and tucks himself underneath the blanket. Settled in the darkness, Jericho stares up at the ceiling and muses on the memory of Harinder's slow, shallow breaths until he, too, falls asleep.

Chapter Fifteen

Harinder Drowns in a Pool of Cats

Riding the bus to work is anxiety inducing, but not as bad as it could be. Jericho gave him such methodical instructions, Harinder started to believe he was five years old and going to kindergarten for the first time. He clutches the pink Post-it note as the bus jostles over a never-ending gauntlet of potholes and refuses to let himself feel.

On the way back, he gets cocky.

More specifically, he panics.

Ten minutes before closing, Harinder texts Mint asking if he can come over. Before she has a chance to respond in the affirmative (because there's hardly any chance she'll say no), he puts the address into the maps app and muddles through the intersecting bus lines.

Harinder has never used the bus system. Once he turned sixteen, he started driving his dad's car. When it finally quit, he sold it for scrap and bought a bike. It was a good bike. He got custom decals in honor of his dad and rode it everywhere for five years. Aside from the delivery job that required him to drive the company truck, Harinder relied on his bike exclusively.

Now his bike is gone, and he's shivering on a street corner because he made it about three-quarters of the way to Mint's loft and then got on the last bus going the wrong direction and had to call her to rescue him.

It's encroaching on seven thirty by the time Mint gets him safely into her loft. The living space is surprisingly cozy, considering the external suggestion that the building has sinned in the eyes of every god in existence, and is also going through a rough divorce. The neighborhood isn't great, but both she and Darren are tough as nails, so it doesn't seem to bother them.

He is immediately greeted by an entire herd of cats and feels no shame about falling to his knees, already fighting tears. Mint isn't as tactful as Jericho. She stands in the hall, half smiling and watching as he scratches every cat that can fit in two hands while at least four others rub against his body. Their purring is the best therapy.

Then, Sir Charles comes sauntering up, and that's it, he's bursting into tears. Around the cat's throat is a crisp safe-release collar, proudly displayed. The color is a nice match for his fur. A brushed copper tag dangles from the nylon, light glinting over the engraved letters. Chauncy, it reads. The new moniker is close enough to Harinder's chosen name that he doesn't have the energy to make a snarky comment. Instead, he scoops the Abyssinian into his arms and gurgles quietly.

"Mint, what were you— Oh. Hm. You brought company."

And that would be Darren. Harinder keeps his face hidden behind as many cats as he can manage.

Darren is Mint's asexual life partner. He's a tall white man who stands at six feet and change, with short blond hair and the specific shade of blue eyes people describe as "striking." He would make an intimidating jock, but he's actually a standoffish geek. The two met as roleplay partners on LiveJournal back in 2008 and have been inseparable ever since.

"Hari's having a rough day." Mint gently ushers Darren out of the hallway. "Make yourself comfortable, Hari!" she calls as they disappear around the corner to whisper about him where he can't hear.

That's fine. This is fine.

Crying is much better when one is not frozen on a public park bench, trying to find shelter against the vindictive wind. Harinder stumbles to the cat room. It's a majestic wonderland, and if Jericho could only see it, he'd know why Harinder adopted a cat out to Mint with minimal mind tricks and bullshit.

Harinder can't find anything wrong with this expertly crafted feline haven. He does his best to let the cats out to play during the day, but no cat should be locked into a kennel with only a few toys for the rest of their life. This is leagues better, and he should wish it for every animal who passes into his care. He just needs to make sure they will be safe in their new homes.

Mint and Darren's loft only has one bedroom, which they converted into the cat room. The rest of the space is divided by strategically placed furniture, and privacy curtains conceal their bunk bed from unfamiliar visitors.

Harinder still has trouble believing that two fully developed adults sleep in a bunk bed, or even fit in one. Mint is only a few inches shorter than Darren, and they both have solid frames.

Whatever. Harinder isn't concerned with their sleeping habits when the cat room is the true holy grail of pet ownership.

The room houses several massive cat trees, all designed and built by the pair themselves. The walls are installed with ramps, and there are fresh, cat-safe plants in a large windowsill planter. Toys scatter the floor, along with food and water dishes for daily grazing. The cats roam freely, but the room is a holy homage to the most pure, intense love of animals Harinder has witnessed, off the internet, in anyone but himself.

He lies on the floor and cries until he can't cry anymore—not just about the housing situation, but because he misses his dad. Because he liked his bike. Because he wants his own animal to cuddle and obsess over, one he isn't expected to say goodbye to after a few days/weeks/months. Because he doesn't want to take the bus everywhere, and because it's hard pretending everything is normal at work when he's homeless and distraught.

Because he didn't expect Jericho to be so nice to him, and he has no idea how to go back and face him. After a rough trial period of several years, Harinder has come to accept that his *friends* care about him, but he doesn't know how to deal with an almost-stranger treating him with such fucking unbelievable kindness.

He also cries because the cats are soft, and because there's hair on the floor that gets in his eye, and because he completely forgot to eat, despite the remaining hot pocket in the freezer at work.

When Harinder runs out of tears, Mint shows up with a mug of hot chocolate that smells like peppermint and tastes like vodka.

"Darren is making dinner," she says in a chipper voice. Darren is vegetarian, too, and a surprisingly good cook. He and Harinder might not get along, but a home-cooked meal sounds amazing right now. Harinder hopes Mint doesn't hear his stomach gurgle.

"Okay." His voice is raw and scratchy. She shoves a box of tissues at him, which he accepts.

"Sooooo," Mint says, preparing to tactfully pry.

"I got kicked out of my apartment, and a weird hot guy who stalks me at work saved me from losing everything I own and sleeping on the streets. Instead, I only lost about half of what I own, and am sleeping in his bed."

Mint opens her mouth, then closes it. "With him?"

Color rises in Harinder's cheeks. "I'm not peddling my ass for housing, believe it or not. I'm not quite that desperate and hopefully will continue not to be." She snickers. "No, he let me sleep alone in his room, and he slept on the couch."

"That was nice of him," she says. "You said he was hot?"

Blinking, Harinder says, "No I didn't."

Mint narrows her eyes and leans in toward him. "You absolutely said he was hot. I don't make mistakes like this." On cue, one of the cats rubs against her elbow. She welcomes the purring body into her lap, stroking it like a very confident supervillain.

"He isn't hot; he's a fucking loser," Harinder stresses. "I'm not attracted to him. At all."

"There's something here about ladies and protesting too much."

Harinder narrows his eyes right back at her. "I'm not a lady, fortunately."

The few inches between them practically crackle while they lock gazes, before Mint breaks off, snickering. "Whatever. You're still totally into him."

"Not!"

"What's his name?"

Harinder wracks his brain for pros and cons to telling her, trying to remember if he ever let anything slip about Jericho before. He's pretty sure he doesn't talk about Jericho to any of his friends because Jericho isn't... wasn't...isn't?...a friend. Shit.

Jericho's a stranger, except, no, he really isn't. He's been coming around for weeks, and Harinder has told Jericho things he hasn't told people he's known for much longer and been much more friendly with. Harinder has a feeling some of the things Jericho has told him were extremely personal, too, as far as one can accurately measure when Jericho purports to not have any friends.

Harinder doesn't know what Jericho is, and he's so distracted puzzling over it that he ends up answering Mint honestly.

"His name's Jericho." Silence. Harinder distractedly glances at Mint, who's patting the cat in her lap. "Mint? Did you hear me?"

"Jericho?" she wonders.

"Yeah."

"You mean that one guy who came in and argued with you because you wouldn't let him have a cat?"

Oh, shit. Harinder forgot they'd met.

Oh shit.

"I guess so," Harinder hedges before rushing on to explain. "I do this with everyone though. He's just—he's really fucking persistent. I scare everyone away, except for you; you're an exception. Only, he's so fucking mediocre, but he won't leave; he insists on accepting every heap of shit I hurl at him. Mint, I got him to agree to a goddamn background check."

She nods enthusiastically, not speaking as she processes the information. He expects— Harinder isn't sure what he expects from her. Commiseration, maybe. He should have known better.

When she finally speaks, it is with perfect confidence. "You absolutely have a crush on him."

"Fuck off," he spits.

"No, listen," she insists, flapping her hands in the air with excitement. "You're enamored by his persistence. You find it attractive that this boy who is otherwise a loser is so desperate for your validation that he will endure your constant abuse and work hard to change your opinion of him! It's basically your romantic dream."

"Nightmare," he corrects through gritted teeth.

"You like it," she asserts smugly.

"I cannot stand him."

"And yet! You're sleeping in his bed."

"I was desperate."

"You called him hot."

"You imagined that."

A voice calls from the other room, but Harinder is so heated he misses what it says. Mint only grins, scooping the cat in her lap into her arms as she stands.

"Whatever you need to tell yourself, Hari. You'll figure it out eventually. The foundation is already there." Then she cackles as she leaves the room, cat draped over her shoulder. A second later, she sticks her head back in. "Dinner's ready, by the way."

Harinder rolls his eyes. "I'll be there in a second." She smirks at him as she slips through the door.

He doesn't have a crush on Jericho. That he knows for sure. Jericho is a nuisance. A better person than he thought, yes, but still a huge, gigantic pain and also a fucking loser nerd. Harinder isn't attracted to him at all, but Mint might not be wrong about one thing. It burns him to think, and yet... It does help that Jericho isn't running away. It *does* mean something that this stupid kid keeps trying to meet his demands even if they're deliberately set up to see him fail. It's not endearing or inspiring, but it reminds Harinder a lot of himself. The desire to meet an impossible odd.

He might have to accept that he does want to be Jericho's friend.

There's a knock on the doorjamb.

"Ahem, Harinder," says the intruder. Unlike Mint, Darren doesn't know how to handle Harinder's unpredictable moods. "I don't know if you realize, but it's impolite to keep your hosts waiting when you've been informed that a meal is ready."

"Can it, Darren," Harinder says, brushing the cat hair off his jeans as he stands. "I'm coming."

"Don't forget to wash your hands," he says.

"Daaaarren," Mint calls from the kitchen area. "Harinder isn't five. Stop nannying and get to the table!"

"Yeah, Darren," Harinder mimics, tone malicious. The giant man looks completely out of his depth, which is hilarious because Harinder is well over a foot shorter than him.

"He's right, though, Harinder; we're hungry!" Mint scolds.

Harinder sneers in her direction as he approaches the kitchen sink. "Be patient, Mint. I mustn't forget to wash my hands because, apparently, I'm a dirty heathen who eats after touching cats or something."

He does, and he knows Mint does, too, but he's not going to get into an argument about it. Not right now. He has too much to think about.

Chapter Sixteen

Harinder Gets Pushed from a Moving Car (and Deserves It)

After dinner, Mint insists on driving Harinder home rather than leaving him to endure the bus system. The drive is about twenty minutes as opposed to over an hour bussing. He doesn't know how to tell her he was counting on the extra processing time, so when they arrive outside Jericho's apartment building, Harinder promptly has a panic attack.

"Oh my god." Mint drops her phone in her lap when he starts to hyperventilate. "Hari, are you okay? What's wrong? Do I need to call EMS?"

Harinder holds up one hand, wheezing between the fingers of the other one. "I'm fine! It's, it's, fine, it's—"

"Harinder, slow down." Mint grabs his wrist to keep him from flailing and pats his back. The touch isn't gentle or soothing, but it's grounding, and that works a little. "What's wrong?"

He doesn't know. He doesn't have a way to put it into words and didn't have time to figure that out. Mint's expression grows increasingly more worried, so Harinder manages to force out the words: "Why are people nice?"

Mint drops her hand, brow furrowing. "Is that what this is about?"

Face crumpling into a scowl, Harinder turns on her. His nails dig into his palm. "Of course that's what this is about! That's what everything's about! People aren't nice, especially not strangers, especially not people who have every reason to resent me and revel in my pain! People do not just enjoy my company, nor do they want to help me."

"I both enjoy your company and want to help you," Mint says.

Harinder bulldozes past her, not because he doesn't care, but because he is incapable of stopping. "You don't count. You know me. You know..." He deliberates. "...how I am."

"Harinder," says Mint carefully, the tiniest hint of sadness in her voice, "I thought you were past the thing where you pushed people away because you hate yourself too much to allow someone to genuinely like you." It's blunt because Mint is not a delicate person, no matter how much she cares. She is sensitive in the way a lion is sensitive as it rips out your throat and then asks you about your cold.

"Jericho doesn't like me," Harinder says reflexively, although the signs would point to that statement not being entirely true.

Mint rolls her eyes. "Whatever you want to say, Harinder. I, for one, am not going to sit here and enable your pity party."

Harinder looks up at her in alarm. His lungs are still tight, and his hands are shaking even if he got distracted from his short-of-breath ranting.

"Especially not while you insult both yourself and everyone who actually cares about you!"

"Mint, wait—"

"Nope," she says and, in a swift motion, unbuckles her seatbelt so she can reach over him to unlock his door, then shoves him out of the car. Harinder scrabbles at the window, seconds too late to shove his body back inside the protection of the cabin.

"Mint!" he wails, already shivering.

"No," she calls through the now locked car. "You're going to deal with this on your own since you obviously don't want help! Call me when you stop being a jerk."

The car lurches into motion, and Harinder flings himself back to avoid his toes being crushed. Then she's gone, and it's freezing, and Harinder doesn't want to go inside and face Jericho. It's way too cold for stubbornness, so he gives in and approaches the building, only to find out there's a lock on the door, and he doesn't remember Jericho's apartment number.

Shit.

He could hit the closest number he remembers on the buzzer and hope they take pity on his soul and let him in, or he could throw himself under the nearest bus. It takes five additional minutes of panic before Harinder realizes he has Jericho's phone number. He doesn't want to call because that would involve some awkward explanation, but he realizes, with no small amount of horror, that he's going to need to explain no matter what he does.

Throwing himself under a bus sounds better and better, but he doesn't want to die an icicle. Mr. Kulkarni would have a hard time replacing him, and Harinder doesn't trust the man to maintain the standard of upkeep the store pets need to live a comfortable life.

Harinder closes his eyes before pressing dial and holds his breath the entire time it's ringing.

It goes to voicemail.

Oh god. Is Jericho ignoring him? Maybe he doesn't remember Harinder's number, fuck, he should have texted, stupid idiot— Harinder hurriedly texts him: *i'ts hharinder 'm outside.*

His fingers aren't quite working right from the combination of frigid air and screeching anxiety. Harinder holds his breath for additional seconds, and...nothing. Fuck. Jericho really is ignoring him. He fucked up.

Mint was right and he knows it. He pushed too hard with his ungrateful ass and now Jericho's not going to let him in; he lost all his stuff after all and his phone is barely half charged, and what about his T shot—

Goddamn it. Maybe if he explains the situation, Mr. Kulkarni will let him sleep in the back room for the night, and then tomorrow he can find a hotel. He has some money. It'll be fine. It's gonna be fine. He just—maybe Jericho will at least curb the rest of his stuff instead of throwing it straight in the garbage, so he can get some of it back—

"Young man. Excuse me, young man." The stern voice at his back makes Harinder jump.

"IpromiseIwasn'tbreakingin!" he shouts in one breath before realizing who's addressing him. A small, straight-backed Black woman stands on the stoop, inspecting him over the rim of her glasses. She's holding a large bag in her arms. Harinder recognizes her after a few minutes as Jericho's neighbor, but he can't remember her name.

"Oh, uh. Hey, Mrs...."

"*Miz* Watson," she stresses, clucking her tongue with displeasure. "Jericho seems to have forgotten how to introduce people because I don't know your name either."

She recognizes him. Harinder doesn't know how to feel.

He clears his throat. "I'm Harinder Mangal, ma'am."

She nods. "A pleasure. Could you carry this bag for me, Harinder?"

When he realizes she's going to get him inside, whether she knows what she's doing or not, Harinder springs eagerly forward to grab her things. She inspects him critically and doesn't relinquish her possessions until he swallows down his awkward overenthusiasm.

With her hands free, Ms. Watson steps up to the buzzer and slides a key card through the reader, unlocking the door. She holds the door open for him, which makes him feel ashamed and uncharitable despite the fact that he's carrying her bag. In his best attempt at charitable behavior, Harinder awkwardly finagles the second door open. She says a brisk "thank you" as she passes.

Harinder follows her up the stairs. She walks powerfully despite her small stature, not seeming winded in the least. "Isn't there an elevator?" Harinder asks without thinking.

"There is," Ms. Watson says curtly. "But I prefer to stay trim and exercised."

"Got it," Harinder says, trying to hide his face behind the bag. It succeeds to a point since it's a large bag, but then he can't see and trips over the stairs. Ms. Watson throws him a skeptical look over her shoulder but keeps walking.

As they're ascending the final level of stairs before what Harinder belatedly recognizes as Jericho's floor, his phone beeps. His arms are too full to check, but that was his text alert. It's probably Mint making sure he isn't dead on the side of the road, no thanks to her. He's trying to figure out how to get his phone out of his pocket without dropping the bag when a door in front of him flies open, and Jericho bursts out.

Upon seeing his neighbor, Jericho hesitates. "Oh, hey, 'sup Ms. Wats— Harinder!"

It's an exclamation. Like, an honest-to-god exclamation, emotion and everything. Did he really just hear that? Jericho doesn't do the whole "yelling" thing, even when he's distressed. No matter what Harinder's thrown at him, he's always been restrained in his responses. Now, he looks manic.

"*There* you fucking are."

"I, uh, got sidetracked—"

"Gentlemen," Ms. Watson says, jangling her keys, "I hate to interrupt, but here is my door."

"Of course," says Jericho, immediately stepping forward. "Here, let me help—"

"That won't be necessary," Ms. Watson says. "Harinder has assisted me just fine. You can put the bag on the counter, then have yourself a nice night, Mr. Mangal." She gestures into her open apartment. Kimchi is shuffling at the dog gate, but Harinder doesn't risk stopping to say hi, much as he wants to.

Nodding awkwardly as he exits, Harinder mumbles, "You, too, Ms. Watson," and passes into the hallway. The door closes behind him, leaving him alone with Jericho. He should have stopped to pet Kimchi and put this moment off, even if only for a few minutes.

"Uh." He swallows hard. "Hey."

Jericho's mouth tightens at the corners. "Hey."

Harinder doesn't know what to say. He fully expects Jericho to tell him to get his shit and fuck off. He's waiting for it, watching Jericho's forehead scrunch, and then he opens his mouth and something Harinder doesn't expect comes out.

"Dude. You're, like, crazy shivering."

Surprised, Harinder looks down at his hands. Huh. So he is.

"It's cold outside," he says, not mentioning the panic attack.

"How long were you out there?"

Harinder doesn't know. "Long enough."

Jericho sighs. "Come inside, man, let me get you some hot cider or something."

"What is with you and juice?" Harinder asks, although he doesn't mean to complain. It just comes naturally.

Throwing a reproachful look over his shoulder, Jericho says, "I like it. Do you want something else instead?"

"No." Harinder already feels like an ungrateful shit. "That's fine."

He follows Jericho into the kitchen, not wanting to see the living room where Jericho slept, or the door leading to his bedroom. Mentally, he's calculating how best to get his stuff and leave before Jericho throws him out. Maybe if he cuts it short without making things hard for Jericho, he'll at least let him sell his remaining furniture and keep the money.

There's silence as Jericho putters, and it lasts until he gets the apple cider into the microwave.

"Where the fuck were you even at?" Jericho asks, half under his breath. Harinder barely hears him over the whirr of the microwave.

"I stopped by a friend's house on the way back from work."

Jericho hunches his shoulders, staring at the spinning mug. "And you couldn't, like, text me to let me know?"

Harinder bristles, leaning into his familiar state of indignant fury. "I'm sorry. I forgot that I miraculously grew another dad. Do I have a curfew now too?"

"No, but I know there's people out there who want to fuck you up, and suddenly you're out and I don't have any way of contacting you because you never gave me your personal number, and I got a little freaked out, okay?"

He's floored. "Do you think I need you to protect me?" It sounds ridiculous even to his ears, but Harinder can't stop. "Is this some kind of sick charity fetish, or what? I don't need you to be my guardian fucking angel. Just because you housed me for a night does not mean I'm now your devoted little pet. I can take care of myself; I don't need anyone to look after me or worry about me, especially not fucking *you*. I don't even fucking like you!"

Jericho stills. The microwave beeps. He doesn't move to retrieve the mug. "Okay." His voice is flat and painfully empty, like Harinder confirmed his worst fear.

Fuck. How could he? After Jericho showed such kindness, despite Harinder being an utter twerp, here Harinder is, throwing it back in this kid's face. What a classic act for the most undeserving piece of shit this side of New England.

He desperately wants to apologize, but the word dries up in his throat. He doesn't know what to do or how to fix this.

And then his body moves on autopilot.

Harinder grabs the front of Jericho's shirt and yanks the taller man around to face him. Jericho's body coils defensively, ready for a blow, but he doesn't need to because when Harinder pulls him down, the only thing smashing into Jericho's mouth is his own.

It lasts. The kiss is chaste, but Jericho immediately melts into it; barely a second, and he's pressing against Harinder's lips. His body stays tense and rigid, but he doesn't pull away. Doesn't move at all, until Harinder leans away and lets him straighten.

Harinder clears his throat and looks aside.

"Okay," Jericho says again, his voice funny.

"Right." Harinder elbows his way past Jericho, focusing all of his attention on the microwave and showing no reaction to whatever the hell just happened. The mug is scalding hot, but he grabs it anyway, ignoring how his palms smart as he makes a beeline across the kitchen and toward Jericho's bedroom. If Jericho wants to kick him out tonight, it can fucking wait. He closes the door behind him and locks it as if that will somehow hide his shame.

Chapter Seventeen

Harinder's Life Is an Off-Brand Princess Movie

When he comes out much, much later, Jericho is sitting on the couch. Harinder winds the long way around so he can sit as far from Jericho as possible, still not managing to meet his eyes or look directly at him. He tries to tell what Jericho's thinking from his posture, but Jericho isn't giving anything away. He sits casually, but maybe too much so.

Okay, maybe his brain is getting ahead of him. It's not like Jericho has a crush on him. Jericho is a really chill person—maybe a little desperate—and he's okay with letting Harinder fuck up like that because he's...nice. Nicer than Harinder expected or was willing to accept. Just because Jericho didn't freak out doesn't mean they get to make something of this, or anything else that Mint was implying.

"So," Harinder begins, swallowing past his oppressively dry throat.

"Yeah?"

"So. Uh."

He's pretty sure he hears Jericho snicker, and tosses a scowl at him, but all he sees is a patient barely there smile. There's a coppery beauty mark above Jericho's lip.

This close, Harinder can see Jericho has faint blotchy spots high on his cheeks and temples, mixed in with a few acne scars. Harinder doesn't know why such things would be considered blemishes—they're unquestionably adorable.

Wait. Holy shit, what?

"About. About what I said earlier." Harinder is pretty sure that's what he's attempting to say.

Jericho waves a hand, flippant. "Don't worry about it, man. You were stressed; I get it. We're cool."

Fuck.

"Alright," Harinder hedges, staring at his fingernails and picking nervously at the polish, chipping away at the black over his thumb. "And, uh." Jericho hums in acknowledgment. "What happened after that." Jericho hums again, quieter. Shier. "Would it be okay if we didn't make a big deal about it?"

Jericho's face twitches. He turns away, shoulder lifting casually, putting a barrier between Harinder and any revealing expression that might cross his features. Against his better judgment, Harinder leans forward in an attempt to see him.

"Yeah, that's fine. Don't worry; I won't bring it up. Like it never happened." Jericho sounds completely cool, unbothered, even.

Harinder's back straightens. "Why would you do that?"

Jericho sends him a reproachful look over his shoulder. "You literally just asked—"

"Not what I meant."

"Enlighten me, then."

"Not making a big deal out of it doesn't mean it didn't happen." Harinder ignores the way his palms are cold with sweat. "I just don't want you to think it means something you don't want." That sounds...weirdly ambiguous, and also not what Harinder is trying to say. "I'm just, I'm trying to..."

Fuck. Why is being sincere hard? He gives up, blurting out, "I don't even know if you're gay!"

Jericho whirls around. For a sick, terrifying second, Harinder thinks he's about to get punched.

"What do you mean, 'don't know if I'm gay'?" Jericho all but yelps. "Holy shit, of *course* I'm gay."

Harinder's mouth hangs open, lax. He didn't expect this at all, even after Jericho showed no qualms about kissing him back. "Jericho," he says slowly, "you've said 'no homo,' like, eight times since we met."

Jericho's lips purse. His eyes flick down, freckled eyelids lowering in thought, long white lashes brushing the apple of his cheeks and what the fuck is wrong with you Harinder, *stop this.*

"I guess I don't have an excuse," Jericho says eventually. "Mostly, I think it's funny, and also don't want to get the shit beat out of me if I'm too queer at the wrong guy."

Arching an eyebrow, Harinder says, "You think I could beat anyone up?" It's not self-deprecating. He knows his limits. He's five foot three. Harinder is capable of punching someone in the nose and booking it, but actual ass kicking is beyond his skill set.

"Look," Jericho says flatly.

Harinder snerks. "I'm listening."

"*Look.*" Jericho squeezes the corners of his mouth down as he tries not to smile.

"I'm pretty sure your shitty poker face has given up, and you should just stop trying already," Harinder says, hoping his intentions aren't obvious.

"Is that what you think, huh."

Harinder rests his chin on his palm. "Yeah, it is. You are way more transparent than you think."

"Speak for yourself."

"I do," Harinder says. "I couldn't repress my feelings about the mismatching patterns on someone's pajamas even under the tenderest interrogation method. If you asked me to think of a number between one and one hundred and then ordered me not to tell you what it was, I'd say you could go fuck yourself with exactly five iterations of the number seven."

Jericho laughs. "You're too much."

"You have, like, eight desks in your house and you're trying to tell me what's too much? I don't think I've ever owned this much furniture in my life."

"I've got a thing about filling up space. The apartment I grew up in was so small...too much extra room makes me feel twitchy."

"You're like a gerbil that's spent its entire life in a single-level critter trail," Harinder says mournfully.

A pause. "Don't bring your weird animal fetish into this."

"How about you don't pervert my completely pure-intentioned empathy for our nonhuman cousins?"

He snickers again, and Harinder betrays himself by thinking he likes Jericho's laughter a lot more than he likes seeing him miserable. Harinder genuinely isn't sure why it took him so long to figure that out, but there it is.

"Sorry, Hari. Perversion is kind of a thing that I do. Nothing is allowed to be pure or wholesome in my presence. I'm the blue chaos alien from that one Disney movie—"

"God, you absolute shitwheel. I know what *Lilo & Stitch* is."

A moment later, Harinder blinks. Aside from Mint, who gets away with it because he's too scared to stop her, people who presume to refer to him as "Hari" get their heads bitten off for the audacity. Jericho, whose neck is fully intact, somehow just managed to escape that fate.

"Okay, but the real question is— Can we watch *Lilo & Stitch*?" Jericho bounces on the futon in something Harinder refuses to believe is excitement, because if it *is* excitement, that would be cute, and Jericho is not cute.

Harinder eyes him warily. "Don't tell me you actually own that movie."

"All the original videocassette tapes, bitch."

"No. You don't."

Jericho has already launched himself up and is rummaging in a closed storage cabinet on their right. He withdraws a large box from the cabinet and, true to his word, there are at least twenty VHS tapes in there, all different animated movies, though not all of them Disney.

Harinder spies one in particular and picks it up. "We're watching this one."

Shifting the box in his arms, Jericho cranes his neck to see what Harinder picked. "*Anastasia*?"

"Yeah," Harinder says, holding the movie tenderly. "My dad and I watched this together all the time. It was our favorite. I watched it a lot in foster care after he, uh...died." Every time Anya described lying on the peppermint-scented rug, missing her grandmother, Harinder had clutched a pillow and sobbed. He never accepted comfort, and after a while, the members of his foster families stopped trying.

"The romance was also quality," he says hurriedly. "I get really fucked up by couples who start out hating each other and come out the ass end of the story madly in love."

Jericho eyes him, a smile curving the corner of his mouth. "Do you, now."

It takes Harinder a second. There's so much he could say and nothing that seems right, so he turns his face away and doesn't quite hide his smile.

Aside from teasing Jericho a bit about owning a VHS player, Harinder doesn't talk much, although Jericho rambles throughout the movie. It's a very gentle stream of consciousness commentary and even makes Harinder laugh in a few places, so he doesn't eviscerate Jericho for interrupting. It doesn't ruin it. Harinder's seen it so many times the quips enhance it. Jericho's funny, and when he's not awkwardly losing his shit, his verbal shitposting might be described as graceful.

Harinder doesn't realize the implications of Jericho not tripping over himself around him until the credits are rolling, "At the Beginning" is playing, and he notices they're so close their thighs are brushing. When the fuck did that happen?

When Harinder lifts his head, Jericho is looking at him. Their faces are a little too close for their status as not-friends.

"Hey," Harinder says, voice husky. He doesn't know why he's whispering.

"Hey," Jericho murmurs back.

"I, uh." Harinder fumbles, eyes flicking over the planes of Jericho's face. "I think I made a mistake earlier."

Jericho's lip quirks. "Yeah?"

"I dislike you a lot less than originally advertised."

His laugh is a breathy gust that traces the contour of Harinder's lips. Something he can't identify churns in his belly. "Believe it or not," Jericho says, low and smooth, "I kinda got that impression."

Harinder elbows him lightly and absolutely is not blushing. "Shut up."

"Somewhere down the line, there was a very subtle hint—" Jericho continues, then laughs again as Harinder shoves him a little harder. He flows through the gesture, and Harinder is amazed at how fluid he is when he isn't strung up in his own ribcage, choked with anxiety and loneliness.

Jericho's cheekbone is full, lit in the TV light, the rest of his face shadowed by the room's late-night darkness. Harinder gives in and crosses the distance, setting his lips very lightly against Jericho's cheek, as if to make up for his roughness earlier. Jericho goes suddenly still.

When Harinder pulls away, Jericho shifts to face him, turning his entire body. Opening up. Harinder watches him in the low light of the darkening credits and hazards a small, hopeful smile.

Chapter Eighteen

Jericho Calls off Sick

"Where the fuck are you?"

Jericho shifts his phone in his hand, rolling his weight onto the balls of his feet. "I'm in bed sick," he says and punctuates it with a very delicate cough.

On the other end, Harinder breathes a displeased huff through his nostrils.

"How did you fucking get sick?" he asks, not whining at all, but Jericho hears the petulance anyway. It's kind of nice, so he plays up the next cough.

"It was all the bus trips I took in the dead of winter to come visit you," he says melodramatically, keeping his voice breathy and weak.

"Fuck you," Harinder snaps.

To his credit, Jericho doesn't laugh, but it's a huge struggle. "Wow. See if I risk pneumonia for your ungrateful ass ever again." He waits for Harinder's reaction, but Harinder is squinting at his phone suspiciously instead of acknowledging what Jericho said.

"Is there something wrong with your phone?" he asks. "I keep hearing—"

Jericho clears his throat again, loudly. "An echo?" he says, stepping closer. "Yeah."

He makes eye contact with Harinder from across the store and is lucky he doesn't get a phone thrown at him.

Harinder hangs up when he sees him, and Jericho barely has time to hold up his hands in surrender as Harinder storms toward him, a scowl etched on his face.

"Are you kidding me right now?"

He smirks. "I mean, maybe." Harinder fists a hand in Jericho's shirt, pulling him down an inch or two so Harinder can frown closer to his face.

"What are you doing here?" he demands.

"Visiting you." Jericho says crosses his arms over his chest like Harinder doesn't have his shirt wrapped around his hand, tugged away from Jericho's pale chest. He's still wearing a single shirt and jacket, which makes it genuinely surprising he's only faking sick instead of living it. "A second ago, you were complaining that I wasn't here," he continues. "I'm all confused now."

Not indulging that with a response, Harinder instead narrows his eyes as he inspects Jericho. "You aren't really sick, are you?"

"Nah," Jericho says easily, dropping his hands and switching to shoving them in his pockets as Harinder's grip on him loosens.

"Good." Harinder tugs until he can catch behind Jericho's neck. Jericho bends the rest of the way down, obliging as Harinder pushes himself up to kiss him. He doesn't think Harinder has noticed how he's still too nervous to initiate the contact, even after over a week of eagerly submitting to Harinder's insistent and sometimes confusing whims. This time, Jericho is prepped and ready and indulges him with a soft and wanting mouth.

Harinder pulls back, voice gruff as he mumbles, "Happy birthday, assface."

Jericho knocks their foreheads together for a fraction of a second before straightening, breathing out a silent laugh. "Thanks."

Harinder surveys him with something that's almost a smile and then clears his throat, glancing away. "How the fuck did you even get in here without me noticing?"

"Didn't you hear? I'm a fucking ninja."

"A shitty ninja, who is also terrible and gay."

"There's one part of that I won't argue with," Jericho quips, wearing a fond smirk.

"Hmmm."

Jericho meets him halfway when he leans up for another kiss.

Someone clears their throat behind them. "Excuse me, gentlemen, I don't mean to interrupt but—" Harinder whirls around so fast he damn near takes Jericho's lips with him.

"OhmygodMr.KulkarniI'msofuckingsorryIdidn'tmeanto—"

At least, that's what Jericho approximates, because what actually happens is a mash of incoherent syllables exploding from Harinder's face in the span of two seconds. He falls silent when his boss holds up a hand to stop him, then turns beet red and hangs a left, shooting down the aisle where he's going to, presumably, curl up in the fetal position behind the counter.

Jericho looks back at the older Indian man. "Hey, I'm Jericho."

"We've met. Ajit Kulkarni." He extends his hand for a shake. Jericho doesn't want to be rude, but he feels awkward literally the entire second and a half his palm is touching Mr. Kulkarni's.

"Oh yeah," Jericho says, recalling the ferret incident. "No ferrets this time, fortunately."

Mr. Kulkarni raises his eyebrows but doesn't comment, nor does he acknowledge what he interrupted.

"I've seen you here quite a bit, Jericho. Do you have many pets?"

"Naw," he says, waving a hand. "I just like pestering Harinder about the adoption." It comes out without him thinking—rather, he figured it was a neutral enough topic that he wouldn't have to explain why he was sucking face with Mr. Kulkarni's employee. Until he remembers that adoptions usually don't take an entire month to go through.

As predicted, Mr. Kulkarni's face turns confused. "I haven't signed any paperwork about a discharge. Why has it taken so long to complete after I approved the application?"

Jericho panics, scrambling for an explanation. In all truth, they haven't discussed the adoption at all since Harinder came to stay with him. It's become a stalemate of sorts while Jericho waits for Harinder to say something about the results of the background check.

"Weeeell, there was a problem with my, um, apartment?" Yeah, okay. Keep going. "And Harinder had to reevaluate my suitability, and then I had to fix some stuff up—all my fault, don't worry—but I'm still planning on going through with it, just waiting on the final repairs to be complete, you know how it is—"

"I see," Mr. Kulkarni says. "Well, I wish you luck. In the meanwhile..." He looks at the counter. Surprisingly, there are no sounds of mournful wailing or clothes being rent, so Jericho hopes that Harinder's doing okay. "I have to go talk to my employee."

Mr. Kulkarni takes two steps and then Jericho chokes out, "Wait." He pauses, looking over his shoulder in question. "He's not in trouble, is he?" His face goes hot and red. "Because that was, like, totally my fault, he didn't— I can stop coming here if you don't want me distracting him, like..." He fists his hands to keep them from shaking.

"Jericho," Mr. Kulkarni says slowly, turning to face him again. "Harinder is, bar none, the best worker I've ever employed here. He gives most of his time to this store and doesn't complain about the hours or the workload, and saves me hours of daily trouble with his competence. I am well aware he's not the perfect model of professionalism, but business hasn't been impacted, so I have trouble motivating myself to do anything about it." Clearing his throat, he turns away and starts down the aisle again. "Just make sure no customers see you."

It's a while before Jericho can compel his body to move. He sneaks into the next aisle so he doesn't pass Mr. Kulkarni, emerging beside the ferret cage. The plan is to sneak out while Harinder and Mr. Kulkarni are talking, to spare himself an awkward conversation, but he's distracted by the sound of Harinder's raised voice.

"Is this the supervisor finally?" Harinder growls into the phone, his eyes flicking to Mr. Kulkarni before he frowns back down at the paper in front of him. "Yes, I waited all yesterday for you to return my call, and I don't appreciate that I had to follow up myself— Yeah, well, we're all busy. Cry me a river.

"Look. Wednesday's shipment was unacceptable. What? Yes, this is Aquariums & More, owned by Ajit Kulkarni—" Harinder glances at Mr. Kulkarni again, unsure. "Yes, it's a private business, not a chain. Look, that's not important, you should have our address on file. It's on— yeah, okay. Listen. I have a standard to uphold. I have customers, just like you do, who expect a certain level of quality from the wares we sell. The large comet goldfish we received in our latest shipment were barely bigger than the small feeders.

"What? Excuse me, I have *pictures*. Don't act like you personally oversaw this shipment. My customers come from all around the county expecting healthy, size-appropriate feeder fish for their pets, and I don't know how you expect me to sit here and sell them this subpar merchandise with a straight face. They're half the size you usually send!"

He throws a hand up in the air, and Jericho covers his mouth. Holy shit. All this with his boss standing there? Poor Harinder must be experiencing some kind of fit. Jericho can only see the back of Mr. Kulkarni's head and thus can't gauge his expression, but he wonders what the man is thinking.

"If you knew that your stock was not up to standard, it's on your company to compensate your clients for the mistake. Sir, I understand there are no constants with animals, but that isn't my problem, and it certainly isn't my customers' problem. I can't even charge twenty-five cents for these, and that's already a five cent loss per individual. Yeah? Well it's too late, the damage has already been done, and I wouldn't want to be running your company when the rest of your clients notice your slipping quality.

"I patronize your business because you set a standard that you're now refusing to meet, so either give me a discount on my next order to compensate from the money we're going to lose by dropping the price on these so-called 'large' feeders, or you can kiss Aquariums & More's business goodbye. Unless you think I should call that vendor you just mentioned to check those accusations with them that the lacking quality of this batch is their fault— No? Hmmm, yeah, twenty percent sounds fine. I'll inform my manager to look for it on the next bill. Thanks for your patie— Damn, this fucker just seriously hung up on me." Harinder scowls at the phone.

It takes all of Jericho's power not to slow clap. Let it never be said that Harinder Mangal takes anything in the way of shit, except from maybe his boss, which…

"Thank you for protecting the quality of our product, Harinder," Mr. Kulkarni says as Harinder walks back to the cradle to hang up the phone. (He was pacing around the cashwrap during the whole rant.) "If you don't mind, could we hold the next call so I can speak with you for a moment?"

Harinder "Take No Shit" Mangal looks scared for once, but Jericho, peeking out from around the ferret cage and safely out of Mr. Kulkarni's view, waves his hand to get Harinder's attention. He gives a double thumbs-up and mouths, *It's okay* at him, gesturing at Mr. Kulkarni and making a don't-worry-about-it motion. Harinder scrunches his brows dubiously and gives a barely perceptible nod.

"Yeah," he says, turning his face to Mr. Kulkarni, even though his eyes keep twitching back to Jericho. "What's up?"

I'm gonna go, Jericho mouths, stepping back toward the exit to indicate his intention. Harinder's eyes follow him before snapping back to Mr. Kulkarni, who has (obliviously) started to talk.

Only hanging around for a second longer to determine it is, in fact, not a big deal—sounds just like business bullshit—Jericho finally does slip out the door, breathing a deep sigh of relief the moment the cold air hits his face.

Chapter Nineteen

Jericho Learns About Chain Emails

Harinder gets home late again, though he texts him this time. It hasn't even been two weeks, so Jericho reprimands himself for thinking of the apartment as Harinder's home. It's just a transient space for him until he can find a better apartment. It only has one room, anyway, and Jericho can't sleep on the couch forever. Obviously.

Mint picked me up I'll be in late, he texts.

Jericho sits on the couch and fidgets, trying to figure out how to fill the time. He's already finished his livestream and got a bunch of extra donations and shit on account of it being his birthday. He's tired of the internet now. Jericho has no idea how he spent all his day fucking around online before. Before there was someone else in his apartment to bother, before he had somewhere to go every day.

Huh.

Jericho nervously reaches for his phone, runs his fingers around the case. He hasn't tried this in weeks, but it's his birthday, and...Shiloh hasn't said anything yet. He's empty-handed. Harinder still hasn't approved the adoption; they just stopped fighting about it entirely.

Jericho doesn't know if making out with Harinder every night will compel him to give in, but until then, he assumes Shiloh will stay angry. He's hurt that she'd shut him out indefinitely over a fucking cat, no matter how much she loved Mephi. Jericho is her *brother.*

He hypes himself up and pulls up her contact, staring at the picture of them together, neither of them facing the camera but caught in a rare moment of mutual laughter. Layla sent it to him. Jericho screws up his mouth, feeling vulnerable. His sister fit perfectly against his side, his arm draped across her shoulders. They don't usually touch. The half hug was mostly a fluke coinciding with a particularly witty joke.

Before he can talk himself out of it, Jericho hits the call button. He holds his breath all the way through the ringing, all the way to the voicemail message. "Good day, you've reached the cell phone of one very absent Shiloh Ker—" Jericho hangs up.

Then he gets his shoes.

He doesn't take the bus to Shiloh's house, though sometimes she makes him take a cab. It's less than fifteen minutes away on foot and barely three minutes driving. She lives on the top floor of a duplex; the lower apartment is inhabited by a deaf couple and their hearing child. Layla is fluent in ASL and has interpreted a few conversations between Jericho and the couple. Mostly simple stuff, but it was cool.

Today, Jericho doesn't see anyone. They must be out.

He goes around to the back door where Layla and Shiloh always enter, and stops dead when he sees a note taped to the inside of the door.

Dear visitor,

I regret to inform you that I am out of the country until December 21st. Please leave any packages up front with my downstairs neighbors.

Regards,

Shiloh Eliot Kerekes

For several minutes, Jericho doesn't know what to think or do. He stands at the door until his feet freeze, at which point he staggers off the porch and makes his way down the driveway. His chest is cold in a way that has nothing to do with the early December chill.

She left town without messaging him. She left town without telling him she'd be gone for their birthdays. She left town without making up or forgiving him or anything, not even a threatening message written in pig blood. He feels like shit. He feels abandoned, and he can't even message Layla about it because he suspects they went together, and they might even block him if he tries.

He walks with his hands in his pockets, brooding, until his phone rings. Despite himself, he gets excited, yanking his phone out of his pocket. It's Harinder, not Shiloh, and while Jericho is a bit disappointed, he eagerly accepts the call.

"Where the fuck are you?"

"Déjà vu, man. Aren't you sick of wondering where I am yet?"

He can practically hear Harinder roll his eyes. "Aren't you done not being where you're supposed to be?"

"Where am I supposed to be?" Jericho wonders, not mentioning that despite his teasing he was exactly where Harinder wanted him at the time of the first phone call.

"At the fucking apartment. Where else would you be? I forgot the key on the kitchen table, and I'm locked out, so get your ass up and let me in."

"Got some bad news for you, babe. I'm currently at least ten minutes away."

Harinder groans, long and loud. "Since when do you leave the apartment?"

"Fuck off, I go outside all the time."

"Only when you're harassing me. Who are you harassing now?"

"Chill out. I'm not harass-cheating on you. I went to see my sister."

Harinder pauses, then asks, "How'd it go?"

At some point, Jericho let it slip that she wasn't talking to him, though he doesn't exactly remember when. "She's out of town, apparently," he says, feeling helpless. "She'll be back on the 21st."

There's silence, and then an incredulous sound. "She's missing your fucking birthday?"

"Looks like it."

"Did she at least call?"

"Nope. Probably forgot." He doesn't bother speculating on whether it was accidentally or on purpose.

"Forgot her own brother's birthday?!"

"Yeah," Jericho says, then rolls his neck. "Look, I'm gonna hang up. I gotta get this existential crisis out sooner rather than later. I'll see you in about ten minutes, aight? Don't freeze to death."

Harinder grumbles but acquiesces. "I'll try."

"Cool," Jericho says, then hangs up.

Fucking sigh.

Contrary to what he said, he doesn't have much of a crisis on the rest of the way there. He's somewhere between resigned and realistic. It is entirely possible that Shiloh is in an area without service, or just got intensely wrapped up in something like she does sometimes and will call him tomorrow, or in a few days, or even later tonight to make up for the earlier infraction. Shiloh can be passive-aggressive and petty, but surely she wouldn't lock him out forever.

He's bullied himself into a slightly better mood by the time he gets to the building. Harinder is nowhere in sight, so Jericho assumes he managed to bribe his way inside. True to his expectations, he climbs the stairs to find Harinder balled up in front of the apartment door, staring at his phone.

"Hey," Jericho says.

"That was eleven minutes," Harinder says.

"I'm sorry for my betrayal. I offer you my left hand as penance."

"Fuck no," Harinder says, scowling at him. "I don't know what you've touched with that thing."

"Probably for the best." Jericho nudges his hip with the toe of his high-top. "Move so I can unlock the door, doofus."

"Don't tell me what to do." Harinder rolls out of the way and climbs to his feet.

Snorting, Jericho unlocks the apartment and pushes the door open. He gestures inside. "My liege."

"Watch it." Harinder slips past him, heading straight for the bathroom.

When he emerges, Jericho is trying to organize the futon area and, as such, takes a few moments to realize Harinder has parked himself in the middle of the living room and is staring, brows drawn.

Wait. Holy sh—

"You cut your hair?"

Holy *shit*.

Harinder's face reddens, and he grimaces at the mixing desk. "Yeah, Mint suggested it when I was over. Darren was trimming her hair, and it just seemed convenient."

His voice is so deliberately careful Jericho is ninety-six percent sure that wasn't how it happened at all. He doesn't challenge him. That stupid little piercing is visible below his cropped bangs, and although his hair still looks puffy and crazy, the curls are easier to see when they aren't snarling around his ears—instead, kind of haloing him just so, and damn.

This fucking loser looks good. Like, Jericho guessed after a while he was attracted to him, but that was kind of a— He knew he wasn't ugly, but Harinder is...stealth hot.

Holy shit times three.

"Stop staring," Harinder snaps.

"Everyone can see your Hot Topic jewelry now."

"I hate you."

Jericho swoops in like an owl on a soft, vulnerable mouse and ignores the squeak of indignation when he presses a quick peck to Harinder's now exposed forehead. "You look great, Hari." He tilts his head to the side like he's inviting a punch.

"Thanks, I guess." Harinder goes even more red and stares at their feet, which are way too close. Jericho obliges him by shifting back.

"Hungry?" Jericho asks, tossing his head toward the kitchen. He's hyperaware of his own hair, curls flopping over his eyes with the movement. Usually, Shiloh maintains his hair, but he's not going to think about that. He can always go to a salon...if he can find a salon around here that works with Afro-textured hair.

"Not right now," Harinder says. "I ate at Mint's."

Jericho pauses. Harinder's eyeballing the door to Jericho's room again, looking like he's about to bolt. Jericho doesn't know if Harinder didn't get what he wanted, or if he did and doesn't know how to handle it. Judging from experience, it's probably the latter. He doesn't know what to say to make Harinder stay, but he knows he doesn't want him to go just yet.

"Hey," he says, even though he doesn't have a follow-up planned. Harinder's eyes snap to him, expectant. "Uh, do you wanna..."

Eyebrows creeping up his forehead, Harinder shifts his weight until he's rocked completely back onto his heels, then drops so he's flat on his feet again. "Wanna...?"

"...go swimming?" Jericho asks, then winces.

Harinder looks around the apartment. They aren't by a window, so it's a useless gesture, but Jericho knows what he's thinking. "It's December," Harinder says in a flat voice.

Jericho clears his throat, finds the inside of his mouth sticky and dry. "The apartment building has an indoor pool."

Harinder blinks very slowly. "I don't have a bathing suit."

That seems like a plausible roadblock until Jericho remembers— "Maxx left his last time he visited. You can wear that."

"Who's Maxx?"

Huh. "My best friend. He still lives in De Queen. Whatcha say?"

"Well." Harinder's face crumples in thought. "I guess my day can't get any weirder."

"Especially not after this morning," Jericho snickers.

"We're not gonna talk about that," says Harinder firmly. "Get me the bathing suit."

*

"Well, this is disappointing," notes Jericho of the giant sign attached to the tape around the pool. CLOSED FOR MAINTENANCE it says, and both Jericho and Harinder exchange looks. "We could shower together—" Jericho jokes and is cut off by Harinder elbowing him in the stomach.

"No decency," Harinder says, sounding scandalized. "I walked down all those stairs for nothing."

"Stop complaining." Jericho surveys the abandoned recreational room. There are a couple people working out, visible through the glass partition that separates the pool from the exercise equipment. "Look, hey. The hot tub's still running."

"That's a way better idea than swimming in a cold pool," Harinder comments.

"Shut up." Jericho pulls his shirt off. He pretends Harinder isn't looking at him as he does it, pretends he isn't preening when he drops his towel and kicks off his sandals. With a little bounce, he jumps into the hot tub, then goes on to pretend his skin isn't being scalded. "Aren't you gonna get in?" He ignores Harinder's nasty little huff of amusement in response to Jericho's pain.

"Yeah, yeah." Harinder pulls off his shoes and folds his towel on top of them, then...hesitates. His fingers pluck lightly, absently at his collar, eyes unfocused.

"Everything okay?"

Harinder's gaze snaps back to Jericho. "Yes. Yes, I'm fine." He swallows and pulls his shirt over his head so quickly it gets stuck coming off his shoulders.

They've shared kisses that were a little more intense than pecks and involved a little more skin than not, but Jericho has yet to see Harinder shirtless. Before he gets lost wondering about it, Harinder straightens, and Jericho thinks *holy shit* directly related to Harinder for the fourth time that night.

"You have nipple piercings?" Jericho doesn't know how he missed that before, but he regrets it intensely. (He wants to put his mouth on them, oh god.)

"Yes."

"Why?"

Harinder gives him a speculative look. "That's a weird question. I have them because I wanted them."

As he slides into the water, Jericho also notices he has a circle of tiny red stars around one areola, and what looks like a constellation on his bicep framed by a couple strings of numbers. He's getting the impression that Harinder likes stars.

"What're the tattoos, then?" he asks, nodding to them just as Harinder's chest disappears under the water. Harinder pushes himself back up, so his nipples are exposed. Jericho tries not to feel a little thrill about it, and fails.

"I got this one on a dare," he says, touching the red stars encircling his areola. "Sam, one of my online friends, put down money that I wouldn't."

"And you did."

"Yes, I did."

"You're way more contrary than I initially realized," Jericho observes, smiling faintly. "And I knew you were pretty goddamn contrary from the start. What's the other one?"

Harinder freezes, and that's the exact moment Jericho connects that those strings of numbers he saw were dates.

"Um," he says hurriedly, "you don't have to—"

"My dad liked stars." Harinder stares blankly into the water. Not at Jericho, but not exactly away either. "He was into everything to do with them. He liked astrology and was really geeked out that I was born in Leo season like him, so that's what the constellation is. He even had a really expensive telescope, which he left to me after he passed away."

Something about that statement seems off to Jericho. He's seen all Harinder's stuff, and there wasn't a telescope anywhere in—

Oh. No. "Someone stole it when they kicked you out," he says, horrified.

Harinder swallows audibly. "Yeah. Someone did."

Jericho rubs a wet hand over his face, smearing his bangs off his forehead. "Fuck. I'm so sorry, Hari."

Following his example, Harinder pushes his own hair back, then gives Jericho a sidelong look. "You don't have to be sorry. Like, I know it's typical and annoying to say when someone apologizes for a situation, like 'oh, it's not your fault.' Well, no shit it isn't, but they still feel bad for you. But you shouldn't. Feel bad." He puts a finger in his mouth, chewing on some dry skin. "You're the best thing I've got going for me right now, so."

It punches him in the heart with more force than an actual punch would (and Jericho's been punched before, but he doesn't think about that).

He doesn't know what to say, so instead, he cautiously pushes himself up and glides through the water until he is perched awkwardly on the space between two seats, right next to the one Harinder is sitting in. It's weird with him half out of the water and Harinder in up to his neck. Harinder notices, and he scoots over, tugging Jericho by the elbow until Jericho slides into the seat, his hip slipping below Harinder's.

When Harinder settles back down, he's in Jericho's lap.

Jericho swallows and licks his lips, aware that Harinder is examining him for signs of discomfort. He very carefully winds an arm around Harinder's back. Their foreheads touch. For a while, they don't talk.

"Do you remember when you got your first chain email?" Harinder asks.

Jericho lifts his head. "What?" He processes what Harinder said, confirming that it is, in fact, what he heard, and says, "No, I guess I don't. Why?"

Harinder takes a long breath. "My dad got cancer when I was ten years old. Throat cancer, though he never smoked or anything. He'd done some voice acting for, like, kid's cartoons? And had to stop because of it. I was so fucking scared of losing him, but three years later, doctors said he'd probably survive."

"I mean, he...didn't, right?" Jericho asks, squinting. He's wondering if this is related to one of those emails that purports to have the cure for cancer in flying to China and not drinking milk or something.

"He definitely died, but it wasn't from cancer," Harinder says.

Jericho doesn't speak; he just waits.

Harinder takes a shuddering breath, presses his head into Jericho's shoulder, and continues. "I got an email address when I was twelve, and didn't have much to use it for. Eventually I amassed a small collection of fuckheads to be friends with, and one day, someone sent me one of those shitty urban legend chain emails that promises to kill your family if you don't forward it."

"Your dad did not die of a chain email," Jericho says, incredulous.

"Shut up and let me finish," Harinder snaps. "I deleted it, and nothing happened. Weeks later, I had a nightmare and woke my dad up, hysterical, convinced everyone around me was gonna die because of this fucking chain email I didn't forward to everyone on my friend's list."

"Right," Jericho says, rubbing his arm a bit.

His lips twist, and then he sighs. "There was a gas leak in the house one day. The kitchen exploded while I was at school."

He knew Harinder was building up to it, but the reveal is so blunt and unexpected Jericho loses the ability to breathe. After several moments of silence, he accepts that he has no idea what to say. Harinder saves him the trouble.

"I blamed myself, of all fucking things. Because it was so—fucking out of nowhere. How? How could that just happen? He was making dinner so it'd be ready when I got home, just like any fucking day, and then suddenly he wasn't fucking there anymore." Harinder's voice starts to crack, but he forces through it. "He survived three years of cancer treatment, and then one day, the fucking kitchen explodes. And I was thirteen, and all I had to justify that even happening was a stupid fucking chain letter I deleted a month prior."

Jericho says nothing, so he should probably expect what comes next.

"How did your uncle die?"

His throat ties itself in a knot, and Jericho thinks if he tries to speak, all that's going to come out is a sob. He does anyway, and what issues forth is dry and hollow.

"Overdose."

"Oh."

"Yeah."

Harinder plays with the baby hairs at the back of his neck.

"It was weird, because he didn't use when I was living with him."

Harinder reads between the lines. "Did you ever blame yourself?"

Jericho wants to tell him to fuck off. He really, sorely does. But he sees where this is going, and he looks at the fucked up, emotionally raw person in his lap and can't find it inside him to refuse.

"Yeah. All the time."

Then it's Harinder wrapping his arms around Jericho, and if there's some unusual wetness on his neck and cheeks, Jericho doesn't mention it. Neither of them say anything more as they sit together in the hot tub, hands petting idly until the light flickers to let them know the rec room is closing soon.

"We gotta go," Jericho says, his voice a quiet husk. Harinder nods, wordless.

It takes them a bit to pry themselves apart, but they do, and climb out to grab their respective towels. They're so mutely miserable that Jericho struggles in his brain to find a solution as he physically struggles to shove his still-wet torso back into his shirt.

Harinder dries himself more thoroughly, then wraps both their wet towels across his shoulders after he's put his shirt on again. Jericho thinks it's probably to simulate the feeling of that sweater he's wearing all the time. Safe. Covered.

Harinder hangs back until Jericho is ready, and then they walk toward the exit together, not quite touching.

A thought strikes. "Hey, Hari?" Harinder hums in question. "You said piercings—plural."

"What?"

"You said when you first moved in that you had more piercings than just your eyebrow. I feel like nipples only count as one."

Harinder looks at him weird, pausing in the doorway. "There's two holes, dumbass."

"But an industrial has two holes, and it's still just one piece of jewelry."

"Okay, but even that doesn't follow. A different piece goes into each hole."

"Conceptually, it's the same. You get your nipples pierced, people perceive them as two halves of a unit. Who has just one nipple piercing?"

A slow, reluctant smirk creeps across Harinder's features. "That's dumb, but I guess you're right." He opens the door leading out of the pool area and starts toward the stairs.

Jericho pauses, trying to figure out what just happened. "What. Hey, Harinder. What?"

Harinder reaches the base of the stairs and breaks into a run.

Chapter Twenty

Harinder Meets Mr. Titanic

Jericho catches him before he makes it up the second flight of stairs, but Harinder has a tactical advantage and whaps him in the face with the wet towels. He makes the most of Jericho's temporary incapacitation and bolts all the way to the apartment door, at which point he realizes Jericho has the key in his swim trunks, and he's trapped.

"Put your hands in the air an' surrender without a fight," Jericho twangs as he ascends the top of the stairs, a towel in each hand like he's approaching some comical Old West–style shoot-out. "We've got you surrounded."

Harinder makes a show of looking around, genuinely searching for Jericho's so-called entourage. "Wow, it seems like your army is nowhere to be found, much like my reason for living," he deadpans. He gets a wet towel to the face for his trouble.

"No, wrong," is all Jericho says as he unlocks the door to let them in. He's still holding the other towel in his left hand, so Harinder doesn't push it because he knows better than to look down the barrel of a loaded gun and call its mom ugly. Or, as it were, make depressing fatalistic jokes in front of the boy who likes him and is making his life slightly easier because of it. (Okay, a lot easier. The kissing helps.)

Speaking of kissing, Jericho is taking off his shirt again, and Harinder doesn't remember what he was thinking about anymore.

The attraction hit harder than he was expecting. It swarmed him all at once when he realized Jericho had somehow shimmied up the ranks of people Harinder was barely tolerating and proved himself worthy of Harinder's trust. Now here he goes, swooning all over him while divulging the juicy details of his tragic past. Harinder would be disgusted with himself if he wasn't too busy eyeballing Jericho's naked torso.

"God," Jericho says, stretching his shoulders. "I hate being wet."

Harinder smiles despite himself, but doesn't say anything.

"Y'know, I'm glad we didn't go swimming. Then I'd have had to wash my hair." Jericho ruffles his fingers through his wild Afro. "I'm gonna shower anyway though. BRB. Unless you wanna join, that is." He disappears into the bathroom, still talking out loud as he closes the door. The water begins to run.

It takes a moment for Harinder to remember his body. Jericho's casual suggestion that they shower together hit him hard in the diaphragm, and he would have accepted in half a heartbeat if Jericho hadn't obviously been joking. Sighing wistfully, he accepts he'll have to shower later and wanders into the bedroom.

He switches into a pair of old and worn jeans and a baggy shirt with sleeves so long they cover half his hands. He's warm from the hot water inside, and wearing comfortable things outside. Overall, he notes a distinct lack of his usual ever-present pain.

Despite it being universally horrible to talk about his dead father, it's as if Harinder has been cleansed. Now it's out of the way. There isn't much more they can say about their respective guardians, and even though Harinder is paranoid and precious about his personal life, it feels nice to have shared mutual catharsis with someone. For now, his inner demons are at rest.

In other words: it would be absolutely, disastrously dangerous to go out and be around people right now, even the exact person who enabled him feeling so good in the first place.

Chewing his lip, Harinder deliberates. Active discomfort and aggression are the tools with which he navigates most of his life, even around people he likes. He's painfully aware of that. He's also aware that his rare moments of happiness engender a vulnerability he hates revealing. Harinder's soft squishy underbelly is a map to his own personal city of gold, and no one is plundering those riches today, or ever, thanks.

Which is why it's so weird that when he goes to lock the door to his (no, Jericho's) room, Harinder ends up twisting the knob instead, letting himself out.

He goes to the bathroom and hangs the borrowed swim trunks in the shower next to the towels and Jericho's trunks.

Harinder stares at the tile wall through the clear shower curtain. Small illustrations of sushi rolls impede his view. "What the fuck am I doing?"

"No clue. You've been in here for five minutes."

Jericho reclines lazily against the doorjamb, still shirtless, and. Smiling. This heartbreakingly small, uneven tilt of lips. Those lips are full and soft, Harinder knows from experience, especially when they're moving from his mouth to his throat. Especially when they break away to breathe, and Jericho nuzzles behind Harinder's ear, laughing softly.

Harinder still remembers the first time he ever heard Jericho laugh.

And so, he smiles back.

"I was just thinking."

"Oh yeah? About what?"

Harinder contemplates him—at a few paces closer, he can smell him: warm, hand lotion and chlorine, coconut oil (he uses it on his hair) and chai-flavored lip balm (winter hates his skin, especially his lips), and lavender deodorant (his sister makes body care products).

Eventually, he opens his mouth and says, voice troublingly husky, "About how much of a giant, repulsive nerd you are."

Repulsive, he says as he lets himself orbit a little closer. The hot tub was the first time he's seen Jericho shirtless, and he wasn't exactly getting his hands all over that gorgeous alabaster torso while gross crying on his shoulder. Without that barrier, it sounds incredibly tempting.

"Aw," Jericho says. "I totally believe that. Sincerely."

His upper body is fairly average. Not especially toned or chubby or skinny in any direction. He has soft pectorals and a smooth stomach, no chest hair, nothing until the little trail below his navel.

Those *hips* though.

The sexiest aspect of Jericho's half-naked image are his hipbones, teasingly revealed by a loose pair of sweatpants, riding low. Beautifully defined, they arc out in a way that begs to be grabbed and squeezed.

To stop himself from wondering what's going on in the places he can't see, Harinder mutters, "Shut up," and faceplants into Jericho's chest.

He's finally, at last, not angry about the eight inches Jericho has on him, because it's so easy to fit his head into the crook of Jericho's neck and let his callused palms drag slowly as he wraps his arms around Jericho's back, tracing every inch of skin in his path.

Jericho consumes him, more fervid than a swarm of angry bees.

Warmth surrounds Harinder like—*like a worn comforter...like his dad's yellow sweater...like a long-distance friend he hasn't seen in years...like a hot bubble bath...like the smell of fresh bread...like holding someone's hand for the first time*—and oh, god, he hasn't been hugged in so long, not properly.

Side-hugs, maybe a quick squeeze, post-makeout cuddles, but not...

He shivers, there in Jericho's arms, and Jericho draws him in him closer, rubbing his nose through Harinder's wild hair. Harinder makes a soft sound he won't admit to. It's relief and stress and terror and darkness and blinding fucking light, like the way Jericho's curls reflect when he's lounging in the sunbeams from the window.

Harinder melts. Jericho kisses the top of his head, strokes between his shoulder blades. Jericho is trembling too.

After a time, Jericho gently insinuates a hand between them, cupping Harinder's jaw and turning his face until they can look at each other. His face twitches in clear apprehension, and the vulnerable parts of Harinder that prey on other people's weaknesses so they won't notice his own strain to come up with something teasing or mean to say. But he doesn't. He hides it behind his teeth with a mental click and pushes up on his toes to kiss the corner of Jericho's mouth.

If Jericho, this terrible, obnoxious kid who annoys the shit out of him and doesn't seem to understand how to give up on a person, can trust Harinder, he thinks it should go both ways.

"I was wondering if I could draw you," Jericho says finally.

Harinder raises his eyebrows. "Like, in a Titanic kind of way?"

Despite himself, Jericho dissolves into snickers. "Shut up. I make my living writing and drawing indie comics, if you didn't know."

"Oh, wow." Harinder has seen the art supplies laying around, and there was that day with the paintings (Harinder cringes at the memory), but he never went so far as to ask more about Jericho's artistic background. Is that rude of him? Probably. "So this is more of a 'Mister Titanic' situation. Professional."

Jericho snorts as he laughs, full-throated and impossibly nerdy. "Oh my god. You're killing me. I'm never going to be able to pick up a pencil again."

"That's going to make it pretty hard to draw me."

"Yeah, totally," Jericho says, trying to quell his laughter as he nods his head. "You'll just be sitting alone in my room pretending to ignore the ashamed sobs."

"That's okay. I already ignore my own internal screaming. This'll be easy."

"Are you challenging me to an anguished self-loathing match? Because you're so on."

"I will beat you into the ground." Harinder jabs a finger at Jericho's face.

Jericho contemplates the digit, then darts forward and bites it. His tongue drags as he pulls back again, teeth scraping, and smirks in self-satisfaction at Harinder's surprised squeak.

His smugness is infuriating (and sexy) and when he tosses his head in the direction of his bedroom, Harinder is pretty much powerless to refuse.

"I hate you," Harinder says as he crosses the threshold, despair and anticipation wrapped around a weight in his stomach. Jericho laughs like he means it.

"Go get cozy." Jericho pulls out a box of art supplies. From the box he withdraws a sketchbook. Harinder doesn't know much about art, but it looks more sophisticated than any sketchbook he's seen before. The cover is a buttery golden-brown, and when he opens it to flip through the pages, Harinder notes that the paper is thick and textured.

Harinder goes to lie down on the bed. He takes out his phone, but his eyes remain on Jericho, watching him intently until the screen goes black from disuse. He gives up on pretending not to care.

Jericho is pretty. It's a weird way to describe him because Harinder wouldn't necessarily say "handsome," or even "attractive" at first glance. Intimately, though, when Harinder studies the slope of his back or the knobs of his knuckles, the way his muscles flex as he digs through the box—

When his wet hair is slumped over his ears, and his mouth is twisting with concentration, and his entire body is a mess of careful shadows on ice-white skin—

When he isn't being awkward and shy and hostile, isn't nervously choking on words, isn't being defensive. When he looks comfortable in his environment and rolls his neck fluidly, thumbs hooking under the waistband of his pants so he can tug them a bit higher on his hips—

When Harinder realizes that it's been only a month, and he already feels like he knows Jericho, and likes him, Jericho morphs from an awkward socially-isolated dork into the man that turned twenty-one today. A man who is far more considerate than he lets himself appear to be. Jericho cares. He cares a lot, and Harinder remembers his snowy eyelashes touching flushed cheeks as he tried not to cry in Harinder's store.

It's those details that turn Jericho from gawky to graceful, rhythmic in his movements. Before Jericho's pencil even hits the paper, Harinder swears he already hears the scratches of graphite sketching out his thoughts.

"How should I... What should I do?" Harinder asks, unsure of how this is supposed to work.

Before him is Jericho's setup: He's sitting on the floor with a short easel propped in front of him to hold the sketchbook level with his face, just low enough that he can peek over it with his thoughtful gray eyes. Next to him is a laptop that he stops fiddling with to look at Harinder.

"Uh. Whatever's comfortable?" He scratches the back of his head. "If you could pose, that would be cool, but you don't have to."

Harinder has never tried to look attractive, not once his entire life. He wears mom jeans and his dad's old sweater, which is getting so ratty he'll have to let go of it soon if he doesn't give it a break. The yellow—a shade he hated even when it was new—has grown even dingier over the years. His dad insisted it was goldenrod. Harinder compares it to the foamy bile people spit out when they're dry heaving.

Everything he wears is baggy and comfort oriented. He hopes Jericho likes drawing folds.

In the end, he doesn't come up with anything spectacular. He settles on his side facing Jericho and pulls his knees up like he wants to curl into the fetal position but not quite. The pillow under his head is folded in half so Jericho can see his face.

Well, that's the effect anyway. Harinder mostly wanted an unobstructed view of *him*.

Jericho hits a button on the laptop, and chill music begins to play. The notes are minimal but meaningful, and the beat is soothing enough to be a lullaby, but he keeps his eyes open, devouring every detail.

Sometimes when Jericho looks up, he meets Harinder's gaze, but only for a second. The rest of the time, he's intent on capturing the authenticity of Harinder's image. His focus pulls taut like a string, a solid thing that Harinder could pluck and make music from.

After about twenty minutes, Jericho purses his lips and puts down the pencil. He stares at the sketchbook. Harinder can't decide if the look expresses satisfaction or disappointment.

Jericho rubs his palms on his thighs. "Hey," he murmurs. He's not smiling, but his mouth is gentle, face relaxed.

Harinder shifts onto his stomach, folding his arms under his chin. He kicks his feet in the air, scratching one ankle with the toes of the other foot. "Hey."

"Are you alright?" Jericho asks, a hint of concern in his tone.

"Yeah, minus one thing." Jericho's eyebrows crumple with worry. "You're over there."

Jericho's mouth opens, then closes it. He snorts, twisting his mouth to obscure a smile. Harinder wonders if Jericho has a smile quota like Harinder does. Positive emotions are exhausting.

"Gimme a sec." Jericho pushes his easel out of the way, grabs his sketchbook and little tray of different pencils, and crawls across the floor until he can press his back to the side of the bed, balancing the sketchbook on his thighs. His bare shoulders are so close Harinder could touch them.

Now he can see Jericho's drawing. It's loose and gestural with rough, bold strokes intermingling with delicate details, so minimal yet confident that Harinder's curiosity gives way to amazement. All this time this fragile person has spent around him, he's been hiding the beauty of his personhood, the depth of his sensitivity and skill. Harinder has never seen himself as beautiful, so he has no idea how another person managed to turn him into something that could be called art.

He reaches for Jericho's arm, stroking the skin with feather-light fingertips. Jericho shivers but continues to work on the drawing, refining the details. Harinder watches it transform from a suggestion to a mirror of himself that somehow accentuates features he didn't even know he had.

The music pulses. So does Harinder.

Jericho lets him explore his body, though he doesn't take his attention too far from the drawing. It's fine because Harinder can feel him clench and hum as he kisses up his neck, brushing dry lips behind his earlobe to make him twitch. His hand charts a map of his upper arm, the muscles in his chest, his clavicle. Studiously gentle. His jawline, the whorl of an ear, the texture of his tightly coiled hair.

An index stroking the dip below his bottom lip, middle finger tracing the peak of his Adam's apple, palm flat against his sternum, matching the beat of his heart to the rhythm of the music.

Finally, Jericho sets the sketchbook aside. The music plays on. He shifts, still on the floor, until he can look Harinder in the eyes. Harinder touches his face and tries to see into him, read what he's feeling.

The pads of his fingers stop at Jericho's temple. They contemplate each other for a long, sweet moment.

He slides his hand into the back of Jericho's hair and tightens his fingers, suddenly overcome with conviction. "You're fucking beautiful, you goddamn asshole."

Jericho doesn't even laugh. His face scrunches up, emotional and raw, and Harinder wonders what he's been missing all this time. Harinder is agonizingly tender as he kisses him, lips fitting between Jericho's and rubbing, chapped bits scratching together, pressing then retreating. His heart flutters madly in his chest.

A couple seconds later, Jericho's phone goes off, and they both freeze. "'m gonna ignore that," Jericho mumbles against Harinder's lips, but Harinder draws back an inch.

"Just see who it is. It could be your sister."

Jericho blinks like he didn't consider that, then scrambles to pull his phone out of his pocket and turn it on. He blinks in surprise when the screen lights up. "I'll be damned."

It's almost one AM, and Harinder sneaks a glance over his shoulder at the display advertising one text from Shiloh. Jericho doesn't try to hide the screen from him, so Harinder sees: *Sorry about the late text, dear. Time zones got in the way of my promptness, but happy twenty-first nonetheless.*

Jericho stares at it for a long time, then turns off his phone. He sets it aside and lets out a long, shuddery breath.

Harinder drums his fingers against Jericho's collarbone. "Sleep, maybe?"

"Nah," Jericho says, twitching his head to the side. He reaches his empty fingers up to twine with Harinder's. "Not yet."

Chapter Twenty-One

Harinder Regrets Making up His Mind

He's made up his mind.

Harinder scuttles through the aisles of the store, squinting at prices, fidgeting with a calculator. Everything works out, especially once he factors in his discount, and it's not like he has to pay rent this month. He's got extra to spare.

When the elevator doors open, he has to hit the Open Door button twice before he can get everything out on his own. Most of it gets piled in the litter pan—bag of food, toys, dishes—but the actual tub of litter stays in the elevator room because he is far too fun-sized to carry everything on his own. His legs strain as he tries to navigate to Jericho's apartment door with his arms so full, but he doesn't regret his decision. In fact, as he frees one hand just enough to knock, he finds himself feeling proud.

"Jeez," Jericho says through the door. "Are you ever gonna remember your—" Jericho stares at Harinder and the carrier under his arm.

"My hands were occupied." Harinder cracks an unsure half smirk, trying not to vibrating from excitement and doing a poor job of it. "Happy birthday. I hope you don't mind that it's a day late."

Dumpling scratches at the grate and meows.

Jericho looks stricken. "What?" His voice wavers.

Harinder shifts, starting to lose his spark. Discomfort begins to twist in his gut. His good moments only go so far, and this one is almost up.

"She's yours. I was a being a dick before, and while I maintain that some of it was warranted, I'm willing to come out of my cave of hatred and fuckery long enough to admit that after a certain point, I was just being an irreconcilable shit-tit, and my punishment would be admitting it before the world. Or at least you."

More silence. Harinder feels his hackles creep up even though he should be giving Jericho time to process. He wanted grateful tears, damn it. "Earth to fucking Jericho. Say something."

Jericho grunts and clears his throat. "I don't know what to say."

Incredulous, Harinder lifts the crate higher as if Jericho might have somehow misunderstood his meaning. "I'm approving your application, fuckwit. You get the cat. Hurrah. An entire month of annoying me has paid off, along with, like, maybe some of the other stuff, too, but we won't talk about that because it could legally be constituted as a bribe, and then I'll have to eliminate any and all witnesses who might be privy to that particular weakness of mine."

Jericho is silent for another beat, and then: "Please don't kill Ms. Watson."

Despite himself, Harinder spits out a laugh. "I'll try to restrain myself, but no promises." Pause. "Are you gonna help me bring this shit inside?"

It takes a second, but Jericho nods and takes the pan from Harinder, then walks into the apartment like he's in a daze. He sets Harinder's purchases on a plot of empty desk space.

"Is this why you bitched that the apartment was dirty and told me to clean it while you were at work?" he asks.

"Yeah. Also, it was a mess."

"Half your fault."

"It's *your* apartment. I keep the room perfectly neat, thank you very goddamn much. Now watch the cat." It takes a lot of unappreciated effort for Harinder not to emphasize that Dumpling is now, officially, also Jericho's. "I have to grab something else from the elevator."

"How much shit did you bring? How did you get this all home on the bus?"

Harinder rolls his eyes. "I called for a car, dumbass."

Then he's off, down the hall so he can yank the litter tub back to the apartment door that he left open. He should have made Jericho do it, but he's hoping by the time he comes back, Jericho will have adjusted to the proper level of gratitude Harinder was expecting.

He regrets the decision later. It's not that it's hard for him to move heavy things; he has to move some of the smaller tanks himself at work. Still, he's tired from the day, and after expending all that energy, he finds Jericho sitting at the end of the couch, Dumpling's carrier on the coffee table as far away from him as he can get it. He's staring moodily at Dumpling as she meows, displeased about not yet being freed from her plastic prison.

It occurs to him, very briefly, that Jericho might be overwhelmed in the emotions department. He obviously has issues with people doing nice things for him—not that Harinder is one to talk—so maybe he needs a cooldown. What do normal people do to make situations less awkward? Isn't there a thing where people talk about their day at work or school or the gym or something?

Clearing his throat, Harinder attempts to launch into a conversation that isn't primarily based on his hatred for the world. "So, uh...how was your day." He forgets to make it sound like a question.

Jericho looks at him, pursing his lips. "It was aight. I just cleaned, and drew some. Pretty typical Friday."

Typical. Right. "I, uh. Finally gave that kid his gecko."

"Oh, yeah?"

"Yeah." Harinder messes with the cat accessories. He should get the litter box set up, at least, before letting Dumpling out. "I thought he wasn't coming back after the second week, but turns out he was focusing really hard on being sober when he showed up."

Harinder pauses. "He was a fucking wreck, hands shaking all over the place. If you quote me on this, I'll kill you, but...I think he'll be fine. He seemed really invested in doing the right thing for a pet, so maybe it'll get him onto a better track than, uh." He doesn't want to be denigrating, but being an unwanted ward of the state with a drug addiction at seventeen isn't exactly the best situation to enter adulthood from.

Jericho grunts an affirmative, like he understands Harinder's unspoken thoughts, but he doesn't say anything. Harinder crushes a plastic wrapper in his hand and refuses to lose his cool.

"So, I'm starting to get the dreaded Christmas calls," he says because that's another thing that happened today.

When he turns to look for a response, Jericho has his fingers halfway shoved in through the bars of Dumpling's crate, which is a good step. Then Jericho notices him looking and pulls his hand back, tucking it awkwardly between his knees. Harinder pinches his lips down on a frown.

"Christmas calls?" Jericho asks.

"Yeah, like, people wanting to get animals for someone as a gift." He drags a hand down his face. "It's goddamn terrible. 'Do you carry puppies?'" he mimics. "'Will you have kittens available at Christmas time? Can I get a fish tank, slash hamster, slash miniature pig for my child for their sixth birthday?'" Harinder scoffs. "I hate people like that. A pet is a responsibility, not a whim or an accessory or a fucking gift. Animals shouldn't be a surprise; they're a commitment."

Harinder's hand balls up in a fist, but when he looks over at Jericho it uncoils. Jericho's face is some mixture of green and red, like he's both sick and embarrassed at the same time.

"Are you...okay?" Harinder wonders if he should be more concerned than he realized.

"Yep, I'm totally fine," Jericho says, suddenly standing. "I'm gonna go shower. I'll talk to you later." Without waiting for Harinder to respond, he disappears into the bathroom, quickly shutting and locking the door after him.

Harinder balls his hand back up into a fist. He looks over at Dumpling in her crate. She yowls at him.

"He didn't even say thank you," Harinder bemoans.

Let me out, Dumpling meows back.

Goddamn it.

*

Harinder sets everything up. He wants Jericho to be there when he lets Dumpling out and she starts to explore. Maybe it'll trigger something nurturing in him. Then, he thinks maybe he should let her out so Jericho emerges to find her already comfortable. Harinder doesn't know which would be better. He ends up hemming and hawing so long that when Jericho finally comes out of the bathroom, nearly an hour later, he looks at him weird and asks, "Why is the cat still locked in the crate? She's havin' a fuckin' aneurysm, and you're just sitting there staring at her."

And...he's not wrong.

"I uh," Harinder starts. "Wanted you to do it."

Jericho blinks, then scrunches his nose. His hair is dripping in his eyes. "Alright, I guess." He acts like the cage is on fire when he walks over and sits on the couch, contemplating it like a vat of actual fucking lava instead of a fluffy, adorable cat who really badly wants to scratch up his furniture and sit on him at inopportune times.

"She's not going to bite you," Harinder says crossly.

"Didn't think she would." Jericho throws him a narrow look. "Just wanted to...make the most out of it, I guess."

Harinder doesn't know how to interpret that, but before he can think about it too hard, Jericho is unlatching the crate and swinging open the door. Dumpling goes rocketing out of the crate and promptly disappears under the couch. They both stare at the empty space.

"Well," Jericho says. "That happened."

Harinder stands to try to coax her out, but Jericho waves a hand.

"Don't bother. She'll come out when she wants to. You hungry? I'm hungry." He walks over to the kitchen without another word.

He makes scrambled eggs and fries slices of tomatoes to put on top. He gives Harinder a plate. It's got mozzarella cheese and cracked pepper sprinkled over the top. Cooking pretty things is already not Jericho's style, but then he sits in silence and eats while staring morosely at his plate, and eventually, Harinder can't handle it anymore. For one: the eggs are delicious, but he still hasn't gotten a thank you, or even a reaction, and his grace period is fucking over.

"What's your goddamn deal?" he bursts out with no warning. Possibly not the best approach. Definitely not the best approach, judging from Jericho's expression.

"My deal is...I wanted food?"

"So you make fancy breakfast food?"

"Fuck off," Jericho says. "Eggs don't have to be breakfast food; they're a completely versatile part of a balanced diet and also don't go bad fast, so when I eat Chinese takeout five nights in a row, they're still there for me when I run out of cash before my next Patreon drop. By the way, I'm not proud of that and don't plan on repeating it, but it's good to be prepared for these kinda mental—"

"Jericho." He stops, going immediately silent. Usually Harinder has to say his name at least three times to get that effect. "What. The fuck. Is wrong."

The apartment creaks. Jericho is frozen and not saying anything, staring at his half-empty plate. Abruptly, he stands up and walks out of the kitchen. Harinder follows him, despite an initial moment of hesitation because he's too stubborn to let it go. Jericho stops at the bedroom door, the weird threshold where their energies mix. He feels safe in there, which is why when Jericho refuses to go in, Harinder mentally starts preparing for a fight.

"I gotta tell you something," Jericho says after a long pause. Harinder tenses but doesn't interject. "It wasn't something I ever— Like, I don't even know how to..." He runs a hand through his wet hair. "I never could have anticipated shit happening like this and everything is wrong and I promise I didn't mean any harm by it."

"Please tell me you're not the one who robbed my house and stole my bike," Harinder suggests, half joking.

Jericho looks back at him, brow furrowed. "What? No. Dude, what the fuck."

"I'm just saying, there are a lot of ways to piss me off, but I can't think of anything you could have done in recent memory that could be that life ruinin—"

"I lied to you."

At first his hackles raise. Harinder mentally prepares to get indignant and angry and defensive, but then he still can't think of anything Jericho's done aside from being overwhelmingly annoying and also the nicest person he's met in ages, so. Uh.

"Are you not really an artist?" Harinder asks, wearily sarcastic.

Making a frustrated sound, Jericho turns on him. "I literally cannot believe you're missing a great chance to get angry at me. What's wrong with you?"

Harinder throws his hands in the air. "I just can't fucking think of anything you could have done that's that bad, you horse's ass! Excuse the fuck out of me for not being ready to draw and quarter you over something I don't even know yet."

Jericho's face is pained. "I can't believe this. You like me too much to hate me for no reason." He drags a hand down his face. "This fucking sucks."

Harinder is at a loss. "How the fuck does that suck?"

Does Jericho not...like *him?* Did Harinder get himself attached to this weird, wonderful, irritating boy—this boy who is compelling and beautiful at the oddest of angles and kind where no one can see—only to discover that the feeling isn't mutual? A bright-yellow pang lances through Harinder's chest at the thought.

Then Jericho turns away, and his voice is pitifully small when he creaks out, "Because you're gonna fucking hate me when I tell you."

Chapter Twenty-Two

Harinder Goes Through Phases, Like the Moon or Something

"What in Satan's balls could be this fucking important?"

"I didn't actually plan on keeping Dumpling when I wanted to adopt her, is what."

The silence hurts. Harinder is a foot farther from Jericho than he was a second ago, but he doesn't recall taking the steps back. "What...the fuck."

Jericho squeezes his eyes behind his fingertips. "I fucked up, Hari. I... It's a long goddamn story? I just thought..."

"Explain. *Now*," Harinder demands, harsh and low. Jericho has the grace to flinch, but it doesn't make Harinder feel better—rather it makes him feel quite worse.

"Can we sit down?"

"No."

Swallowing hard, Jericho mutters, "Okay," then raises his voice, still avoiding looking at Harinder. "My sister, Shiloh, she had this cat." At the "had," Harinder's stomach drops. "I went over one day, not knowing... He was scared of the vacuum, y'know? Like lots of cats are, but... Shiloh was vacuuming, and he was hiding by the back, and the door was unlocked, and I was really excited, and he just. He just ran."

Breathe in, through your nose. Breathe out, through the—

"Between my legs. He got out. We looked for hours, but it was dark, and he's a black cat."

Silence falls.

Harinder scrubs a hand over his eyes. "What next?"

Jericho shrugs with one shoulder. "Not much. Shiloh stopped talking to me. She was really mad. That's why—"

"Yeah, I can put the fucking pieces together, Jericho."

He licks his lips and clenches his fist. "Yeah. Well, I...thought...I could get her another cat, and...maybe she'd. Stop being mad at me."

And there it is, out there in the open. The last month of Harinder's life. A critical decision on his part. Not just a gesture of trust, but a gift, as little as he likes pets as gifts, but. It was an olive branch, if the making out itself wasn't one already. The little *I like you. Here, please be happy* that Harinder gave in the only way he could. And now.

Now.

"You don't want her."

"It's not like that," Jericho says.

"Did you just let me stay here so I'd—"

"Fuck no!" Jericho whirls to face him. "That's the fucking unplanned part!"

"You're a fucking asshole," Harinder says quietly.

"Harinder—"

"Shut the fuck up," Harinder snaps, voice climbing. "How fucking dare you? How fucking dare— I cannot goddamn believe I— You— *All this time*, you were trying to manipulate me to fix your shitty mistake, and I..." Fell for it. He slept in Jericho's bed and opened up about his past and let his heart grow fond of the sight of him, the sound of his voice.

And it was all a goddamn lie.

Jericho slumps bonelessly against the doorjamb, still not entering the bedroom. Not that Harinder could stop him. (Just last night, they sat together in that room and Jericho showed him his art and they touched without words and it was sincerely, painfully beautiful.)

"It wasn't supposed to turn out like this. I didn't mean to..."

"Kiss me? Invite me into your home?"

Jericho's lips form the start of a *no*, but no sound comes out.

Harinder knows their tentative start of a relationship wasn't Jericho's fault. Harinder kissed *him*. Jericho helped Harinder because he had no other options. It wasn't in the script for them to actually— to actually—

"I didn't plan any of that. You weren't supposed to know that I gave Dumpling away, but since you're here, I couldn't just."

"Give her away and hope I wouldn't notice?" Harinder supplies dryly.

"It's not like I was gonna sell her to a circus or anything. My sister loves her cats."

"I don't have any issues with your sister's petkeeping skills. I have issues with you tricking me into thinking well of *your* petkeeping skills."

"It was an accident!"

"An accident you tried to dodge accountability for!"

"I'm sorry, okay?"

"It's too late for sorry! I already gave you the fucking cat! I—" He won't cry. Harinder doesn't cry much anymore, and he refuses to cry over Jericho *motherfucking* Adams. "I'll just. Make sure to be out of here by the end of the weekend."

There. Jericho finally crosses through into the bedroom. He looks around, not touching anything, not even sitting on the bed. It takes Harinder a second to realize Jericho is looking not at his own belongings, but Harinder's, scattered through the room like equippable items in a videogame.

"You don't have to," he begins.

"I do."

Jericho trembles, standing in the middle of the room. "I'm sorry," he squeaks out.

Harinder curls his lip. "No, you're not."

Looking over his shoulder, Jericho frowns. "Look, I get you're mad, but...don't. C'mon."

It sounds like it should have been said defensively, but he just sounds sad, and worn, and tired. Pleading.

"Don't what?"

"Don't act like I don't care," Jericho says, waving a hand in a chaotic loop. "I get that I fucked up, and you can feel free to punish me for that as you're already fucking doing, but don't act like you can just write my feelings out of existence just because you're mad at me."

Harinder snarls, "*What* feelings?"

"The ones where I fucking like you, jackass." The yelling stops. Harinder isn't sure how that happened, but it does. "I didn't mean to hurt you. I keep talking about a plan, but there never was a plan, not really, I just; I was fucking lonely, and worried, and it seemed like the only option I had, and I was stubborn, and then I." His voice catches. Jericho clears his throat. "Started to."

"Started to," Harinder repeats slowly.

"Enjoy your company, I guess? I don't fucking know how to say it. I like you. I like that you're here. I'm fucking sorry I fucked that up, okay? At least let me have that." He plunks himself down on the edge of the bed and buries his face in his hands.

Harinder props himself against the doorjamb, frowning at Jericho. "Why should I? Genuine question."

Jericho shifts. "I don't know how to answer that."

Harinder doesn't know whether to start flailing or roll his eyes or scream and stomp his feet or what. In the end, he doesn't do any of those things.

"You know how important this is to me," he says slowly. "And you're saying you're sorry and that you want me to believe you. Why should I believe that?"

No one says anything for a few minutes, and then Jericho whispers, voice scratchy, "You should take her back."

"What?"

"The cat. Dumpling. I didn't... I don't deserve her, or your trust, or my sister talking to me, or anything. Take her back when you go to work tomorrow."

Harinder sighs heavily, then moves until he's in front of Jericho and drops to sit on his heels, peering at Jericho's half-obscured face. After a moment, he pulls one of Jericho's hands away so he can look into the other man's eyes. "That isn't what I wanted to hear."

Blinking, Jericho says, "What do you want to hear?"

Harinder purses his lips. "I don't know. You're supposed to figure that out. Tell me you like me again."

Jericho snorts very quietly. "I like you."

"How much?"

"More than either of us deserve?"

"Mm," Harinder hums, thinking it over. "Try again."

"As much as you deserve, not that I'm worthy of your presence," Jericho tries.

It wins a soft snicker. "Getting better." Harinder allows them both a moment of silence, if not peace. A contemplative pause, and then: "You're a fucking dumbass for doing this, you realize." Jericho nods mutely. "You could have just nixed the idea and pretended it was never a thing, at least until I moved out."

He shrugs. "But you didn't." Harinder touches his knee. "You told me the truth even though it made you look like the biggest dumbass on the entire East Coast and knowing I was probably going to kill you and hide your body in the basement storage while living off your resources until they were gone, at which point I'd disappear to find a new life."

"Yeah, well, I did guess all of that," Jericho says. "Though I thought you'd just steal everything and get to your new life so you'd have all my savings and stuff."

"No. I'll still work, saving up my paychecks while I live off your money." He clears his throat. "Anyway."

"Anyway."

"I literally can't believe you were stupid enough to tell me about this, but I guess if you were less of an idiot, I wouldn't like you as much, for whatever unfathomable reason."

Jericho looks up at him through his (long, white, ridiculously pretty) eyelashes. "You like me?"

"Still. Again, I couldn't exactly say why, but. Yeah."

The corner of his mouth quirks up, weak but hopeful. "You're way too nice."

"You first," Harinder says, then stands up. "Scoot over."

"What?"

Harinder finally gives in to the urge to roll his eyes. "You heard me. You're taking up half the bed, you ridiculously, unnecessarily tall jackwagon." Jericho stares at him like he just grew a dick on his forehead, but slowly stands up. He doesn't move after that though, so Harinder takes it upon himself to throw his body on the bed, scooting over until he reaches the wall.

Jericho is still standing there like a powered-down robot, so Harinder gives a helpful pat to the mattress next to him. "You coming, or am I going to sleep?"

Like coming to life, Jericho scrabbles beside him, eyes wide and shocked as he lays himself next to Harinder, taking pains not to touch. Harinder rolls over onto his side, tugging Jericho's arm until he does the same.

"Hey," Harinder murmurs.

"What's up?"

"If you ever do something like this again, I really will kill you and steal all your earthly possessions. You know that, right?"

"I don't know that I *could* do something like this again, but deal anyway, I guess."

"You get what I mean."

"Yeah." Jericho pauses, looking down at the mattress. "Arrre...you still moving out?"

Harinder looks down as well, bites his lip. "No, I guess not. I don't really have anywhere else to go anyway. Besides, someone has to be around to watch Dumpling while your incompetent ass is bumbling around fucking shit up."

"I won't take offense to that because it's true," Jericho says primly.

"Good." Slumping onto the pillows, both of which he's stolen to his side of the bed, leaving Jericho with nothing, Harinder huffs a deep breath through his nostrils. "That conversation was exhausting."

"I was expecting worse," Jericho admits. "But yeah."

Harinder eyes him speculatively. "Why did you tell me?"

Jericho meets his gaze after a brief hesitation. His eyes tremble like he wants to look away again. "Because I...if I wanted to keep you around, you'd have to know eventually. Like, I couldn't keep it a secret forever, and you'd hate me more if you found out after I'd done it."

Despite himself, a slow smile spreads Harinder's lips. "You want to keep me around," he repeats.

Jericho goes red and looks away. "I guess I do."

"Then I guess I'll stay," Harinder says, inching a bit closer into the space between them. "But I'm going to be extra annoying about it."

He watches Jericho's lips press together, repressing a smile. "I'm okay with that."

Harinder grins, fierce and awkward but honest, weirdly happy even after the emotional rollercoaster. "You'd better be." Then he touches Jericho's face.

Then Jericho kisses him.

It's the first time Jericho has initiated intimacy between them (he probably hopes Harinder hasn't noticed), so for a short second, his reaction is surprise. That's all Jericho needs to crumble in insecurity though. He jerks back, already turning bright red.

"Wow," Harinder says, blinking.

Jericho clears his throat and talks with that forced apathetic tone as if his voice isn't wobbling and his skin isn't flushed with embarrassment and fear, which he probably doesn't realize is unfounded. "What."

Harinder shakes his head. "You're such a baby." Before Jericho can react, Harinder pounces. Jericho hadn't squirmed back that far after all.

Propped on one arm, Harinder leans over Jericho with a fist in his shirt. Jericho flops onto his back, gasping in quiet shock in between returning Harinder's kisses, lips fumbling, hand fidgeting in the air like he doesn't know what to do with it. Harinder helps.

Loosening his fingers from Jericho's shirt, Harinder threads them instead through Jericho's, squeezing until Jericho responds. Harinder guides his hand to his hip, silently telling him it's okay to touch. Then he slides his palm up Jericho's forearm and tugs until Jericho takes the initiative and winds it up his back, sliding under his sweater but still over his shirt.

They stay like that, mouths hungry, until Harinder's arm tires. He prods at Jericho again, fussing incoherently. Jericho gets the hint and shifts onto his side, so he's rolling on top of Harinder and their thighs slot together in the most satisfying way; he can't help but arch, rumbling in his throat.

Jericho makes A Sound, and Harinder smirks against his mouth, then bites him. He gets a whimper for his trouble, Jericho's lips parted and his breath heavy. Harinder licks over his bottom lip with his tongue, soothing away the sting of teeth, and Jericho crashes against him with not a second to spare.

Last night Jericho was shirtless and vulnerable and pretty, and right now he is desperate and needy and not shirtless, and one of those things needs to change. Harinder goes for it: palms flattened, coursing down Jericho's front, taking in the planes of his chest. He gives in to an earlier desire to squeeze at his hips, and it's just as nice as he imagined—even more so when Jericho whines and bucks, mouth falling a bit too far open.

Harinder coaxes him back into motion, humming in encouragement. Harinder's fingers find a sliver of skin and seek more, pushing Jericho's shirt up as they chart the length of his sides.

Eager and squirmy, Jericho rears onto his knees and rips his shirt over his head, shaking the wayward curls of his Afro from his eyes. Harinder gazes, appreciative, gnawing on his lips.

He takes back his earlier thoughts about Jericho not being especially handsome. Here, he's flushed and straddling Harinder's thigh, pants tight, the waistband low, and... *Shit.* It takes massive self-control on Harinder's part to bring his hands to Jericho's shoulders instead of his zipper. He weaves his hand into the thick coils of Jericho's hair, holding the other man steady while he methodically sucks a dark, massive hickey into the crook of his neck. Focusing on the task when Jericho is keening like that and squirming beneath him is just as challenging as not reducing himself to begging for his dick.

Speaking of which.

"Don't freak out," Harinder rasps, lips brushing Jericho's throat.

Jericho gasps something that might be a laugh. "About?"

Harinder doesn't let himself hesitate. He really should have brought this up sooner, but the vast majority of the time, he forgets it matters to some people. So, he unbuttons his pants with perfunctory speed, reaches inside, and yanks his packer from the confines of his jock. "This was getting uncomfortable," he explains, hoping he isn't turning bright red. He hates when people make his being transgender into a *thing*.

With the casual air of someone who's trying his best not to freak out, Harinder angles his body so he can throw the squishy silicone penis into the laundry basket across the room, by the closet. He'll fish it out later.

Then he returns his focus to Jericho, brows knit with worry. Jericho did say he was gay, after all. What if this is a dealbreaker?

Jericho stares in the direction of the flying dick. "You're a really good throw," is all he says. "We good?"

Harinder's lips part silently. He briefly loses himself in the soft angles of Jericho's smile, accepting and amused. "Yes." Harinder's heart is going to beat out of his fucking chest. "Come here."

With the barrier of his packer gone, Harinder feels so much more when Jericho settles between his legs, grinding experimentally so they both shudder. Impatient, Harinder shoves his hands down the back of Jericho's jeans, grabbing his ass through his boxers, and yanks so they're flush.

He knows Jericho isn't experienced. While he never asked directly, Harinder is fairly sure Jericho is a virgin, and so he resolves to proceed gently and with caution. It's a little awkward because Harinder is unquestionably a bottom, and Jericho is unquestionably shy about his desires, but Harinder has no problem being bossy, has no qualms showing Jericho exactly where to put his hands.

With the passing of several luxurious minutes rich with hot tongues and playful nips, teeth tugging and lips seeking, Jericho's confidence grows. Emboldened, he rakes one hand through Harinder's thick hair while the other settles on his hip, fingers drawing a nervous circle before Jericho pushes Harinder's shirt and sweater all the way up to his armpits.

Harinder gasps, eyes wide, gut tense with excitement, lower body throbbing. Jericho devours him with his eyes, blinking rapidly as he takes everything in. Without warning, he descends.

Jericho kisses up Harinder's sternum, sliding a hand under the small of his back, holding him still so when he lowers his mouth to one of Harinder's nipples, Harinder has nowhere to go except closer.

"*Ffffuck.*" Harinder writhes; if Jericho hadn't been holding him securely, he probably would have taken himself right over the edge of the bed.

It doesn't take experience to know piercings in erogenous zones are to be played with, and sweet blistering hell on a popsicle stick, does Jericho get the message. He flicks the tip of his tongue over the pebbled nub, teasing the bar for additional friction.

Harinder has lived his entire life as a trans man, having come out to his dad as a tot, to complete acceptance. Puberty blockers prevented him from growing breasts, sparing him the hellish ritual of binding and, if he could ever afford it, top surgery. However, he is both chunky and naturally sensitive. The shallow curves over his chest sing as Jericho squeezes the soft skin, thumb attending to the silver jewelry in Harinder's right nipple while he sucks wetly on the left.

It's so good Harinder thinks he might come in his pants from this alone.

Without meaning to, Harinder rakes his nails from Jericho's shoulder blade up the bare skin of his neck. Before he can apologize, Jericho releases the nipple from his mouth to breathe a long, low groan. He abandons

Harinder's chest, leaving his nipples swollen and painfully hard in the cool air, letting his mouth explore further down his torso. His teeth nibble over Harinder's ribs, provoking a half laugh, half moan.

Then Jericho surprises him as he often does.

He massages low on Harinder's hip before his hand, quite unexpectedly, slips beneath the waist of his unbuttoned jeans. Not far at all—just deep enough to allow the heel of his palm to apply pressure to his aching clit. Harinder wails, hips jerking up to chase more of the sensation.

"Is this okay?" Jericho asks, voice trembling.

Harinder can only nod, whimpering and bucking.

Jericho shifts to bring his mouth to Harinder's, allowing his hand to change angles so his fingers brush the outside of Harinder's jock. Harinder kisses him desperately, wrapping his arms tightly around Jericho's neck. His legs part, knees drawn toward his chest like the wanton harlot he is. Harinder truly could not care less—it gives Jericho space to rub experimental fingers against the damp fabric covering Harinder's snatch.

Until Jericho stops. "Wait."

Harinder makes a displeased noise. "Wait what?"

Grunting, Jericho worms his hand down the front of Harinder's jock, long artist's fingers seeking—

"Oh, son-of-a-*fuck*."

Jericho's middle finger finds the metal of Harinder's one remaining piercing: a vertical curve through the hood of his clit.

"Found it," Jericho murmurs triumphantly.

"Congrats," Harinder wheezes. "Please be nice to it."

Jericho laughs. "Cross my heart."

He starts up a cautious but insightful rhythm, responding attentively to Harinder's cues. The pads of his fingers are callused—molded by paintbrushes and charcoal pencils and, less poetically, his tablet stylus—and they trace Harinder's swollen erection with skillful care. Jericho seems to know when to ease up, eliciting begging gasps, punctuating the desperate beat with sudden pressure, hand moving quickly as he jerks Harinder to near madness.

In the end, Harinder really does come in his pants.

He cries through each spasm, nails digging into Jericho's shoulders. Jericho kisses his jaw over and over again, whispering missives far too sweet for Harinder's ears.

The pressure finally subsides, leaving Harinder a sweaty, panting mess. Every inch a gentleman, Jericho slides out from the cradle of Harinder's legs, gently rubbing his quivering thighs as he lowers them to a more comfortable position. He settles next to him, fingers stroking Harinder's side, soothing him as he rides out the last few aftershocks. Harinder shivers, breath slowing.

Rolling to his side, Harinder inspects Jericho. He brushes his fingertips over the bright red divots in Jericho's pale shoulders, imprints from Harinder's nails. Jericho smiles crookedly.

Harinder drops his hand lower, to Jericho's thigh, dangerously close to his apex where he's still hard and impossibly warm.

Jericho presses his lips together, cheeks flushing. "Not this time?" He speaks as if he's asking permission.

Smiling, Harinder flutters a kiss over Jericho's brow. "Of course. Never anything you don't want."

Their foreheads meet, mouths doing the same a moment later. Sweet and soft, they kiss until Harinder is convinced they've melted into a gooey puddle, neither of their edges discernible from the other's.

With a final sigh, Jericho smooths Harinder's sweater into place over his belly. He gathers Harinder in his arms, burying his face in the crook of his neck, and draws in a shuddery inhale.

Harinder gently pets his hair. "You okay?"

"Mm," Jericho responds, muffled. "Just glad you're still here."

Anything he could say would ruin it, so Harinder hums and is otherwise quiet, lightly trailing his fingers up and down Jericho's back. Nothing else needs to be said; Jericho already knows Harinder's decision.

Chapter Twenty-Three

Jericho Should Probably Explain the Cat

Despite spending the first twenty-four hours in the apartment hidden under the couch, Dumpling settles in well. If by "well" Jericho means: she establishes a ritual that somehow involves waking both him and Harinder up at the same time.

Harinder feeds her before going to work, but he also locks the door to the bedroom every night. Even though Harinder is regular and gets up at eight every day (it used to be much earlier) and puts her bowl down at eight thirty on the dot, Dumpling has decided that seven sounds better. It makes no sense—at the store, she didn't get fed until after nine—but there's no reasoning with her.

Precisely seven o'clock every damn morning, Dumpling climbs out of whatever hole in which she was conducting her usual cat business and scratches at the bedroom door, meowing plaintively until one or both of them starts begging for mercy. Usually it's Jericho.

Harinder starts sleeping with the door cracked.

The week leading up to the twenty-first passes in anxious increments. After the fight, Harinder and Jericho sorted things out, mostly by dry humping a lot, but the next day was still awkward, and it hasn't changed much.

On top of lingering disappointment that Shiloh missed their birthdays *and* won't be back until nearly

Christmas, Jericho has no idea what to do about the cat. He's beat his head against the wall, agonizing over every available-seeming option, yet still has no idea how to handle the situation. Harinder gives away nothing, and Jericho is too scared to ask what he's thinking or, god forbid, *feeling*.

When the twenty-second arrives, no decisions have been made.

If nothing else, Shiloh is talking to him again. She texted yesterday to let him know their flight landed safely. Jericho can't guarantee she isn't just pretending to be okay and waiting for him to notice, but hopefully Shiloh will pick up on his exhaustion and be honest about her feelings for once.

He loves his sister. Normally, he would never think this, but under the circumstances, it's starting to feel like he might have to choose between Shiloh and Harinder, which he desperately would prefer to avoid. How does one put value on one's sister versus...whatever Harinder is to him, expressed in fewer words than "someone he likes a lot and would prefer to keep around"?

How is Jericho supposed to make sure Shiloh is okay and that their relationship isn't permanently damaged without alienating Harinder to the point where he applies for some human experimentation research in the Netherlands just to get away from him, and they never see each other again, except perhaps thirty years in the future when Harinder is a mutated horror who recognizes Jericho in a dark alley, reaching out to him, caught in nostalgic desperation for one last dreg of human contact—?

Okay, Jericho, calm down. The chances of that happening are much less likely than Harinder slowly growing to resent Jericho for lying, their comfortable companionship withering more and more until one day Harinder leaves, too tired to deal with any more bullshit, and doesn't come back.

A shudder runs along his spine. They haven't talked about it since Jericho's initial confession. He doesn't want to bring it up again, but time is running out. Jericho never would have guessed he'd be this torn up over a simple fucking cat. Especially not a cat who scratches at the door when he and Harinder are making out—the lesser of two evils because if they don't close the door, she jumps on the bed and no, no, no.

Nowadays, they can't keep their hands off each other. It's a poor substitute for talking about their problems, but Jericho figures their fight maxed out the Difficult Conversation meter, and now they're waiting for it to come back out of the red.

Speaking of red... A big maroon blob enters his vision, turning into Harinder, who is wearing one of Jericho's big hoodies. He moves between Jericho and the television, presently paused on a frame of this indie animation series Harinder introduced him to. The plot is pure cringe—deliberately so, or so Harinder claims—but the bizarre art style is unexpectedly compelling. Jericho has it playing (muted) at 0.25x speed and is doing gestural studies on his tablet.

He sets the tablet aside in the nick of time because Harinder lands in his lap a second later.

"Hey, buddy."

Harinder slings an arm around his neck and kisses him instead of responding. Jericho melts helplessly, hands slipping up the back of his shirt. His core temperature is ridiculously high—great for winter snuggles, particularly ones that involve being half naked under a blanket, ignoring the movie in the background, just skin on warm (*warmer*) skin, Harinder's hips glued against his, chest swelling rhythmically as he sucks at Jericho's clavicle— Hey wait, what?

Jericho is no longer being kissed, and even worse, Harinder knocks Jericho's hands free of his clothing and stands, crossing his arms and scrunching his nose.

"Why aren't you ready to go yet?"

Jericho blinks owlishly. "Ready for what?"

Harinder just got home from work an hour ago—heh. There it is again. *Home.* Like this is Harinder's living space and not a temporary shelter while he looks for a better apartment. Jericho is crossing his fingers for Harinder to find something on this side of town, mostly so Harinder can get to his job without trouble, but more selfishly, so Jericho doesn't have to travel too far to see him.

Regardless, it's seven PM on a Friday, and Jericho doesn't have plans. Unless one counts "drawing and fretting" as plans, which Jericho doesn't.

Rolling his eyes like he's being done a great disservice, Harinder says, "Gee, I wonder. Like you haven't been a ball of fucking anxiety all goddamn day over your sister getting home."

Tensing, Jericho shrinks into the couch cushions. "Yeah, but—"

"Look, assface, it's getting dark. There's no reason to pay for a cab both ways, so I assume we're walking back, and I don't need that to happen at two AM. Forecast says it's going to snow at least three to five inches overnight."

"You listen to the weather?"

"I have a smartphone, dicksore, there's an app—"

"Wait... We?"

Finally, Harinder's rigid, aggressive stands goes a little mushy at the edges. He bites the inside of his lip.

"I figured you'd want some help transporting Dumpling, considering what a gangly fuckup you are. You'd probably drop the carrier, and she'd escape right in front of your sister. Not that I want that to happen, mind you, but if it does, I need to be there to witness your utter humiliation after the fact. Maybe I'll even have my phone out, just in case, so I can relive the moment of devastating failure again and a—mmph."

Using a kiss to stop someone from talking is so misogynist-romcom, but in the midst of Harinder recounting how badly he wants to revel in Jericho's pain, he picks up the subtler cue: Harinder is giving Jericho his blessing. He is also accompanying him, so he'll get to meet Shiloh, and then they'll walk back together, snowflakes glittering under the streetlamps, and maybe they'll even hold hands. That is, if Harinder doesn't complain about the cold and insist on shoving his hands in his pockets.

Jericho's pockets. He's wearing Jericho's hoodie. Jericho bounces on his toes and cradles Harinder's face as he kisses him. Just as he starts to get into it, Harinder elbows him. His attempt to scowl is undermined by the badly repressed smirk fighting the downturned corners of his mouth.

"Stop being sappy."

Jericho calls bullshit. Harinder is the king of sappy; he just hates being caught at it.

"Sure," Jericho agrees, shoving his hands in his sweatpants pockets to stop himself from grabbing Harinder again. "Lemme just switch to the latest action thriller so I can complete my transformation into the heroic, square-jawed Hollywood hunk I was always meant to be."

Harinder raises his pierced eyebrow at Jericho, the smirk becoming a little more prominent. "Does that make me the sidekick or the love interest?" He pauses a beat. "Choose your answer wisely."

"Neither," Jericho says smoothly, walking backward so he can maintain eye contact. The bedroom still houses his clothing—the items that he hasn't been cycling in and out of the laundry basket, anyway—so he shuffles in that approximate direction. "You're my mentor. Like the noble Philoctetes, you will craft me from the finest marble into the spitting image of masculine godhood."

What could have been a derisive snort dissolves into a mess of snickers. "Are you calling me a goat?"

"Only half."

"I'll remind you of that fact next time we make out."

"That could have been five minutes ago, but you're making me put on real pants."

"Don't call those paper-thin, skintight abominations you wear 'real pants.'"

"Oh, I'm sorry. Maybe instead, I should wear the formless dad jeans I got at the Salvation Army for two bucks after they were donated by someone's mom."

"All I'm saying is that when you get hypothermia from wearing practically no clothing in the middle of December, don't blame—pfffft."

Jericho misses the doorway by a few inches and runs his head into the doorjamb. Harinder doesn't kiss it better, but he does ogle him while he changes, which is half as good. Jericho doesn't complain.

Correction: Doesn't complain until Harinder reveals his evil plan and makes Jericho put Dumpling in the carrying crate without assistance.

"I'm going to get tetanus," Jericho whines.

"She's had her vaccinations."

"I'm bleeding out."

"I have 911 on speed dial."

"Does 911 even need speed dial? It's not like it's hard to—"

"Shut up and knock."

Beside him, Harinder shifts the crate in his arms. The cab has long since driven off, and Jericho's been using the scratches Dumpling liberally applied to his arms to stall. Unfortunately, if he continues fronting, Harinder might actually knock for him.

Jericho stares at the door in terror and confesses, "I'm having second thoughts."

"No, you're not." Harinder punches him lightly in the side while balancing Dumpling on his hip. She mews quietly at being jostled but has otherwise been fairly quiet. Aside from the scratching, she doesn't make much noise unless she's about to be fed. "You're just scared of rejection."

Jericho shoots him a dry, miserable look. "Thank you, Captain Obvious. We're all wowed by your unworldly powers of deduct—"

This time, Harinder side kicks him in the shin. "Your sister is not going to reject you."

"You don't know my sister," Jericho hisses weakly, shaking his leg out. It doesn't really hurt that bad, just a tingle.

"I know *you*."

Jericho forgets what he was doing. Harinder's eyes are on him, intense and dark, thick brows low and scrunched over his eyes. Mmmngh. "I know that I've spent over a month wanting to tell you 'no' in various ways and haven't managed to stick with any of them."

Jericho's heart pangs.

"So, you know," Harinder finishes lamely, dropping his gaze to the snowy porch under their feet. "Don't worry, or whatever. I'm sure she finds you as annoyingly irresistible as I do."

A very small, very genuine smile creeps up on Jericho's mouth, and for once, he doesn't try to hide or repress it. He runs with it, letting the feeling flow through him—or is it those happy hormones he's heard about, the ones triggered by facial expressions? Like endorphins, but emotional mind control. He's okay with being mind controlled by happy Harinder feelings.

"I like you too." Jericho delicately removes the cat carrier from under Harinder's arm, holding it to the side while he negotiates through the space between them. A small smile, maybe a bit bashful, plays across Harinder's lips. He leans up when Jericho leans down.

The door opens. It takes him a second to register the shifting light with his eyes closed, and when he hears a voice, he nearly drops the carrier.

"Oh. Hello."

"Shiloh!"

Head jerking, Jericho regards the slender figure of his sister with terror as she purses her lips at him through the screen door.

"Is this some weird door-to-door sales pitch? Because I am definitely interested, if so."

Hi, Shiloh. Long time no see. This is my—uh, this is Harinder.

Jericho gawps and doesn't say a word. The floundering is oh so strong.

Meanwhile, Harinder is looking incredulously between the two of them. Just as Shiloh opens her mouth to (presumably) question why Jericho is kissing a boy on her porch, in the dark, Harinder bursts out: "You didn't fucking tell me you were twins!"

They blink at him in tandem, two pairs of snowy white eyelashes. Shiloh brushes a cluster of tight blonde curls behind her pale ear and clears her throat.

Jericho finally finds his voice. "Why wouldn't we be?"

Harinder takes a step back. "I don't know! That's usually something you mention. What about your birthday?"

"Shiloh was born after midnight," Jericho explains, because duh. He was the twelfth, she was the thirteenth.

"Indeed, I was," Shiloh adds, pushing open the screen door. "Care to come inside, gentlemen, or are you insisting on holding this meeting in the snow?" She's right. It's beginning to snow again, and if Harinder's stupid weather app was right, it's going to be nasty.

Shiloh gives them room to step inside. Harinder takes a step forward, then looks pointedly over his shoulder. "Jericho?"

"Yeah, yeah..." Jericho inches farther into the light, hoping Shiloh doesn't notice the cat carrier. It must be hidden behind Harinder's body because she turns her eyes toward the hallway, unawares. Jericho tries to be subtle about hovering behind Harinder, the screen door falling closed behind them.

"Darling," Shiloh calls. "We have company. Don't come out looking unseemly."

Layla's voice is muffled at first but clears as she makes her way down the hall. "I never look unseemly, Shiloh, shame on— Oh, hello Harinder." She sounds surprised.

Jericho is equally surprised.

"Wait, you know—" he starts to say but is interrupted by Harinder's louder exclamation.

"Layla? *This* is your Shiloh?"

The room goes very quiet. Dumpling chooses that time to make noise. Of course she does. "Miaow!" she implores loudly, scratching at the front of the carrier.

Suddenly all eyes are on Jericho, and he wants to die a lot.

Shiloh peers at the carrier on his hip. Harinder unhelpfully steps out of the way, giving her a better view. He clears his throat, also unhelpfully.

"Hello there," Shiloh says.

"Wait, before we discuss why I'm holding a cat," Jericho blurts. "How the fuck do you two know each other?"

Layla and Harinder exchange odd looks.

"We dated in high school," Layla answers crisply.

Jericho scrunches his nose. "But you're—"

"She didn't realize she was a lesbian yet," Harinder says.

Layla sniffs, brushing her hands over her skirt. "The relationship was very chaste, and it helped form a lifelong friendship that I do not regret despite its awkward beginnings."

"What about its awkward right-now?" Harinder wonders, glancing back at Shiloh in a way he probably thinks is sneaky.

"That I do regret," Layla says. "Good evening, Jericho. It's been a while since I've seen you. Is everything okay?"

Harinder chokes on a laugh, then *he* gets to be the center of attention. Serves him right.

"Fuck off," Jericho tells him.

"This is approximately zero percent my fault," Harinder answers, gesturing as if pushing the Awkward Attention Volleyball back to Jericho. He's glad it's only metaphorical because if an actual volleyball were rocketing toward him, his options would be "drop the cat" or "get hit in the face," and Jericho has no plans to drop a cat while standing in a room with both Shiloh Kerekes and Harinder Mangal.

The room at large seems to expect Jericho to respond, but he doesn't. His vocal cords fail him, and he stands there opening his mouth like a dying fish. When he finally speaks, bullshit pops out.

"My arm's getting tired. This cat is heavier than she looks."

Harinder snorts.

"We should all go sit down," Shiloh suggests, leading the way into the living room.

Chapter Twenty-Four

Jericho, Get Out of the Bathtub

The apartment his sister shares with her fiancée is a lesbian DIY paradise. It gracefully combines classiness with nerdiness and superimposes the resulting image over a 3D-printed vagina, which Shiloh would nitpick was actually a vulva, and he should know better, blah blah blah.

Jericho has always liked being here. It's clean but not tidy, and despite the motif, the decor is more welcoming than pretentious. It feels lived in. He likes it better than his apartment, stuffed tightly with bullshit in hopes that it'll squeeze out the loneliness.

Or, at least, he did before. Harinder's there now, and the space feels a little less Yawning Maw of Emptiness. He's even straightened the desks up a bit. Consolidated.

Jericho sets Dumpling on the coffee table. Layla thrifted it, calling it vintage. Shiloh shellac-printed screenshots from old B horror movies all over the surface. They're a good team. Both of them are sitting on adjacent overstuffed chairs while he and Harinder share the loveseat, although there's very little love happening right now. They aren't even touching.

They're all waiting for him to speak, so Jericho takes a deep breath, and—

Mrrrow.

—something rubs against his leg.

Jericho jumps. He can't imagine what would be touching him except for the all-seeing elder god Shiloh allows to live rent-free under the couchhhhholy fuck it's Mephi. Either that, or Mephi's clone. Jericho supposes there isn't a shortage of black cats out there, but he also doesn't take Shiloh for the "get an identical-looking animal to replace the old one" type, so what...the hell.

"What the fuck is *he* doing here?" Jericho yelps, gawking at Mephi, who now looks affronted.

Everyone in the room is staring at him like he's crazy, Shiloh most of all.

"That's Mephi," she says patiently, as if fearful he suddenly regressed to preschool-level understanding.

"No shit," Jericho snaps. "That's why I said 'what is he doing here.'"

"He lives here, Jericho," says Layla.

Harinder doesn't say anything; he's watching the shitshow with rapt fascination.

"I," Jericho chokes. "I got you a new cat."

The room goes very, very still.

"Oh," says Shiloh, breaking the silence. "I...Jericho, we found Mephi two days after he got out. He was hungry and came right to the house."

Jericho is standing up, but he doesn't remember getting off the couch. Mephi puts his ears back, deciding he doesn't much care for this weird and unpredictable human and his very sudden emotions.

"Why were you ignoring me, then?" Jericho's voice cracks a tiny bit. Behind him, Harinder makes a sound, but Jericho doesn't look back. His eyes are fixed on Shiloh.

Shiloh, whose eyebrows are crawling up her forehead in shock. "Darling, I...I wasn't ignoring you."

"Like fuck you weren't. Layla said you were going to block me if I didn't...leave you alone..." The steam is starting to hiss out of him; he watches Layla and Shiloh exchange worried looks.

"It was two AM, and you wouldn't stop texting weird rambling apologies," Shiloh says at the same time as Layla offers, apologetically, "It was only a joke."

The couch hits him in the back because he just thumped down onto it. All this time. All this emotional work and...

It was all in his head. A big misunder-fucking-standing.

"Jericho..."

"No, no," he says reassuringly. Not. "It's fine. I'm just gonna go die now."

Harinder immediately puts a hand on his leg. "Like fuck you are," he says in tandem with Shiloh's much calmer, "Jericho, please." They pause, visually sizing each other up.

Oh, hell. He can't handle this right now.

This time Jericho makes a pointed decision to stand. He bolts, leaving his sister, the cats, and Harinder behind in the fucked up, ridiculously cozy room that's full of so much awkwardness it's going to spontaneously combust, and Jericho's not gonna be around for that, nope, he's going to go hide in the bathtub, behind the unicorn-themed shower curtain, yes, that is exactly what he is going to—

"Jericho."

He has a foot halfway into the bathtub, as promised, when Shiloh closes the bathroom door behind them.

"Hey there. Mind giving a guy some privacy?"

"If you were using the facilities for their intended purpose, maybe I would."

Jericho snorts, hoisting his other leg into the tub so he can sit down. "Only maybe?"

"We did bathe together as children," Shiloh says wryly, inching farther into the room.

"Key word—children."

"We aren't much better now." Shiloh primly joins him in the tub, crouching until they're at eye level.

"I would argue, but we're sitting in a bathtub."

"Exactly."

Silence ensues.

Shiloh studies him from under her pale eyelashes. "Are you okay?"

"No," Jericho says immediately, not needing to think. "I thought you'd never talk to me again."

"I'm...sincerely sorry, Jericho." Shiloh bites her lip. "If I had any idea, I would have reached out. It was— I suppose my silence was foreboding, but it was entirely that Layla surprised me with the trip to raise my spirits after Mephi's untimely departure, and then we were so busy getting ready, I just figured I'd let you know when you contacted me. When you didn't, I assumed you were busy yourself."

She gives him a speculative look. "Although, I don't think I was entirely wrong..."

"Grill me about Harinder later," he grumbles.

"Deal." She opens her arms. Jericho stares at the pre-embrace with something akin to terror. "For the record," Shiloh continues, "nothing short of killing Layla and eating her organs could make me stop talking to you."

"What if I ate her organs while she was still alive?" Jericho wonders, already considering multiple other ways he could kill and/or eat Layla without it ending in Shiloh shunning him.

"So long as it was consensual, I don't see a reason for me to be upset."

"Cool." Jericho's throat goes tight. "I'll remember that." He sits frozen, regarding her open arms as one would the serrated jaw of a waiting predator.

Shiloh brushes the tip of one finger along his cheek. When she speaks, her voice is so, so gentle. "Come here, darling."

Jericho crawls into her arms like they're kids again.

*

They don't leave the bathroom until Jericho has made Shiloh pinky swear not to tell anyone how he clutched her while relief crying into her shoulder. She kisses his cheek, reassuring him she isn't mad ("yes, Jericho, *really*") and insisting he come by tomorrow for a haircut. Finally, Jericho believes her enough to release her into the wild living room where Harinder and Layla are pretending not to be ridiculously tense as they catch up.

"So are you two—" Layla is saying as he enters the room. Jericho comes close to running back into the bathroom, but Shiloh greets them both in a loud voice.

"Everything alright out here?"

Layla turns to her. Harinder goes red and looks at his knees. "Yes, Shiloh, thank you. Harinder and I were just— discussing what a coincidence it is that we all know one another indirectly."

"How about that six-degrees-of-separation thing," Jericho jokes, still visibly uncomfortable.

"We do all live in the same city," Shiloh responds evenly, lowering herself into a high-backed chair. She pats the armrest. Jericho props himself on that instead of walking over to the loveseat. Harinder might make fun of him later, but fuck him. "I've invited Jericho to brunch tomorrow." She glances at Layla. "Harinder, you're more than welcome to accompany him."

Harinder twists his mouth. "I work until six on Saturdays."

"Dinner, then. Or whenever you're next off."

He shifts. "I'm not."

Shiloh blinks, shoots a look at Jericho, then seems to think against searching him for answers. "Pardon?"

Shrugging, Harinder says, "I'm the only employee, and we're open every day. I don't have days off."

Layla clucks her tongue in disapproval, and Jericho flinches when Harinder's face turns stony.

"Sorry that we can't all have cushy jobs and a Master's degree, but I—"

Shiloh waves her hand, standing up. "I'd appreciate if we didn't get into fights about classism in my living room. Please."

Harinder silences. Jericho is secretly impressed. He's only seen Harinder's boss shut him up so quickly. There've been times where Jericho kissed him, and Harinder tried to keep ranting in between smooches.

Harinder watches Shiloh like a caged animal, ready to bolt if given the chance. Jericho wants to go to him, but forces himself to stay put. They size each other up. Finally, Shiloh speaks in a calm, even voice. "Seven thirty tomorrow. Is that manageable?"

There are a few seconds of agonizing tension in which neither of them speaks. Harinder's eyes shift toward

Layla, who is looking away, visibly pouting after having being snapped at.

"That's fine," he agrees at length. "I'm a vegetarian."

A faint smile curves Shiloh's lips. "I'll keep it in mind."

The coffee table yowls. Dumpling is done being ignored and follows with another, more plaintive miaow.

"So, onto more pressing matters," Shiloh says brightly. "Thank you for the birthday present, my darling twin, but I'm going to have to refuse."

Jericho's spine goes straight. "What?"

"As you can see, Mephi is fine." She gestures at her leg, which the cat is currently rubbing against and purring.

"You can have two cats," Jericho hedges, because he's pretty sure people can do that. Like, he's seen it on television. People have more than one cat.

Layla makes a warning noise; Shiloh flaps her hand dismissively. "Some people do, but our lease only allows for one, and furthermore, Mephi doesn't get along with other cats. Remember Lacrimor?"

Jericho wasn't in the city at the time, but he does vaguely recall when Shiloh plucked a three-legged, one-eyed stray off the streets and attempted to make it her own. She had to send him to live with her adoptive mother a short while after, citing trouble in paradise between the two males.

"Not really," Jericho says, watching as Mephi negotiates his way between the coffee table legs over to Harinder, whose lap he immediately jumps on. Jericho notes the subtle ways Harinder's body relaxes. He likes being able to read Harinder's more opaque tells.

"Mephi is extremely territorial," Shiloh explains.

Jericho looks on helplessly, not sure what to do or how to convince Shiloh to change her mind. Maybe Dumpling will be different since she's a girl cat—isn't there a thing about animals working better in different sex pairs? Maybe? He'll google it real quick—oh.

Before Jericho has a chance to reach for his phone, Mephi and Dumpling catch sight of each other through the carrier grate. Mephi does a classic cat arch, digging his claws into Harinder's thighs and hissing. A displeased rumble issues from the carrier.

Shiloh strides quickly over to Harinder and plucks Mephi off his lap as carefully as she can with his stupid toe-hooks clinging to Harinder's jeans. She doesn't seem particularly bothered when the beast immediately latches onto her front, nails embedding themselves in her shoulders.

Jericho winces.

"As you can see," Shiloh says, turning to display Mephi, her arms spread, illustrating how he clings (fucking ow?). "I don't think it's going to work. Sorry, dear." She wraps her arms around Mephi again, stroking and soothing him and making little coo noises as though the matter has been solved, just like that.

Jericho flounders, eyes flicking between her and the cat carrier. "Wait, though— What am I supposed to do with her?"

Harinder fixes him with a vicious look, mouth sneering in a weird display of vindictive delight. "No returns," he says, then brushes his pants off, stands up, and walks out of the room, leaving Dumpling sitting on the coffee table.

Jericho watches him go, mouth hanging open like a suffocating fish.

*

Layla drives them home.

Harinder makes Jericho hold Dumpling's carrier for the ride back, which is mercifully short and unmercifully silent. He's in the front, Harinder having elected to slump into the back seat without any protest. Jericho is a tangled ball of nervous energy, clenching his fingers in the sides of the crate until they're bee-sting red, stiff when he tries to unhinge them.

The moment the car slows, Harinder jumps out and slams the door. He doesn't say goodnight to Layla and doesn't wait for Jericho. Turns out he remembered his key this time. Jericho watches, slack-jawed as Harinder stomps inside without looking back.

With a tired "good night" and an appreciative smile, Jericho bids Layla goodbye and, lacking the energy to climb with a cat carrier in his hand, shuffles to the elevator. When Jericho makes it inside, he is greeted by the sight of a closed bedroom door, leaving him standing in the doorway holding a cat and no longer sure of the direction his life has just taken.

The last several weeks have been thrown into confusing ruin. It was all a misunderstanding. Even more than that, it was all a misunderstanding of his own manufacture. The entire thing was his fault. He'd let the cat out; he'd bugged Shiloh into telling him to leave her alone; he'd interpreted that as sincere rage and didn't follow up on the situation at all, only to find out the problem corrected itself.

He'd then proceeded to lie about his intentions to a person who only wanted to see the cat end up in a good home rather than in the hands of some incompetent shitheel who couldn't even talk to his own twin sister.

And yet, if he hadn't done any of that, he'd never have met Harinder. Or, he would have run into "the obnoxious guy at the pet store" once every couple of months when he stopped by Aquariums & More to buy food for Kimchi. They would've orbited around each other, completely ignorant to what could have been.

Jericho lets Dumpling out of her crate. She runs immediately beneath the couch. It's fine. She'll come out when she stops being mad.

So will Harinder. (Haha. The jokes write themselves.)

He doesn't want to wait that long.

His sneakers are soaked from walking through the snow to get inside, so he takes them off and pulls his rarely worn boots out of the closet. Crusty old socks have been shoved in the toes—gross, but dry, so he ignores the puff of sweaty fabric dust as he shakes them out and tugs them on. There is other weather-appropriate wear in here too. He grabs a boring gray coat and slides it over his arms, covering the Ninja Turtles hoodie he finally washed, and digs a pair of gloves from the front pocket.

Finally, he grabs a hat, but doesn't put it on. Instead, he twists it between his hands nervously as he walks over to the bedroom door, and knocks. There's no noise inside.

"Hey, Hari?"

Shifting. Footsteps.

Harinder opens the door and peers out. "What?" He blinks twice at Jericho's unusually warm getup.

"So," Jericho says, propping his shoulder against the doorjamb. "I'm a little sore about missing out on walking back with you." Harinder raises his eyebrows. "I was looking forward to it. Winter is supposed to be romantic at night, and I even—" He reaches into his pocket, managing to grab only one of the gloves. The other falls on the floor. "I even brought gloves so you wouldn't bitch about your hand being cold when I tried to hold it."

Harinder's lips part noiselessly as he stares at the glove in Jericho's hand. Slowly, he reaches out and plucks it from Jericho's fingers and inspects it. He looks back at Jericho, lips quirked. "You're a fucking loser, you know that?" Then, he stuffs the single glove in his pocket and extends his other hand toward Jericho. "Let's do this."

Chapter Twenty-Five

Harinder Confesses His Crimes

"I said 'take a walk,' not 'make out for an hour on a park bench,'" Jericho comments, breath husky.

"Oh well," says Harinder. "At least it's not snowing. We'd be covered."

Jericho gives him an amused look. Harinder watches his eyes move down from his face to his knees, which are quite comfortably settled on either side of Jericho's hips. His eyes gleam in the light from the streetlamp a couple paces behind the bench.

Okay, yeah, the bench on which Harinder is currently straddling him. Whatever. His neck was getting sore. Sue him.

"*You'd* be covered, you mean," Jericho comments, running his hands up Harinder's back. It's cold around the edges of their little gay cocoon, but inside, it is warm and soft and uh, tingly, in. Places. Yeah.

Harinder snuggles closer to Jericho's front, forcefully shoving his head under his chin so he can nuzzle his nose against a small sliver of Jericho's exposed throat. "I'd live."

"Bet we'd get covered in snow and would still be making out." Jericho snickers softly.

"Mm. The heat generated would form a perfect halo of ice around us."

"Instant igloo."

"The gay Captain America."

"Wait, Captain America isn't actually two queers fucking under an American flag?"

"I was shocked too."

They dissolve into awful, nerdy snickers. It's perfect and overwhelming in the best way.

Harinder is abruptly overwhelmed by the force of his relief. He mashes his face tighter against Jericho's neck, trying to fight the prickling of his eyes. He surreptitiously rubs them off on Jericho's coat, and if the other man notices, he'll go to his icy grave insisting they were produced by the laughter, not anything so vulgar as *an emotion.*

"You alright there, buddy?"

It's been three minutes, at least, spent clinging to Jericho. Fortunately, he doesn't seem to have picked up on the fact that Harinder was crying. "Fuck off," he mumbles harmlessly into Jericho's shoulder, reveling in the rumble of his quiet laughter.

"You're the one on me, like, literally *on* me. I can't get off anything—other than the obvious, I guess, if you really want me to—"

"Jericho."

Chuckling again, he kisses Harinder's temple, hands smoothing down his spine. "Fine, fine. I'll just sit here while you use me as an emotional vibrator, it's cool."

Damn him for being way more perceptive than he seems. Harinder won't complain. He's comfortable in Jericho's lap, their arms around the other, enshrouded in the peace of a dark winter night.

Then Jericho squirms, whining a bit in the back of his throat. "Okay, I can't feel my legs, sorry— Cuddles are great, cuddles are the best, but."

Harinder pulls back and gives him an exasperated smile, then rolls his eyes when Jericho makes a face at him. "You're weak," he says, climbing off his lap.

"You're heavy," Jericho parries, immediately grabbing for his hand.

"How rude."

He snorts a quiet laugh; Harinder grants him his hand when Jericho fails to take the bait. It's instinctive for Harinder to start completely unnecessary fights. Fortunately, Jericho has learned better.

Not that mindless arguing isn't fun, but they're both exhausted by the night's emotional demands. For once in their lives, they stay silent, hold hands, and walk through the sparkling carpet of snow.

Until Jericho ruins it, of course.

"So," he says, voice casual and light, like something just occurred to him. Harinder gets a bad feeling. "How did that background check ever turn out?"

Oh. Fuck.

Harinder's internal clock shudders and skips several seconds. Breath comes with difficulty because his lungs passed out from shock. The hamster wheel in his head catches fire, and he abruptly stops walking.

"Harinder?" Jericho asks, looking back at him. Their arms are stretched at an angle, hands still linked. "Did you find out about the murders?"

Swallowing, he lets out an uncomfortable, raspy laugh. "Yeah, and the arson and copyright infringement."

"Damn," Jericho deadpans. "Recreating Jackson Pollock's last masterpiece on the side of City Hall with jizz and a broken can of spray paint was my best performance piece to date."

Okay, this is fine. He can totally get out of this by just playing along. Harinder scoffs and evens his pace out with Jericho's, urging the other man into motion once more. "You sound like a frat boy who had to take art history once five years ago and now only remembers buzzwords."

"Mesopotamia," Jericho says amicably. "Something about Etruscans."

Harinder gives him a bland look. "Yes, thank you, very good."

"I actually read the entire SparkNotes page for the *Epic of Gilgamesh* once because I needed to one-up myself during a running gag of historical gay jokes."

"You're a true scholar, Jericho."

"One time, I spent two months studying cuneiform syllabary so I could write a bunch of dick jokes on the wall behind two characters in a panel that had nothing to do with early civilizations. People went absolutely apeshit when someone finally recognized it, then there was this mad frenzy to be the first person to translate everything. One person was an archaeology student and asked their fucking professor to help them. That was probably my best joke since painting a dildo sticking out of the eye socket of a human skull."

"I hope you're not expecting me to be proud of you for any of this."

"Aw," Jericho says, looking up from his feet to give Harinder a fake pout. "I thought you liked the dildo skull painting."

"I said it was evocative," Harinder grumbles, "not that I wanted you to hang it over the television."

"Hey, I took it down!"

"Only after I threatened to enhance it like the 'Monkey Christ' fresco."

"I still maintain that was cruel."

"I am a ruthless sadist and show no mercy. What can I say?"

Jericho laughs, and Harinder slants him a crooked half grin because he's genuinely goddamn thrilled to hear this stupidly anxious dork laugh freely. God, he really has it bad, doesn't he?

Their hands come unlinked, but Harinder doesn't get a chance to complain. Jericho winds around his back, chin hooking over his shoulder and hands tucking up under his arms, squeezing him. They take a few staggering steps forward like that, and then Harinder dissolves into annoyed snickers and says, "This is not fucking sustainable, douchewagon."

"That sounds like something a quitter would say." Jericho drapes more of his weight across Harinder's upper back. "Hey," he continues, not waiting for Harinder to respond. "For real though, what dirt do you have on me?"

Harinder's shoulders tense a bit, and he blurts out, "Nothing!" Shit. "You came up totally clean." He immediately melts into the coziness of a convenient lie until he considers everything that has happened this past week. When he next opens his mouth, it's to add: "At least, I assume you would have if I'd actually requested one."

Now Jericho goes tense, stopping whatever comeback was brewing on his tongue. He slips off Harinder's shoulders and hovers awkwardly behind him, uncharacteristically silent. The back of Harinder's neck burns where he assumes Jericho is staring at him.

"I'm confused," Jericho says finally.

"About what?" Harinder asks, brows furrowing as he stares at a foreign set of footprints in the snow before them, perpendicular to their current path. "The fact that I made up the whole thing, or?"

"Define 'the whole thing,' unless we're doing, like, an 'I accidentally the whole bottle' rehash. Not a bad meme for derivative jokes, but when it comes to callbacks, you could definitely do better."

Harinder snorts, rolling his eyes. "There was a verb in there, you obnoxious meme-loving fucktrain. If we absolutely have to talk syntax—which, by the way, I hate that you're making me do—a more accurate translation would be 'I accidentally the whole *thing*,' which is nowhere near as funny or surreal, and I will fight you if you argue that it is. So, yes, I did make up the whole thing, except it wasn't accidental. I was just practicing my horse's ass impression in hopes that I'd win at the Biggest Horse Ass competition in July."

"You've got a lot of work ahead of you," Jericho says evenly. "You're a pretty small horse's ass. From my vantage point, at least."

"I cannot believe you are crushing my dreams like this, Jericho," spits Harinder humorlessly, hands fisted at his sides.

"Sorry," says Jericho, tone dispassionate. "So, like, indulge me. What was the actual adoption procedure?"

"Personal information, short interview, care release contract."

Long pause. "That's it?"

"Yeah, that's all the rescue requires."

"So... Everything you made me do..."

"Was just me trying to get rid of you, yeah."

Longer pause. Harinder wants to turn around and look at him, find out what he's thinking, but he can't make himself. He suspects his feet have frozen to the ground, and he will be a statue of regret here forever, and then he hears laughter.

"That's cool. I lied about doing the community service anyway."

Harinder whirls. "You did *what*?"

Jericho tsks. "You think I actually washed all those windows? I don't even know who the landlord is. I don't know the first goddamn thing about community service or how to sign off on it or whatever. It was pure dumb luck you didn't ask to see the signature I forged on the community service form I found off Google because I don't know if it would have held up under scrutiny. Fortunately, you were too mad at me being around to care about logistics, and probably too caught up in your own dishonest bullshit to look that far into mine."

They stare each other down for a few intense moments, and then Harinder cracks a small smile, just a twitch out of the corner of his mouth. "No fucking kidding."

The pale man before him, silhouetted in the yellow light, smiles hesitantly. "We're literally a textbook misunderstanding in the gayest romcom ever written."

"Misunderstanding? More like willful fucking deceit."

"There are plenty of romcoms with that plot device too."

Harinder rolls his eyes. "Okay but consider: You'd have to be an idiot to waste precious time watching a story about us, much less enjoy it."

"Total dunderfuck," Jericho agrees, nodding. He examines Harinder for a few more seconds and then half lifts a hand. "C'mere?"

And really, that's all the incentive Harinder needs to tip forward and body slam him very gently in the chest. Jericho's arms tuck around him until he is warm and ensconced in puffy insulating fabric and also the skinny limbs of a huge loser whom he likes a metric fucktonne.

"Should we be apologizing?" Jericho wonders.

"More like congratulating each other," Harinder muffles into his chest.

Jericho thinks about it. "If you'd have just given me the cat, we never would have become friends."

"I would never have just given you the cat, Jericho."

"Except you totally did. Like, I didn't even ask. As a present, too, and then you reamed me for even considering giving an animal as a present. Did we ever establish how fucking ironic that was?"

"Shut up."

"Admit it."

"I will punch you in the dick."

"You'll regret that later."

"As if."

"Okay, fine, but if you break it, I'm renaming Dumpling to Master Splinter."

Harinder pulls his face back just enough for Jericho to see when he narrows his eyes. "You will not."

"You don't get to decide that. She's mine."

"I'm taking her back!"

"You and what army?"

Shoving him lightly, Harinder huffs, "I am the only goddamn army I need, fuckface. Just try me."

"I'll wait until you're gone, then I'll change it." Jericho doesn't bother pretending to stagger backward from Harinder's push.

"Then I'll never leave," he says, crossing his arms and jutting out his chin in noble defiance. He expects a snappy comeback. When they get into the swing of things, Jericho never has to think about what he's going to say; he spits out whatever pops into his head, and often the funniest part is how it wouldn't be funny coming from anyone else.

Instead, Jericho is staring at him. He blinks his light-gray eyes like a terrified stray, tentatively reaching toward trust. "You promise?"

Harinder falters. "What?"

Jericho's expression changes—for a second, he looks nauseous, and then he laughs, but off-key. "Better idea—She's yours. Happy birthday."

"You, what," Harinder says, floundering. "You can't just give my birthday present to you back to me! It's not even my birthday. I'm a fucking Leo."

"Merry Christmas three days early. Hey," Jericho says, no longer looking at Harinder.

Harinder still has no idea what's going on. "What?"

"I'll race you to the slide."

"*What*?" Harinder is starting to feel like a broken record.

"One-two-three go!"

Chapter Twenty-Six

Harinder the Snow Prince

Jericho is no longer in front of him. In fact, he's bolting through the snow-covered grass, plunging into the darkness of the park. The light from the streetlamp reaches just far enough to kiss the gaudy metal and plastic play equipment, their child-friendly colors washed out. And there's Jericho, long limbed and quick as he makes a running jump for one of the uneven wheels suspended from the monkey bars.

There's a pained *screeeeeel* as it oscillates, stopping with a barely there wiggle when Jericho's weight lands at its lowest point, leaving him hanging, feet pulled up so they don't drag on the ground.

"Are we ten?" Harinder calls from a distance, approaching him at a much slower pace, mostly so he has time to hide his perplexed smile.

"Times two and add one, yeah," Jericho says, rocking his lower body so he can propel himself forward, launching toward the second wheel in the row of four. He catches it, but when it twists in response to his weight, his attempt to reach for the next one fails, ending up with him stumbling a few paces on the ground.

Harinder smirks. "Good job."

"My hands are cold," is Jericho's excuse, delivered alongside a very put-on sulk.

"I wonder whose fault that is."

"Yours," Jericho says graciously. "You didn't hold them tight enough."

He rolls his eyes. "Next time I'll sit on them."

Jericho starts climbing the side of the structure, gripping frigid metal despite having complained about cold hands literally a moment previous.

"Oh, baby," he deadpans. "If that's what I gotta do to get my hands on your—hey!"

The handful of snow Harinder lobbed at him dissolves long before it reaches its target, but a few flurries ghost past Jericho's defenses. "Keep talking like that." Harinder makes his usual attempt at sounding menacing, but he's grinning too hard. "Your hands are getting nowhere near my ass."

"Aw, my fingers are gonna fall off. What if I was hypothermic and letting me grope you was the only way you could save me?"

"In that case, we would revisit the scenario where you die and I live in your apartment, draining your resources until someone reluctantly notices you're gone."

"Okay, but how would you even get access to my bank account? Even if you had my ID, no one would look at you and believe you're albino and five foot eleven."

"I will spontaneously grow seven inches purely out of spite."

"And turn white?"

A pause. "Okay, I'm not that desperate. You can grope my ass."

Jericho, now leaning over a rail at the top of the snowy play structure, pumps his fist. "Score."

Jericho shuffles around the platform, kicking tiny puffs of snow up in the air as he runs his fingers around the neglected equipment. He stops at the faded yellow-orange covered slide, seems to size it up. Probably trying to gamble on whether or not he'd get stuck if he tried to go down.

Harinder shakes his head, refusing to admit amusement.

"Hey, Hari," Jericho calls.

"Mm?"

"I made it to the slide first," he says, peering down at him through the shiny red bars. "What do I win?"

"I just gave you permission to grope me," Harinder says, tilting his head at him.

Jericho scoffs and straightens, leaning over the railing again. "That was totally unrelated; you can't use that as two rewards."

"I have two ass cheeks. You get one for each meager accomplishment."

"Man, I totally would have gone to college if they used these kind of incentives," Jericho says.

Harinder throws more snow at him, but it doesn't even reach the platform this time. A bunch of it falls back in Harinder's face. Jericho chokes back a snicker. While he's sputtering and wiping at his stinging eyes, the sound of nylon on plastic assaults his ears. There's a squeaky-scrubby sound, and then with a *wooooosh*, Jericho goes careening down the slide.

A moment later: "Ah, fuck."

Harinder jogs around the structure to better witness the source of Jericho's pain. He is treated to the sight of Jericho shaking snow off his legs after crashing into a big pile that had gathered at the bottom of the slide. *Snerk.* "That's what you get for acting like a third grader."

"All right, Snow Prince, stop rubbing one out to fantasies about other people's misfortune." Jericho brushes a clump of snow off his knee with his bare hand, then clumsily tries to stand up without hitting his head on the slide's low canopy.

Taking mercy on him, Harinder wades over to help, feeling oddly sentimental about disturbing the previously untouched snow. Here it's all shadows, far out of reach from the haloed streetlight. The thick layer of snow reflects the stars, sparkling underfoot. He grips Jericho's hand, pulls him upright, and steadies him with his mouth. Jericho responds with a brief flicker of surprise before dissolving into the kiss, a slow wave crashing down and subsuming him.

He buries his cold hands in Harinder's hair under the hoodie rather than stuffing them down the back of his pants. *Good boy.* Harinder laughs quietly against his lips.

It's like kissing amongst the stars, visceral and safe, and real, and meaningful. Far more important than two queer losers making out in the city playground after hours.

Maybe that is important in and of itself. Harinder commits it to memory for later pondering. In the meanwhile, he seeks heat on the tip of Jericho's tongue, fisting his fingers in the fabric of Jericho's uncharacteristically proper winter coat. His lips were already swollen, and now they are oversensitive and electric, buzzing when the point of contact shifts, tectonic plates shuddering as they meet.

Their bodies are an earthquake at standstill. His molecules threaten to vibrate so hard they'll phase out of existence.

Mouths separate, lips wet, tongues immediately lonely. Harinder whimpers into the darkness. Jericho presses his lips against Harinder's once more and takes them away just as quickly. Harinder watches them curve, slow and sweet and satisfied; aches to return to their stronghold.

Humming, Jericho knocks his nose lightly against Harinder's temple, kisses the apple of his cheek. Murmurs into his skin, "Wanna go on the swings with me?"

Harinder guffaws. "I can't— Fuck. I can't fucking tell if you're the most romantic person in the world or just the most childish."

"Hollywood votes both; I'll race you for real this timmph!"

Harinder gives him a hard shove, knowing he will land in soft snow, and takes off running toward the swing set. His legs are short, but he is fast and determined, and he has plenty of time to select the most appealing swing and flip the seat to get rid of the snow before Jericho even reaches the dug-out hollow marking the structure's perimeter. He regrets sitting down as quickly as he does— the rubber seat is still about as cold as Elizabeth Bathory's vampiric tit—but he didn't want Jericho to have any room to steal his victory from him.

"Were you that eager to win because you were hoping I'd peddle my own ass as a victory trophy as easily as you did yours earlier?" Jericho wonders, selecting his own swing.

It's lower to the ground than Harinder's; his feet are going to drag. Harinder doesn't care. If he wanted the precious high swing, he shouldn't have lost the race.

"I don't need to win a race to get you to peddle your ass to me," Harinder says, dismissive and matter-of-fact.

Jericho hops in his swing sideways and crashes into Harinder as he's trying to build up forward momentum. "Hey!"

"Hey," Jericho echoes, waggling his eyebrows. It's ridiculous. Harinder forces down a laugh.

"Is this a sex metaphor? Because it's not subtle."

"The kind of literature I read doesn't need metaphors for sex, baby." Jericho pushes with his long legs and sails forward smoothly, shifting his weight when he reaches the zenith of the arc. "We say cock and fuck and pussy as much as we want."

"That's not called literature, that's porn."

"Same diff."

"Nowhere near the same diff."

"Look, if you can refer to cleaning tank fronts as an art, I can call my smutty webcomics literature."

"Whatever, Jericho."

"You cannot deny the lasting appeal of alien-robot-tentacle-fucking. They'll be offering college courses on the subject within the next fifty years, mark my words."

"The internet has ruined you."

"No, the extremely lucrative not-safe-for-work commission culture has ruined me. I have no shame anymore."

"I hope the entirety of your career is reduced to the fact that you spent three years drawing low-quality, overpriced furry porn."

"Low-Quality and Overpriced are my middle names."

"Whatever happened to my standards?" Harinder bemoans, finally swinging next to him.

They go in tandem for a while, but Jericho's longer legs win again, and he propels himself higher until his weight makes the chain go slack when it reaches the highest point of every swing. The structure thumps every time Jericho lands back in the seat, tethered by gravity's inescapable whims.

It looks as though he might lift off, like he could hover right out of the seat and fly away.

Harinder doesn't realize he's slowed down significantly until Jericho does the same, peering through the darkness at him with curious eyes. It's snowing again. There are flakes caught in his white lashes. Harinder wants to kiss them away, but doesn't lean forward to do so.

"Can we make a stupid promise?" Jericho's voice cuts into the silence, a pure note against the discordant harmony of creaking chain links.

"Depends on how stupid. For example, I'm not lying to the cops next time you get caught shoving cocaine up your ass in an attempt to smuggle it across the Canadian border."

"Look. That was a fluke."

Harinder leans against the swing chain, then hisses through his nostrils at the cold against his cheek. "So, what then?"

Jericho goes quiet, drops his gaze, fidgets in the swing seat. "It'd be dumb, like..." He halts, pressing his lips together, and makes a sound of frustration. Tries again. "I'm glad things turned out the way they did because I genuinely believe we're big enough assholes that we might not have ever become friends if it hadn't been preceded by three weeks of compulsory harassment along a barely related agenda."

He swallows. "I even think it'll be a pretty hilarious story down the line, now that it's out in the open that we were literally fucking with each other the entire time, and if we'd've been less dickish to each other, we probably never would've given interacting more than a passing thought, and that...kills me, so."

Clears his throat. "So, I'm not upset, and I don't regret it."

"But?" Harinder wonders, sensing the unspoken conclusion.

"But," Jericho agrees. "I don't..." He's visibly struggling.

Harinder stretches to put his feet on the ground— goddamn it, high swing, betrayed by his own hubris— walks himself to the edge of his under-swing divot, and reaches forward to grasp at Jericho's hand. White fingers clench hard around his. The touch burns, but neither of them lets go.

"I don't want shit to continue like this," Jericho finally spits out.

"Lying to each other?"

"Yeah."

Something warm and permanent collects in Harinder's gut. The fear inside him wants desperately to ignore it, but it slowly builds into a crackling fire, musical and persistent. "You think it's stupid to ask that we don't lie to each other for shits and giggles anymore?"

Jericho shrugs one shoulder, not looking at him. "It seems presumptuous, I guess."

"Jericho," Harinder says, still so quiet and gentle it aches in his bones to be producing such a sound toward another person. "I'm not going to lie to you anymore. For as long as we're together."

Together. Not just "friends."

The implications of his wording hit Harinder like a blow to the solar plexus. He holds his breath, dreading a foul twist, punishing him for his insinuation that he and Jericho share something akin to a real relationship.

It is terrifying to acknowledge and at the same time ridiculous not to. Oh, his head is spinning. He might faint.

Then Jericho's lips peel back into the most heart-wrenching smile, eyes crinkling and cheeks going a darker red than they were from the biting cold. He presses his lips back together, trying to hide it, teeth sinking into the bottom one. It's no use; they spread again, and he looks beautiful in the indirect light, a grinning constellation, some kind of etheric sliver hidden in the stars.

Harinder looks for the map to Neverland splayed across his cheeks and hopes fiercely that they be transported to somewhere where they never have to see the end of this moment, never have to give up this blistering second of visceral connection.

Harinder could lose his mind in a smile like that, provided he hasn't already.

He hauls on Jericho's hand, tensing his muscles and pulling their swings closer—gets his foot hooked around Jericho's ankle to steady them, leans in to claim that sweet mouth in a promising kiss.

Their foreheads clunk together, and Harinder lets go, hissing in pain. Jericho is doing the same but also laughing, exasperated and delighted in equal parts.

"Fuck off," Harinder mutters.

"This I solemnly swear, and seal with a kiss—" Jericho teases.

Harinder abandons his swing, stumbling on half-numb legs, and moves as if to tackle him off the swing. Jericho extricates his own self, staggers backward several paces, and then scoops Harinder up before he can Juggernaut his way through Jericho's sternum. They go crashing backward against an incline, Jericho breaking the fall by landing in a snowy heap. Harinder swallows his laugh, then swallows the shriek of "cold!" that follows it.

He kisses Jericho hard and thorough and almost gets carried away until Jericho flips them over, landing Harinder's back in the snowdrift and using his distraction to worm ice-cold hands up his hoodie, sweater, and both his shirts, pressing inexcusably frigid fingers to his vulnerable ribcage. Harinder shrieks and mashes snow in his face and kisses him again and again as Jericho slowly pulls their bodies back into a standing position.

He kisses him until Jericho moans, kisses him until there is winter-defying heat in his lower body, kisses him until the snow caught in his hair starts to melt and drips down the back of his neck.

"Let's go home," Harinder suggests, shivering in horror at the impending promise of "wet and freezing" he's currently facing.

"Motion seconded," Jericho agrees, breathless and red, fresh snowflakes taking up residence on his hat.

Harinder remembers the gloves Jericho offered before and reaches into his pocket to retrieve them. He is immediately disgruntled when he only finds the one.

"Really?" he asks, sighing.

Jericho offers nothing but a sheepish shrug. Harinder shakes his head and slides the glove onto Jericho's left hand, leaving the right one woefully uncovered. Jericho looks at Harinder's hands, but Harinder shoves them both into his pockets. He watches critically until Jericho does the same.

The trip back to the apartment complex is quieter than the walk to the park. They don't speak much, other than soft whispers here and there, mostly bitching about the amount of snow they've absorbed, now melting against their body heat.

There's a preparatory inhale. Harinder waits for Jericho to speak, expecting something jarring, but he's still surprised when he hears what comes out.

"Do you ever stop missing your parent?"

Chapter Twenty-Seven

Harinder Didn't Wish for This, and Yet

Harinder stops in his tracks, heart plummeting to somewhere in the vicinity of his left knee. Jericho pauses, waiting for him, expression solemn.

"Why?" Harinder croaks, not understanding the connection.

Jericho shrugs, stepping away. He looks up at the moon, and his face is...not sad. Wistful, maybe.

"Omar and I did this once. Before he decided he hated me, I guess. I barely remember the details, just that it happened. We walked all over De Queen at midnight. He showed me shortcuts he took around the city, in case I ever got lost. Showed me hideouts in case someone was chasing me. Landmarks." He shrugs. "I dunno. There was a play place then too. He dared me to get into one of the baby swings, and I almost got stuck. I actually heard him laugh." Jericho runs a hand over his thick hair. "I know it sounds stupid. He was a—"

"It doesn't sound stupid," Harinder cuts in sharply. "I've never had an abusive parental figure."

He hesitates, not sure if Jericho is ready to hear that word, considering he's never used it himself. Aside from a small twitch of alarm, he doesn't react. "I can't imagine how you feel, but I do know that it's been eleven years since my dad died. I still cry every anniversary." He swallows thickly. "It never goes away. There isn't a single fucking day I don't..." He clenches his fist, trails off.

Jericho nods, satisfied. "He beat the shit out of me."

Harinder had inferred it, but it still hurts to hear.

"Did all sorts of weird shit to make me scared all the time, always keep me on my toes. Real paranoid guy. I don't think he even liked me, and he sure as fuck never said he loved me. When I was a kid, I think I was, like, funny, or pathetic enough that he found me amusing, but when I got older it was just plain as fuck resentment."

The rant peters out, and Jericho is left looking weak and lost, a babe in the unforgiving cold.

Harinder touches his arm, squeezes.

"I just want to know if I'm a fucked-up freak for still missing him sometimes."

"You aren't," Harinder soothes, hushing him with a chilled-through hand on his cheek. "You're sure as hell not the fucked-up one. Think about it like—" He hesitates. "Like you're not missing what was, but what could have been."

Jericho sniffles, wiping his bare, knobby wrist against his nose, which has started to drip. "That's a good way of putting it, yeah."

"Yeah," Harinder repeats softly. "But really, let's get home. Any more heart-to-hearts can wait until later, I promise. I will stay up all fucking night listening to every wretched confession you can conceive of if you just let me get warm first. Deal?"

Snorting messily, Jericho nods, then hazards a trembling smile. "Sounds good."

They still don't hold hands, but Harinder does shove himself under Jericho's arm (the one with the glove), leaning against him as they walk. It is quiet and peaceful and good in a way he's not sure he even deserves, but he's happy about it anyway.

Around one corner and the apartment building grows visible in the distance, signaling the end of their magically romantic snow escapade. Regret flickers in his chest, but the promise of warmth and hot cider is equally compelling.

Also, maybe taking Jericho's clothes off and cuddling beneath a comforter on the couch. Mm. Or showering together, which they still haven't done despite the jokes. Jericho has yet to get on the "fully naked" train, for either of them, and, despite showing *significant* interest in Harinder's body, still isn't ready to involve his own boner in the proceedings. Harinder is deliciously eager to get his hands on said boner (among other things), but he's content to allow Jericho the lead, following at the younger man's pace.

It's late.

Harinder resigns himself to the fading last wisps of the evening's magic. The hazy glow of yellow streetlamps is replaced with acrid white of the apartment doorstep, stuffed with bug corpses that cast miniscule shadows from inside the fixture.

He reaches for the door, but Jericho tightens his arm, stopping him. Harinder looks up, halfway to irritated. He promised to let Jericho talk as much as he needs as soon as they achieve shelter. The cold and wet is starting to burn his clammy skin; Harinder is officially ready for this to be over. No more blurry-eyed nostalgia for him.

"What?" he asks, trying to keep the edge out of his voice. "Don't you want to go upstairs?"

"Yes," Jericho says, and then doesn't say anything more. He just looks at him.

Harinder sighs and reaches his hands to cup Jericho's cheeks. "Tell me," he instructs, bouncing a little to ward off the cold.

"I want you to stay with me," Jericho blurts, curling his fingers into the front of Harinder's jacket, stroking it fitfully. "Here. Permanently." His pupils are small, eyebrows furrowed. "I—I don't want you to move out." The confession peters out into awkwardness. His gaze falls away, and he scuffs his toe against a bare spot in the concrete, knocking thick chunks of salt aside. "Is that okay?"

Silence. Several seconds of it. Internal contemplation that goes beyond having space of his own, having a cat, having a roommate who doesn't hate him. Harinder thinks of intimacy and movies and apple cider and sex and Dumpling scratching at the door while they try to sleep, Dumpling scratching at the door while they're entwined in Jericho's bed. Stability and convenience and trust.

For once.

He lets out a hollow, tremulous laugh. "Is that okay?" he parrots. "You fucking idiot."

Jericho's chin snaps up, eyes suddenly wide.

Harinder reaches down to yank on his collar. "You just offered me the best thing anyone has ever tried to give me since my dad died, and you want to know if that's fucking *okay*."

Jericho laughs, high and hysterical. They're clutching each other like they're about to fight.

"I'll stay. Fuck. Of course I'll stay."

No longer fisted in his jacket, Jericho's hands come up to knock his hood back so they can wind into his hair, holding but not pulling. "Seriously?" he asks, dazed, as if he can barely believe it.

"Yeah." It's hard to speak past the knot in his throat. Harinder swallows, tries to calm down. Clears his throat, making sure his voice won't come out so squeaky at the next part. "On one condition."

Jericho looks alarmed, but nods. "What?" He seems ready to hear the worst.

Harinder smirks. "We're keeping Dumpling. And you don't get to change her name. And I want you to clear out a bunch of your unnecessary junk so I have room for a fish tank. I've always wanted one."

"What the f—"

His indignant response is cut off when Harinder throws his arms around Jericho's neck and mauls him, mouth a hot counterpoint to the rest of him, which is quickly becoming a very gay popsicle. It's okay, though, because Jericho muffles a sound like a sob into his mouth and clutches him tight and kisses back like he's desperate for air and might find relief in Harinder's own lungs. They share a breath, wordless and intense and dizzying, and don't let go even when there's a sharp click on the pavement behind them.

"Excuse me, gentlemen," a crisp voice intones. "It's not my intention to interrupt, but you are blocking the entrance to the building."

They fly apart like their bodies just transformed into corrosive, acidic sludge monsters who're being forced to do battle.

"Ms. Watson!" Jericho squeaks in the highest register Harinder has ever heard from him. "What are you doing out so—"

"Now, now," Ms. Watson says, her lined face not cracking into anything reminiscent of a smile, but Harinder swears there's a gleam in her dark eyes. "An old woman is entitled to her privacy. Please step aside so that I can bid you both a good night."

Harinder doesn't think about it, just mashes himself against Jericho's chest, both of them shifting as one humiliated being out of her way. They watch her tap regally up the short stairs, swipe her keycard, and step inside. The door closes behind her.

"Damn," Jericho says quietly. "I knew she was gay."

Harinder bursts into ragged laughter. "We'll invite her to the housewarming party. Speaking of—I'm so fucking cold, Jericho."

Jericho takes his hands and chafes them with his one-glove, one-skin ensemble, kissing the fingertips where the limits of water-resistant fabric are being tested. "Me too, but there's no fucking way I'm going inside while she's on the staircase. I will die from embarrassment, just watch me."

"I'm going to die of cold if you don't," Harinder says frankly, scowling despite being nowhere near angry. "Then you will have a dead roommate, and you'll have to apologize to my boss and take care of Dumpling all by your incompetent self."

"Well, shit," Jericho says, shuffling closer. "Can't let that happen." His forehead comes to rest on Harinder's, and they stare at each other like that until Harinder groans, long and loud, and buries his face in Jericho's chest.

"I cannot fucking survive like this; I was not made for this kind of abuse—" he grouses, scrambling like he is trying to actually bury himself in the folds of Jericho's coat.

Chuckling, Jericho squeezes him. "Ms. Watson should be in her apartment by now; we can move, provided our legs haven't frozen in place. Like, that'd suck, right? So close to freedom and yet so far, this is our literal fucking Sisyphus trial, or Loki, maybe. I don't fucking know. What's a good metaphor for someone who's eternally destined to be just out of reach of their— Tantalus! That's the— Oh. Look."

Harinder lifts his head a bit, looking at the side of Jericho's chin because he's staring at something above them. "What?"

Jericho points. "Dumpling's saying hi."

Harinder turns, and sure enough, there's a white fluffy blob pawing at the glass of their window, tucked under the curtain. His lips twitch. Something starts to swell under his ribs, but Jericho distracts him with a nuzzle against the back of his neck.

"How does it feel to finally have one of your own?" Jericho asks, verbalizing Harinder's thoughts.

Fuck. Jericho's right. In the midst of everything, he hadn't really stopped to think about— Dumpling being *his*. It was teasing at the time, but he doubts Jericho would joke about passing Harinder the mantle of ownership.

He chokes up. Viciously triumphant and one hundred percent ready to escape this frozen hellscape before they get distracted by another way-too-late-way-too-cold revelation, he says, "I am going to go inside and I am going to cuddle the fuck out of that cat and you are not going to distract me."

"By all means," says Jericho, kissing behind his ear. He nudges Harinder to get his stiff legs moving.

"You better not have any other plans either," Harinder mumbles gruffly as he reaches his hand out for the door handle while Jericho swipes his keycard.

"Oh, I'm invited to the cuddlefest now?"

"Duh."

"Well, I guess being a second thought is better than being not thought of at all— Hey!"

Harinder hauls hard on Jericho's wrist, pulling him through the entrance, toward this giddily exciting new chapter of their lives. He looks over his shoulder with a crooked half grin and gives him another tug up the stairs to their apartment.

"Shut up and get in here, dumbass."

Harinder's Happy Ending

When Harinder wakes up, he is instantly aware of the unfamiliar surroundings but feels nothing in the way of panic or concern. There is a solid, warm body underneath his. Neither his body nor the other one is wearing very many clothes. Harinder isn't in a hurry to open his eyes, but when he eventually does, he sees the dark blue of the futon cover, followed by the living room rug.

His living room rug, if last night's memory serves.

Bleary snapshots from four AM tell him he and Jericho fell asleep on the couch, huddled together, trying to coax the cold from their bones. He smells sweet. Or, more accurately, like sweat, but Harinder enjoys Jericho's natural scent.

Ten o'clock is Harinder's strict bedtime. He doesn't often break that habit because his work schedule is relentless. True to form, right now it is unusually hard to drag himself upright to start getting ready for work. The warm pressure on his back isn't helping.

At first, he assumes one of the couch pillows fell on him, but the mass seems more solid than a throw pillow. When he shifts on Jericho's chest, so does whatever is on his back.

Harinder is concerned until he hears a soft, grumpy miaow.

Fortunately, Jericho is not awake to witness the embarrassing spectacle of Harinder's heart melting into gooey sludge as Dumpling eases herself onto a couch cushion, then jumps to the floor. She weaves through the legs of the coffee table, rubbing her silky body against the surface, then doubles back to stare at Harinder, hoping to be lavished with affection. And food, probably. Harinder is eager to oblige, stroking her creamy fur. If he had the ability, *he'd* be purring.

He remains nestled against Jericho's chest and doesn't realize he's drifted off again until Dumpling produces a grumpy caterwaul, batting his limp fingers with her paw. Harinder reaches out, but she evades him, bolting toward the kitchen. She stops after a few paces and executes a sharp turn to face him again. She yowls, demanding.

Hungry, right.

It's definitely later than her breakfast time. He should be grateful she let them sleep this long.

Speaking of time. Harinder gropes for his cell phone, but the one that ends up in his hand is much bigger and more beat-up than his. He turns the screen on to check the time and, upon seeing the lock screen, nearly dies on the spot.

The image is of Harinder scrubbing tanks, arm plunged into the water, wearing an expression of pure concentration, his trademark sweater tied around his waist. Such a mundane scene, but the lighting is winter-cool, sun glistening off the snow heaped on the windowsill.

Harinder turns off the phone and drops it on the coffee table. It takes a minute of digging before he locates his own phone, half buried under Jericho's ass.

He isn't late yet, but if he doesn't get his shit together, he's going to be. At least the commute is only a short bus ride now.

Groaning, he stretches his stiff limbs, then contemplates Jericho, still muzzy and grumbling about being disturbed. He typically doesn't budge when Harinder gets ready for work, but even he can't sleep through Harinder squirming around on top of him.

Harinder traces his nose up Jericho's jaw, humming affectionately. "I'd tell you to stay asleep," he murmurs, "But I highly doubt you were planning to get up before noon anyway."

Jericho fails to produce anything in the way of words, but his arms come up around Harinder, fingertips grazing the bare skin of his back before crushing him into a tight hug. He absorbs it like one might a very rich dessert, as if Jericho doesn't offer physical comfort with addictive regularity nowadays.

Dumpling wails. Goddamn it.

With one more kiss, tender against his temple, Harinder extricates himself from Jericho's grip.

He misses Jericho's warmth but doesn't give in to the urge to crawl back under the thick comforter. Aside from holding back from murdering the worst of his customers, Harinder's never had to use as much self-control as it takes to tuck the blanket around Jericho and step away. He grabs the empty mugs they left on the table in one hand to take them into the kitchen.

Dumpling mewls joyfully, wrapping around his legs.

Mugs go in the sink; phone on the counter. He digs Dumpling's food from a cabinet and portions it into her bowl.

Now would be the proper time to get dressed, but Harinder sinks to the floor, ignoring the cold as he sits in his underwear, stroking a hand down Dumpling's back as she eats. She purrs a staccato rhythm as she chews.

When the food is gone, she abandons him, settling some distance away to clean herself. Now it's time to be an adult. Mr. Kulkarni won't care if Harinder is a few minutes late, but he doesn't want to run after a bus.

Harinder slinks into the bedroom to get his clothes, and his eyes fall on the cold, undisturbed bed. From keeping the door locked at all times, Harinder has come to trust Jericho enough to sleep next to him. He wonders how long Jericho will remain sleeping on the futon now that he's asked Harinder to stay, but that's not something he's prepared to confront while wearing nothing but underwear in twenty-degree weather.

Sweater and jeans acquired, Harinder bundles up to prepare for his commute. He lingers in the threshold, looking across the apartment to where Dumpling has rejoined Jericho on the futon.

By the time he makes it to the bus stop, the bus is already pulling up. Massively relieved, he pays and tucks himself into a corner. Only then does he realize he didn't have breakfast. Maybe there's still something in the freezer.

Tonight, they're to spend dinner with Jericho's sister and her prying fiancée, who is going to wring details from his blood whether he consents or not. He focuses on the promise of good food rather than succumbing to dread.

Mr. Kulkarni is at the store when he arrives. Not having to unlock the door and disable the alarm feels strange. Harinder tries not to launch into a fit of suspicion, but fails.

He creeps up to the office, voice quiet as he calls, "Mr. Kulkarni? You're in early."

"I had something to take care of," he says, offering no further detail. "Do you have a moment to talk?"

Harinder refuses to panic. "I'm a little late today, actually," he hedges. "I need to start opening."

Mr. Kulkarni sends a withering look at the clock. "Will you be done by 10:15?"

"I'll have the store open by ten." He's put off by the hitches in his daily routine, but Harinder won't slip on his duties.

His boss sighs but says nothing more. Harinder hoofs it out of his office and makes a beeline for the adoption center. The rescue is scheduled to bring a new cat. He cleans kennels and focuses on excitement instead of the anxiety about an unexpected conversation.

Ten o'clock rolls around. Agitated, Harinder tries to find something else to do. Nearly everything is sparkling. Yesterday was so slow he had to do something to stave away the boredom. Unfortunately, "something" actually meant "everything."

"Harinder."

He jumps. "Yes?"

Mr. Kulkarni levels him with a thoughtful look. "Do you have an issue with the tank wall?"

He starts, realizing he's been glowering at it for several minutes, debating on bringing out the gravel vacuum. "No, I was just thinking. What's up?"

"I want to consult with you about the way the store is currently being run."

Ice solidifies in Harinder's chest. He knew it was only a matter of time until he got in trouble for getting caught with Jericho those weeks ago. Mr. Kulkarni didn't want to give a bad impression in front of a customer, but now that they're alone—

"Harinder."

He blinks, owl-eyed. "Yes?"

Mr. Kulkarni leads the way to the cashwrap, waving for Harinder to follow. He pushes the swinging door aside and seats himself in the chair by the register. Trying to keep his breathing slow, Harinder eases himself into the victim's chair—which is definitely not what he calls it during interviews.

His boss inspects him and thoughtfully rubs his chin. Harinder wishes he'd just drop the damn bomb already.

"You know," Mr. Kulkarni says finally, "I've never been able to figure out what I did to inspire such deference in you. It'd be funny if I didn't feel bad."

"Excuse me?"

He shakes his head. "Harinder, you've been pretending to be a model employee since I hired you. As far as I can tell, you dropped the act for everyone else four months into the job. I don't know if you think I'm obtuse or an asshole, but I would have fired you long ago if it was a problem."

Shell-shocked, Harinder clenches his fingers on his knees. "I don't...understand."

Gesturing at the store, Mr. Kulkarni says, "I'd say I don't get how a person can be so efficient yet terrified of their supervisor at the same time, but that's not what I'm trying to address. I want to reassure you that you don't have to pretend to be something you're not. I know that you take the sign off the hermit crab tank every day when I come in."

Harinder grits his teeth. "They're a very sophisticated species with high care requirements, and it's disgusting that people treat them as throwaway practice pets—"

Mr. Kulkarni holds up a palm. "I've heard the speech. As much as it cuts into pet sales, your dedication to only giving animals to ethical homes is pretty impressive. I can't say it was my priority going in, but..."

"What changed your mind?" Harinder asks, unable to hide his curiosity.

Shrugging, Mr. Kulkarni says, "My custom work connects me with people who are very passionate about what they do. Once you spend an hour talking to a guy who's paying fifteen thousand dollars to turn his mudroom into a walk-in paludarium, you learn more than you thought there was to know."

"Huh."

"You don't give yourself enough credit," Mr. Kulkarni goes on to say, which throws Harinder off again. "You haven't taken a day off in two years. You work constantly, without complaining, and come in early to do extra tasks and still worry if I'll begrudge you the extra time."

Harinder fidgets. "It's not like I have anything better to do..."

"Maybe not before," Mr. Kulkarni says, cryptically, but before Harinder can question it, he's already surging ahead. "It occurred to me that instead of you being constantly afraid of termination, I should be afraid of you realizing you can do better."

"...Mr. Kulkarni?"

"Yes?"

"Why does this sound more like a breakup negotiation than a conversation about the store?"

He laughs. "I'll get to the point. I think I owe you more than what I'm currently doing, and I'm going to make good on that. I want to hire more workers—"

Panic seizes Harinder again; he almost stands up from the chair. Mr. Kulkarni's intentions might be genuine, but Harinder doesn't do well with other people, and he can't afford a pay cut. "That won't be necessary, sir. I promise I can handle the store on my own—"

He laughs again. "Harinder, will you let me finish?"

"Sorry."

"Here's the thing about hiring new people—I'm not around the store all that much. I'll need a supervisor."

The gears slowly click into place inside Harinder's head. He opens his mouth, but no sound comes out.

"Forty hours a week with benefits, and all I'm asking is for you to be available by phone during business hours. You can choose two or three part-timers, depending on how you'd like to make the schedule." Mr. Kulkarni leans back in the chair, inspecting Harinder. "You can write your personal schedule however you want, just remember you can't exceed forty hours while salaried, unless it's an emergency. I assume you'll want to take weekends off so you can spend more time with your boyfriend."

"Jericho's a freelancer," Harinder says before realizing the full implication of what was just said. He sputters. "I mean— We're not, I— Jericho isn't my—"

Mr. Kulkarni levels him with an amused expression. "Excuse me for assuming," he says, and then before Harinder can stutter himself into a further stupor: "So, are you interested?"

The fact that he takes a second to consider it is honestly ridiculous. Harinder gnaws his lip, feeling like a genuine idiot, but the apprehension isn't about the offer— he'd be batshit not to accept. He just needs...a moment. To process. On top of all the other changes in his life, this is near too much good to bear.

"I," he attempts, finally. "Yes. Absolutely." His voice is uncharacteristically quiet.

Mr. Kulkarni slaps a hand on his thigh and stands up. "Fantastic. I'll have some paperwork for you to fill out later, and in the meanwhile, I'll print some hiring signs." He looks around at the store. "With more workers we'll have time to straighten up around here."

The animal enclosures may be immaculate, but the rest of the store is unapologetically grungy. In Harinder's defense, "maid" was not part of the job description.

Now, it doesn't have to be. A respectable amount of excitement at the idea of having cleaning minions surges in Harinder's chest, but he swallows it. "I appreciate this opportunity—"

"Don't. You've more than earned it. I'm just a little late returning the favor." Mr. Kulkarni steps out from behind the cashwrap, inspecting the outside of the counter as he walks along it. "I'd like to see more positive changes in the store once this is implemented. You should have more than enough manpower to make it happen."

"Of course, sir."

Mr. Kulkarni makes a face, and for a moment, Harinder thinks he said something wrong. "I'm serious about getting rid of the ferrets though. Has no one expressed interest, or did you just chase them all off?"

Harinder shrugs weakly. "Eighty-twenty, maybe?"

He snorts. "If you're so picky, why don't *you* take them?"

"My house doesn't allow—"

Harinder stops. It dawns slowly upon him: he doesn't live in that horrible house anymore. No, now he has a home where he's welcome, and a cat of his own, and a full-time managerial job that's only ten minutes down a bus line from the apartment. Fucking hell, this is too much.

He waits for some kind of catch, but nothing appears.

"I'll see what I can do, sir."

"Good," Mr. Kulkarni says, and then he's walking back to his office, all casual as if he didn't just make a proposition that will completely change Harinder's current path of existence.

Harinder spends the next hour or three in a daze. In between customers, he stares at an empty page on his notebook and doesn't write anything. He doesn't even have a film cued up.

Wonder filters into his chambers until he's beyond full. Harinder isn't sure what will happen when the walls grow too thin. There has to be a good-news threshold somewhere, and when it reaches that limit, he's going to fucking pop.

Around noon, his cellphone rings, but the customers have picked up so it's an hour before he gets to check it. There are two texts waiting, one of which is a photo from Jericho. A customer walks into the store while it's still loading. Harinder glances up to see if they need anything, and when he looks back down—

Oh.

Sleek, pale fur mashed up against Jericho's forehead, tinted blue from the lit television. His exposed eye regards the camera with amusement. Dumpling's head is barely in the frame. Only a sliver of her toasted-marshmallow mane is visible, the rest of her face buried in Jericho's messy white hair. Judging by the shadowy angles of his collarbones, low in the frame of the picture, he's still not wearing a shirt.

we miss you, reads the accompanying text.

This has to be the part where he reaches that threshold he was worrying about, but rather than exploding, Harinder feels warm and runny and incorporeal, like wetting oneself but less humiliating. He hopes no one can see him smiling.

The Call button lights up under his thumb.

Harinder Mangal is twenty-four years old, and he feels like Christmas has come two days early. A month and a half ago, some idiot walked into his store, and Harinder made it his mission to scare him off, but it didn't work.

For the first time in his life, he's played a game he doesn't mind losing.

Jericho's Happy Ending

One of Harinder's employees called off, so Jericho is antique shopping by himself. Neither he nor Harinder expected their favorite bonding activity to be arguing over old shit, but it sure happened.

Before, Harinder had no place to put things he wanted. Before, Jericho had far too much space to deal with.

Now, here he is, trying negotiating space and design on his own.

Harinder insisted he consolidate his hobbies into two workstations, which was fair. Harinder claimed the bedroom desk—also fair. He still hides often, and it would be wrong to expect him, in only a couple months, to get over his issues with feeling unsafe.

Jericho's "Cool Things" desk has been sold, replaced with a larger one, boasting high shelves that were an utter bitch to put together. A similar storage technique was applied to the television stand. It's a marvel Jericho never thought to build up instead of sprawling out. The apartment has a lot more room, even factoring in the ferret cage (which fit in the bedroom) and the promised fish tank.

Harinder didn't go crazy with the size, though Jericho suspects he would have if he felt he could get away with it. A respectable twenty gallon sits next to the entertainment center. Jericho was forced to admit he enjoyed watching them, and of course, Harinder has kept the tank spotless.

It's been weird giving up control of his apartment. *Their* apartment. He'd added Harinder to the lease and informed the landlord they were looking for a two-bedroom when the lease was up.

Jericho's been making decisions alone since he was a teenager, something Harinder has never had the freedom to do. The arrangement feels strange, but it works.

It makes him happy.

What doesn't make him happy is Harinder calling him from work when Jericho is already waiting at the downtown market, standing outside the antique store in the early spring wind.

"I have to work a double," Harinder says.

"Oh."

"I'm sorry. Annie says she's sick, and I'm already short-staffed since Josh took medical leave." He sighs. "This is harder than just doing it all myself. At least I knew what to expect."

Jericho thinks it's a massive improvement, though he doesn't say so. Minor frustrations about unreliable employees are much better than only seeing Harinder at night. They can go to the marketplace together next Saturday.

"It'll be fine," is all he says, tone carefully neutral. "What did you want me to look for again?"

"New table for the fish tank—you know the dimensions, right? I'll text them to you just in case. Make sure it has at least one drawer. No light wood; it won't fit with the apartment's atmosphere. Oh, and you should look for a cool lamp. Send me pictures before you buy anything; promise?"

"Promise."

"Good. I— I'll see you when we both get home?"

Okay, there's that flutter in his stomach. It was lost for a second under the disappointment. "Of course. I— yeah. Bye."

They've been dancing around "I-statements" for a while. Jericho feels it's too early for three-word declarations, and he assumes Harinder is in the same position. It's awkward. Four months isn't enough, right? To really grow to love someone?

He scrubs the worry from his mind and walks into the antique shop to browse.

The visuals give him ideas for paintings and illustrations. Harinder bought him a new sketchbook—a small, spiral-bound, pocket-sized thing. It took him a while to start using it. Jericho has always been private about his art; it embarrasses him, but he doesn't know why.

Now, he takes it out and spends a few minutes, here and there, sketching whatever details catch his eye, things that give him ideas and others Harinder might like looking at.

He still wishes Harinder were here to see for himself.

Jericho does find a tank stand with the perfect dimensions, except it has shelves instead of a drawer, and it is a distressed teal rather than natural wood. At least the bits showing through aren't light. He sends a picture to Harinder just in case.

Some other pieces have quality wood, but not the ideal dimensions, and Jericho grows bored. It's hard to decide what Harinder wants without his input, and to make matters worse, all the lamps are ugly. Ugh.

He climbs the narrow, creaking wooden steps to the top floor of the antique shop. He hates this fucking staircase. It'd be perfect for a haunted house. Less perfect for easily transporting delicate antiques. It's not that he has a fear of heights—it's just that dark gaps in things make him feel existential.

Jericho stops focusing on the spaces between the stairs and starts squeezing himself through the tightly packed vendor stations. He wishes he had Harinder's eye. He wishes he had Harinder. He wishes he wasn't so grumpy about *not* having Harinder.

Nothing else stands out to him, and his boyfriend hasn't texted him yes or no on the stand yet, but Jericho expects a "no."

He's about to give up and go back downstairs, maybe get a butterbeer soda from the fancy ice cream parlor across the street to soothe his irritable mood, when he notices a dusty chamber behind the dense line of shelving. It's something he's never noticed before, so he winds around a midcentury dresser and a curio cabinet, emerging into a long musty hall of old doors, windows, and larger items that wouldn't fit on the main floor.

Not a single person is back here aside from himself, which gives it a spooky, surrealist feeling. He hopes this isn't going to turn into some *Cabin in the Woods* shit.

There are wheelbarrows and a chest of drawers with broken legs, advertised "as-is," an entire farm plow covered in rust, and piles of worn wood slabs. It's all cool, but nothing relevant to his goals. He steps around some old bottles and looks for an exit that doesn't require walking all the way back to the corridor he entered through.

While narrowly avoiding a rusty girder, Jericho bumps something with his hip. He turns to steady it and is perplexed by its unusual shape.

It takes him a second to identify it as a telescope.

Jericho has never seen a telescope in person, which is why his first response is shock at the size. He knows the gist from pictures—a long lens with a narrow end and a thicker one, a scope, and a number of fancy doodads he won't pretend to understand the function of. The black exterior has seen a significant amount of wear, but overall, nothing looks overtly broken.

Turns out, telescopes are heavier than they look.

"Excuse me?" Jericho says, searching for a vendor. It's a quiet day and there aren't many people perusing the second floor, and none of them look to be vendors. Even if he could find one, he doesn't know the owner of the telescope or even if it works.

He could just leave it. It's completely reasonable to think, *Wow, this is a cool thing! I'm going to snap a picture of it for my boyfriend and then leave since I did not find what he asked me to look for.*

Jericho heaves a sigh as he approaches the stairs, which seem twice as precarious now that he is holding a large, expensive instrument. He can't see the oncoming steps too well, and descends in abject fear of the spaces between wooden slabs finding a way to trip him up and suck him in.

He reaches the first floor unharmed, telescope clutched safely in his arms. He resists the urge to sag in relief at being free of the evils of elevation. No wonder he never thought to build upward. There will be no Towers of Babel from *this* man.

Once he has collected his wits, Jericho navigates, much more precariously than before, to the desk at the front where the owner and the cashier sit. The owner is a withered white man who speaks mostly of history and doesn't respond well to other topics. He's never treated Jericho like a criminal or tried to follow him (would be a bit hard even if he wanted to), so he's cool in Jericho's book. The cashier is his perky teenage daughter.

Jericho doesn't know her name, but she looks exactly the way one would expect of the daughter of an antique hoarder. Blonde hair with teal highlights, a cheerful disposition, and brown corduroy overalls. She has a nose piercing and bitten nails half covered in chipped black polish. He likes her.

"Hey, is this for sale?"

She blinks owlishly at the telescope. "I didn't even know we had that," she admits. "Daaaad?"

The owner, who was sorting papers at his desk, looks up. "Yes, Jenny? What?"

Jenny gestures. "Is the telescope for sale?"

He leans forward to peer at the item. Uncomfortable with the sudden attention, Jericho places it on the desk and takes a step back, out of the line of focus. He watches as the guy does his thing, looking over the piece with careful hands and a speculative eye. Finally, he puts his palms on the desk, tapping one finger as he levels the telescope with a perplexed grimace.

"This was the one that Archie took in, thinking it was an antique. It's a model from nineteen ninety-goddamn-five." The guy sighs and rubs his hands together. "It has no antique value. Thing's only, uhh..."

"Twenty-five years old," Jenny says for him.

"Yes. If anything, it's obsolete junk. Technology has skyrocketed, not that I know anything about that. No one's looking for these anymore, not even a collector."

Jenny eyes Jericho. "No one?" she asks.

"No—"

"How much?"

*

Aquariums & More is open until eight on Saturdays now, so a double shift could mean Harinder is pulling a twelve-hour open-to-close, or he's going to be there until someone can relieve him. Wanting to be home before his boyfriend, Jericho books it.

It's 2:30 by the time he gets inside the apartment, and Harinder hasn't responded to his text yet. So much for wanting to give input on stuff, Jericho thinks with a small trace of bitterness. What was he supposed to do if he actually found something Harinder liked?

Ugh.

In an attempt to distract himself from the moping, Jericho sets the telescope upright by the largest window in the apartment. He has to shove his drafting desk a few inches over to fit it comfortably, but he manages enough room to not crowd the damn thing. A spare comforter, folded in half so the thick fabric obscures the telescope's shape, drapes inelegantly over it.

Once the gift is hidden, Jericho sits on the futon and fidgets anxiously in his too-neat home.

Times like these, he misses the clutter. Precious stuff to keep his thoughts from running so far he can't catch them.

Dumpling jumps onto the couch next to him and puts a demanding paw on his leg. Jericho smiles weakly as he strokes her back, running his fingers through soft fur that Harinder brushes every night to discourage matting. He's got the greatest executive function skills Jericho has ever seen in a person. Like, damn. Some mornings, Jericho has to sit in bed for an hour before he has the energy to go to the bathroom.

He pets Dumpling, and flips through his sketchbook, trying to get inspiration from any of the day's doodles. That fails.

Finally, he gets up, thinking he'll go to the kitchen and plan dinner for when Harinder gets home, keeping his toes crossed it'll happen sometime before eight. That's when the door opens, and Harinder slumps inside.

"Hey, bud," Jericho says, eyebrows raised in surprise.

Harinder faceplants into his chest, body sagging. "Hey."

"What's up? You, uh. You didn't tell me you were on your way home."

Groaning, Harinder pushes himself upright again. "I dropped my phone in the fucking backstock tank."

Jericho's jaw hangs. "You *what?*"

"Please don't ask how. Shit."

He resists the urge to laugh—not because it's funny, or because it's not funny, even, but because he spent the whole day moping around because his boyfriend wasn't around to look at old baskets with him while Harinder was stranded at work without a phone, more than likely because he was so focused on something he forgot it was in his hand.

"I'm sorry, babe."

"I hate today," Harinder grumbles.

That's when Jericho remembers he did more with his day than sitting around feeling bad for himself.

"I got something that might help you feel better."

Harinder's head snaps up, eyebrows furrowed into a suspicious squint. "What's that?"

Okay, this time Jericho *does* laugh. "Chill. You look like you're trying to shoot lasers."

"Nonsense. I wouldn't fire anything until I knew what you were about to tell me."

"Oh, right. Right."

"Appease my curiosity, you ass. What is the thing?"

"Close your eyes."

"Not a goddamn chance. Tell me now."

Jericho sighs dramatically. "You are literally no fun."

"Zero." Harinder folds his arms and glares until Jericho gives in.

"Fine. Follow me, jackass."

"*Thank* you."

Harinder practically prances after him as Jericho leads him to the blanket-covered gift. Jericho critically looks over the offering, trying to see if anyone could still accurately identify the shape.

He doesn't have time to continue his perusal because Harinder looms over it, performing his own analysis. "Tell me I can uncover it," he demands.

"Go wild, stallion."

Harinder wastes two precious seconds on giving him a withering look, and then he delicately seizes the comforter and lifts it free of the object underneath. Then he stops.

"Oh. It's a— Wait."

Jericho doesn't know what to make of it when Harinder shoves his face close to the lens and scrabbles at the worn surface as if searching for something. Maybe there's a part missing? The antique guy didn't know, nor did he care, if the thing was still in working condition. Jericho paid $100 cash for it and walked out hoping he didn't get scammed.

Harinder finally steps back from the telescope. His face is expressionless and pale. "Where did you get this?"

"Uh, the antique store? I didn't find anything you were looking for, but I ran into this—literally, by the way; they pack things so close in that place. Anyway, I thought you might like it because you said—"

"This is it."

"This is—what now?"

"This is it," Harinder repeats, so intense he sounds angry.

"I don't understand. Is something wrong?"

"You fucking idiot." Harinder's eyes glisten, but before Jericho has time to lose his entire shit, Harinder loses his. "*This is my dad's telescope,*" he says in one long sob, and then buckles against the desk with a hand fisted over his mouth.

Jericho can't breathe.

"This is—the same model?" It's still not hitting him.

"No." Harinder's trying to support himself on the edge of the desk; Jericho finally processes the visual and moves to help him into the chair like a decent fucking boyfriend.

Tears stream liberally down Harinder's cheeks. "It's not the same model," he blubbers. "This is *it*. The one that was stolen."

The words are like getting slapped in the face by a cold, unknown force. It's a refreshing and utterly terrifying smack of adrenaline. Jericho's heart starts to pound. "This is—"

Harinder nods, trying to wipe his eyes with a shaky hand. It's useless. Every patch dried by the corner of his sweater is quickly replaced by a new flood.

"How do you know?"

He flops a hand at the telescope, but it's so uncoordinated Jericho can't tell if he was meant to identify a specific part of it or just consider the whole thing.

"The— There's—" Harinder tries, hiccuping. He swallows, shakes his head, then points with a steadier hand. "There's an engraving. It's old, so you can't really see it, but you can feel it if you know it's there. It's my birth date."

This is the most terrifying thing Jericho has ever accidentally done, up to and including the incident that triggered all this. It's a much better feeling than watching Mephi run into Shiloh's dark backyard.

"Wow," is all he can say. And then: "How would it even have gotten up there?"

Harinder wipes at his face more. The tears have finally stopped flowing. "Who knows? Whoever took it must have tried to pawn it."

Thinking back to what the antique guy said about an employee buying it, thinking it was an antique, Jericho nods, still filled with amazement. "I cannot fucking believe—"

Harinder suddenly grapples for him, seizing the front of his shirt. Jericho doesn't know what's happening until Harinder reels him in, yanks him down, and kisses him hard. He's well used to Harinder's impulsiveness by now, so Jericho tries to reciprocate with an appropriate level of enthusiasm, but the angle hurts his back. He straightens, and Harinder follows like a lichen, wrapping his arms around the back of Jericho's neck to keep him from leaving.

Okay, then. He *did* spend all day bitching about wanting attention.

Jericho gets his hands under Harinder's ass and pulls him flush, then lifts him a foot and a half to the side until he's propped on the back of the couch. Harinder responds to this with a pleased little groan and teeth dragging over the line of his jaw.

After about ten minutes, he runs out of steam, which is good because Jericho didn't drink enough water to be able to survive making out for much longer. His boyfriend's head comes to rest on his chest while Jericho runs his fingers through his messy black curls and waits for him to catch his breath. Harinder mumbles something that he doesn't quite hear.

"What was that?" Jericho asks, worming a hand under the hem of both his sweater and his T-shirt so he can rub at Harinder's back.

Harinder lifts his head off Jericho's chest and looks at him, not yet repeating himself. Jericho stares back, confused.

"I said," Harinder begins, enunciating carefully, "I love you."

Oh.

Jericho's first thought is, *Ah, there it is.*

His next thought is something closer to wanting to cry. He refrains.

"I," he says, but nothing will follow. "Shit. Come here." He crushes Harinder in an embrace, sweater bunched awkwardly between his forearms. He hopes the message will get itself across somehow.

Harinder doesn't produce any angry hissing sounds, so he thinks it does.

"How are you so good at bringing me amazing things?" Harinder asks, fingers fitfully stroking Jericho's jawline.

"I don't know," Jericho says instead of voicing any of his internal bullshit.

"You have given me more good than I can count. You keep one-upping yourself. I'm going to hyperventilate."

"Please don't."

"I don't know if I can stop myself. You're too perfect."

"Stop."

"You can't tell me what to do."

"I will light myself on fire," Jericho threatens.

"That's okay. You don't look very flammable. If you did, I would have tested it by now."

Unable to escape the onslaught of affection, Jericho closes his eyes and hides his face in Harinder's hair. "I'm gonna run out of good ideas someday," he grumbles.

"We'll cross that bridge when we come to it," Harinder says patiently.

"It's going to be a rickety bridge. The kind with fraying rope and rotting wood, and gaps bigger than the ones between the antique shop stairs."

"You're still scared of those?"

"How could I *not* be?"

Harinder shrugs, and smiles, and pushes him back by the shoulders, then taps his fingers on Jericho's cheek until he reluctantly opens his eyes. "Aren't you going to say it back?"

Jericho swallows. He doesn't need to ask what Harinder's talking about. "I'm glad you like the telescope."

Rolling his eyes, Harinder says, "Yes, that's totally the response I was looking for, and one that makes sense as a reply to what I just said. How did you know."

"I'm just magic."

"Magic me some declarations of affection, you goof."

Yes, Harinder definitely likes those. Jericho likes them, too, he just— "I don't know how."

He expects a flippant remark, but Harinder continues to regard him with that small, gentle smile. It's starting to feel creepy. His boyfriend doesn't typically go this long without finding something to snarl at.

"You should try anyway," he suggests. "You get up to three wrong answers before I find Dumpling's spray bottle."

"Dumpling doesn't have a spray bottle. They're inhumane."

Harinder puffs with pride. "See? This is why I love you."

Jericho goes bright red, blood pumping in his ears. His head feels suspiciously like an egg in a microwave, about to messily explode. He tries to force the words out the way he might try squeezing pus out of a particularly stubborn zit. "I, uh. Love you. Also, I mean. This isn't too soon, right?"

"If anyone dares say it is, I will punch them in the tit and then curbstomp them."

"You do that when people mispronounce 'herbivore.'"

"It's fucking annoying, okay? Anyway, this is gay." Jericho snorts. Harinder nuzzles under his chin. "Thank you for the telescope."

Jericho kisses his forehead. "You're welcome, babe— no homo."

Harinder performs an elaborate brutality combo upon him with a throw pillow, but that's okay. Jericho Adams is twenty-one years old, which is more than old enough to not mind losing every once in a while.

Acknowledgements

Great thanks to my sensitivity readers, my amazing editor (who survived many panicked emails), and Reyah Violet, my greyhound. Without y'all I'd still be slumped in the gap between the wall and my mattress.

About the Author

Jem Zero is a disabled lesbian who lives in a house built by zir great-grandfather with zir family and two rescue greyhounds. Zir work is unapologetically queer and strives to communicate the frustration of being limited by one's meatsack & brainjuice.

While arguing zir way through an Accounting Certificate, Jem makes a living as a portrait artist and, similar to most tortured creators, is attempting to establish zirself in creative writing.

Facebook: www.facebook.com/jemzero.art

Twitter: @jem_zero

Website: www.jemzero.com

Coming Soon from Jem Zero

Joints

Moishe Kolton pushes their shaggy black hair out of their face, puffing a gasp of exertion. The box they were attempting to lift sinks back to the floor, slipping from their sweaty fingers.

"Fuck."

Giving themself a break, Moishe approaches a large plastic container, covered in a generous number of FRAGILE stickers. With a grunt of exertion, they scoop it up and plop it on one of the long wooden workbenches. Moishe pops open the handles on either side of the tub, then moves the lid aside. Within, there are numerous black velvet bags nestled in thick foam padding.

Moishe carefully withdraws the topmost bag and unfastens the tie, then eases out a small humanoid figure. They inspect it and sigh.

Claude is a chunky, ten-inch-tall, ball-jointed doll of unspecified gender. This model has oak-brown skin, silver freckles, and ice-blue eyes. There are three more Claudes in this box, two pale and one pink. Moishe morosely runs their fingers over the tinted resin frame, fingertip wiggling into the creases as they pose the doll, manipulating its limbs around the resin balls inserted in each joint.

Crafting ball-jointed dolls is Moishe's *thing*. Moishe sculpts them by hand from resin clay, first creating dozens of parts to make up the doll's figure, then setting them in order to be joined by resin balls, internally strung to allow movement wherever a body would be able to hold a pose. Moishe has been doing this since they were thirteen, after discovering the art form a year prior. Once crafted, the doll pieces are cast so Moishe can make duplicates and sell them online. It's how they make their living, and at over one thousand dollars a head, they're doing alright for themself.

They'd had high hopes for the Claude model. It was the last doll they made in the attic of their parents' Philadelphia home before moving to Burlington, Vermont. In anticipation of how well Claude was estimated to sell, based on social media response, Moishe had made several models before the move, expecting to ship them as they were snatched up from listings on Moishe's website.

Then disaster struck: a much larger rival company released a chubby monster girl bearing four arms and cute little horns. The design was, unfortunately, *fucking adorable*, and it blew Claude out of the water.

The door to Moishe's workshop flies open. "Knock, knock!"

"You know, Tri, people knock *before* they open doors," Moishe says, turning to their best friend with a grin.

Katrina Palamo is a tall woman with brown skin and long, perfectly straight black hair. She and Moishe met online in high school, seven years ago, and have been wildly codependent ever since. When Moishe expressed woeful lament at how dangerous and cramped it was to make ball-jointed dolls in one's parents' attic, Tri was there to suggest, in earnest, that Moishe consider moving to her area. She probably did not expect Moishe to agree, but agree they did.

"Be more flexible, Momo," says Tri, her strides long and purposeful as she moves to enfold Moishe in a fond embrace. "How is my squishy doing today?"

Moishe laughs. "Sulking."

"Stop it." Tri bats their nose gently. "We have to finish getting your workshop set up before game night."

Moishe's laughter turns into a nervous groan.

Elektree, the local game club, is a tax-funded community center located in the middle of a park. The center was constructed snugly beside a massive historical tree whose sturdy branches support the original clubhouse. Access to the tree house is now conducted through the game center itself. Every Saturday night marks the club's weekly board game event, where people from all over Burlington and its surrounding cities gather at the proverbial watering hole to obsess over Magic the Gathering and other cool games Moishe has never had enough friends to play.

Moishe had attended once and met several of Tri's friends before making a slew of excuses about forgetting to turn their parrot off and executing a clumsy escape.

"I don't know," they answer, twisting their hands together. Without thinking too deeply about it, Moishe reaches for Claude and fidgets with the doll's limbs.

Tri extricates the doll from their hands. "You gotta. No freaking out this time either."

"Be gentle with them!" Moishe squeaks, reaching for their beloved creation. Tri relinquishes it, rolling her eyes as Moishe hurriedly returns Claude to the safety of the velvet bag.

"Breathe, kid," Tri says with a snort. Tri doesn't "get" BJDs, which, in fairness, isn't uncommon. People who aren't into them don't tend to understand the hype.

"This doll is worth twelve hundred dollars," they grumble as they settle Claude back into the tub and replace the lid. "Help me finish with these boxes, you jerk."

The tiny vine-covered bungalow where Moishe now lives has neither a garage nor a basement. There are only four rooms—bed, bath, kitchen, and living area—with a tiny porch beside the back door that hosts the cramped laundry units and nothing else. The appeal of this place, outside of the affordable mortgage, is the backyard shed.

"It looks so great in here," Tri says as she effortlessly lifts the box Moishe had been struggling with a moment earlier. As she carries it over to one of the industrial-sized storage shelves, she trips over another box.

"It won't look great for long if you keep running into shit!" Moishe chastises, knowing it's their fault for leaving the box in the middle of the floor in the first place. Tri only laughs.

Renovating the shed into a workable studio took the better part of the two months Moishe has been in Burlington. Transferring the dozens of boxes that were shoved in every corner of the house—including on top of the fridge and inside the bathtub—is the final step.

"Did you see that photo of Little Foot I posted on Insta this morning?" Tri asks in the middle of sliding a tub of molds onto its proper space on the shelf.

Moishe looks away from the label maker. "I did not."

"Look!" Tri thrusts their phone in Moishe's face. Little Foot is Tri's cat—a geriatric gray tabby made of sharp angles and the softest fur Moishe's ever stroked. He is aggressively cuddly and purrs like a power sander.

They smile at the photo. "Cute. I haven't posted much lately."

"Yeah! What's up with that?" Tri reaches for a box containing the molds for one of Moishe's more popular models.

"I've been stuck," they say with a particularly put-upon pout. "Claude is underselling, and I swear to god they put that stupidly adorable monster doll together just to steal my thunder." Moishe clenches their fists. "So I want to go big. I'm going to make a monster doll of my own, and it is going to be bigger than anything they've ever made. It'll be a massive project, and it's going to rock their fucking world."

An anticlimactic pause follows, during which Tri stares at them expectantly.

Moishe deflates. "Except, I don't have a single fucking idea for the design. Having to draw at the dinner table isn't helping either." They cast a meaningful look at the drafting desk against the studio's northern wall.

Tri stops working to pat their shoulder. "You'll get there. In the meanwhile, keep those labels coming!" She treats them to a pat on the ass before returning to unpacking boxes and shuffling materials into their assigned spots.

"How's debate?" Moishe asks after several more minutes of work.

Tri's upbeat personality is basically a superpower. In addition to her SEO marketing job, Tri coaches middle grade debate teams and performs in competitive X-wing tournaments.

"It is what it is," Tri says with a wave of her hand. "This batch of kids isn't as vicious as my last, but I'm trying to bring out their inner predators."

Laughing, Moishe says, "Debate is spicy arguing, not a gladiator match."

Moishe has always been envious of Tri's ability to just...go outside and *do* shit. Meet people, have hobbies, enjoy scenery. Nothing Moishe knows how to do. In high school, they kept their head buried in their sketchbook and relied on the internet for social fulfillment.

That reluctance to socially engage continued into adulthood. Philly was a crowded, overwhelming place, and finding comfort among buzzing leftists, activists, and artists felt more difficult than it should have. Moishe's only external participation was with the Jewish queer Tuesday meet-up their parents insisted they attend. Part of Moishe's resolution for the move had been getting out more, their temperamental chronic fatigue be damned.

"Summer tournaments are coming to a close," Tri says, "and school starts soon. I'm lucky I had enough time to fit in another convention before after-school coaching starts."

"I don't get why you're so into X-wing," Moishe says with a shake of their head, fully aware of the silliness inherent in a friendship involving mutual disinterest in one another's passions.

Moishe is eager to play exciting board games—ones like Dead of Winter and Spirit Island, rather than groaning through fifty rounds of The Game of Life with their parents, rolling their eyes over the marking of success in babies, minivans, and marriage. "How do you get excited about putting Star Wars figurines on a table and measuring flight trajectories for a goddamn hour?"

"It's amazing how hard a set of rulers can get your blood pumping!" Tri protests. "You could come to a con with me; you might like it."

"Oh god. Not with all those people." Not yet.

"You'll get used to it," she says in a soothing voice. "Done with those labels?"

"I think so, yeah," Moishe says quietly. They sweep their gaze around the room, taking in stocked resources and broken-down cardboard boxes, nearly everything in its place. Only one box remains, parked by the east-facing window seat. Wandering over, Moishe begins unpacking the studio's final adornments. A dangling wind chime, hung from the ceiling of the tiny alcove; a blanket tucked into the storage under the seat; a few stuffed animals and pillows, including a prized cross-stitch that reads "Not trans as in FTM, but nonbinary as in fuck off."

"I should go," Tri says, wearing a fond smile. "Tonight at six thirty. No excuses. Do you need the address again?"

Moishe shakes their head. "No, I think searching 'eco-punk game center' will bring Elektree up without issue."

Tri snickers and draws in close for a brief hug before pushing them back to meet their eyes. "I'll be there for you, you know. If you need to step outside for a smoke break, signal me. The safeword is 'manatee.'"

Moishe cracks up. "I don't smoke, but it sounds good otherwise."

Tri smacks a noisy kiss against their forehead before stepping outside. Moishe watches her through the window as she jogs over to the side of the house to unchain her bike. Tri throws a gracefully long leg over the bar and turns around to blow Moishe a kiss before shooting down the street.

Alone once more, Moishe inspects the completed work environment. They want to shriek, *I'm finally an adult!* Instead, they swallow down the excitement. They haven't made it—yet. Tonight will be another challenge to tackle before they can succeed in their dream of living independently.

It'll come. They just have to stay flexible.

Also Available from NineStar Press

Connect with NineStar Press

www.ninestarpress.com

www.facebook.com/ninestarpress

www.facebook.com/groups/NineStarNiche

www.twitter.com/ninestarpress

Lightning Source UK Ltd.
Milton Keynes UK
UKHW011431240621
386089UK00002B/540